The Prairie Mother

Arthur Stringer

Alpha Editions

This edition published in 2024

ISBN 9789361478116

Design and Setting By

Alpha Editions

www.alphaedis.com

Email - info@alphaedis.com

Contents

Sunday the Fifteenth

I opened my eyes and saw a pea-green world all around me. Then I heard the doctor say: "Give 'er another whiff or two." His voice sounded far-away, as though he were speaking through the Simplon Tunnel, and not merely through his teeth, within twelve inches of my nose.

I took my whiff or two. I gulped at that chloroform like a thirsty Bedouin at a wadi-spring. I went down into the pea-green emptiness again, and forgot about the Kelly pad and the recurring waves of pain that came bigger and bigger and tried to sweep through my racked old body like breakers through the ribs of a stranded schooner. I forgot about the hateful metallic clink of steel things against an instrument-tray, and about the loganberry pimple on the nose of the red-headed surgical nurse who'd been sent into the labor room to help.

I went wafting off into a feather-pillowy pit of infinitude. I even forgot to preach to myself, as I'd been doing for the last month or two. I knew that my time was upon me, as the Good Book says. There are a lot of things in this life, I remembered, which woman is able to squirm out of. But here, Mistress Tabbie, was one you couldn't escape. Here was a situation that *had* to be faced. Here was a time I had to knuckle down, had to grin and bear it, had to go through with it to the bitter end. For other folks, whatever they may be able to do for you, aren't able to have your babies for you.

Then I ebbed up out of the pea-green depths again, and was troubled by the sound of voices, so thin and far-away I couldn't make out what they were saying. Then came the beating of a tom-tom, so loud that it hurt. When that died away for a minute or two I caught the sound of the sharp and quavery squall of something, of something which had never squalled before, a squall of protest and injured pride, of maltreated youth resenting the ignominious way it must enter the world. Then the tom-tom beating started up again, and I opened my eyes to make sure it wasn't the Grenadiers' Band going by.

I saw a face bending over mine, seeming to float in space. It was the color of a half-grown cucumber, and it made me think of a tropical fish in an aquarium when the water needed changing.

"She's coming out, Doctor," I heard a woman's voice say. It was a voice as calm as God's and slightly nasal. For a moment I thought I'd died and gone to Heaven. But I finally observed and identified the loganberry pimple, and realized that the tom-tom beating was merely the pounding of the steampipes in that jerry-built western hospital, and remembered that I was still in the land of the living and that the red-headed surgical nurse was holding my wrist. I felt infinitely hurt and abused, and wondered why my husband wasn't there to help me with that comforting brown gaze of his. And I wanted to cry, but didn't seem to have the strength, and then I wanted to say something, but found myself too weak.

It was the doctor's voice that roused me again. He was standing beside my narrow iron bed with his sleeves still rolled up, wiping his arms with a big white towel. He was smiling as he scrubbed at the corners of his nails, as though to make sure they were clean. The nurse on the other side of the bed was also smiling. So was the carrot-top with the loganberry beauty-spot. All I could see, in fact, was smiling faces.

But it didn't seem a laughing matter to me. I wanted to rest, to sleep, to get another gulp or two of that God-given smelly stuff out of the little round tin can.

"How're you feeling?" asked the doctor indifferently. He nodded down at me as he proceeded to manicure those precious nails of his. They were laughing, the whole four of them. I began to suspect that I wasn't going to die, after all.

"Everything's fine and dandy," announced the barearmed farrier as he snapped his little pen-knife shut. But that triumphant grin of his only made me more tired than ever, and I turned away to the tall young nurse on the other side of my bed.

There was perspiration on her forehead, under the eaves of the pale hair crowned with its pointed little cap. She was still smiling, but she looked human and tired and a little fussed.

"Is it a girl?" I asked her. I had intended to make that query a crushingly imperious one. I wanted it to stand as a reproof to them, as a mark of disapproval for all such untimely merriment. But my voice, I found, was amazingly weak and thin. And I wanted to know.

"*It's both*," said the tired-eyed girl in the blue and white uniform. And she, too, nodded her head in a triumphant sort of way, as though the credit for some vast and recent victory lay entirely in her own narrow lap.

"It's both?" I repeated, wondering why she too should fail to give a simple answer to a simple question.

"It's twins!" she said, with a little chirrup of laughter.

"Twins?" I gasped, in a sort of bleat that drove the last of the pea-green mist out of that room with the dead white walls.

"Twins," proclaimed the doctor, "*twins!*" He repeated the monosyllable, converting it into a clarion-call that made me think of a rooster crowing.

"A lovely boy and girl," cooed the third nurse with a bottle of olive-oil in her hand. And by twisting my head a little I was able to see the two wire bassinets, side by side, each holding a little mound of something wrapped in a flannelette blanket.

I shut my eyes, for I seemed to have a great deal to think over. Twins! A boy and girl! Two little new lives in the world! Two warm and cuddling little bairns to nest close against my mother-breast.

"I see *your* troubles cut out for you," said the doctor as he rolled down his shirt-sleeves.

They were all laughing again. But to me it didn't seem quite such a laughing matter. I was thinking of my layette, and trying to count over my supply of binders and slips and shirts and nighties and wondering how I could out-Solomon Solomon and divide the little dotted Swiss dress edged with the French Val lace of which I'd been so proud. Then I fell to pondering over other problems, equally prodigious, so that it was quite a long time before my mind had a chance to meander on to Dinky-Dunk himself.

And when I did think of Dinky-Dunk I had to laugh. It seemed a joke on him, in some way. He was the father of twins. Instead of one little snoozer to carry on his name and perpetuate his race in the land, he now had *two*. Fate, without consulting him, had flung him double measure. No wonder, for the moment, those midnight toilers in that white-walled house of pain were wearing the smile that refused to come off! That's the way, I suppose, that all life ought to be welcomed into this old world of ours. And now, I suddenly remembered, I could speak of *my children*—and that means so much more than talking about one's child. Now I was indeed a mother, a prairie mother with three young chicks of her own to scratch for.

I forgot my anxieties and my months of waiting. I forgot those weeks of long mute protest, of revolt against wily old Nature, who so cleverly tricks us into the ways she has chosen. A glow of glory went through my tired body—it was hysteria, I suppose, in the basic meaning of the word—and I had to shut my eyes tight to keep the tears from showing.

But that great wave of happiness which had washed up the shore of my soul receded as it came. By the time I was transferred to the rubber-wheeled stretcher they called "the Wagon" and trundled off to a bed and room of my own, the reaction set in. I could think more clearly. My Dinky-Dunk didn't love me, or he'd never have left me at such a time, no matter what his business calls may have been. The Twins weren't quite so humorous as they seemed. There was even something disturbingly animal-like in the birth of more offspring than one at a time, something almost revolting in this approach to the littering of one's young. They all tried to unedge that animality by treating it as a joke, by confronting it with their conspiracies of jocularity. But it would be no joke to a nursing mother in the middle of a winter prairie with the nearest doctor twenty long miles away.

I countermanded my telegram to Dinky-Dunk at Vancouver, and cried myself to sleep in a nice relaxing tempest of self-pity which my "special" accepted as calmly as a tulip-bed accepts a shower. But lawdy, lawdy, how I slept! And when I woke up and sniffed warm air and that painty smell peculiar to new buildings, and heard the radiators sing with steam and the windows rattle in the northeast blizzard that was blowing, I slipped into a truer realization of the intricate machinery of protection all about me, and thanked my lucky stars that I wasn't in a lonely prairie shack, as I'd been when my almost three-year-old Dinkie was born. I remembered, with little tidal waves of contentment, that my ordeal was a thing of the past, and that I was a mother twice over, and rather hungry, and rather impatient to get a peek at my God-given little babes.

Then I fell to thinking rather pityingly of my forsaken little Dinkie and wondering if Mrs. Teetzel would keep his feet dry and cook his cream-of-wheat properly, and if Iroquois Annie would have brains enough not to overheat the furnace and burn Casa Grande down to the ground. Then I decided to send the wire to Dinky-Dunk, after all, for it isn't every day in the year a man can be told he's the father of twins....

I sent the wire, in the secret hope that it would bring my lord and master on the run. But it was eight days later, when I was up on a back-rest and having my hair braided, that Dinky-Dunk put in an appearance. And when he did come he chilled me. I can't just say why. He seemed tired and preoccupied and unnecessarily self-conscious before the nurses when I made him hold Pee-Wee on one arm and Poppsy on the other.

"Now kiss 'em, Daddy," I commanded. And he had to kiss them both on their red and puckered little faces. Then he handed them over with all too apparent relief, and fell into a brown study.

"What are you worrying over?" I asked him.

"I'm wondering how in the world you'll ever manage," he solemnly acknowledged. I was able to laugh, though it took an effort.

"For every little foot God sends a little shoe," I told him, remembering the aphorism of my old Irish nurse. "And the sooner you get me home, Dinky-Dunk, the happier I'll be. For I'm tired of this place and the smell of the formalin and ether and I'm nearly worried to death about Dinkie. And in all the wide world, O Kaikobad, there's no place like one's own home!"

Dinky-Dunk didn't answer me, but I thought he looked a little wan and limp as he sat down in one of the stiff-backed chairs. I inspected him with a calmer and clearer eye.

"Was that sleeper too hot last night?" I asked, remembering what a bad night could do to a big man.

"I don't seem to sleep on a train the way I used to," he said, but his eye evaded mine. And I suspected something.

"Dinky-Dunk," I demanded, "did you have a berth last night?"

He flushed up rather guiltily. He even seemed to resent my questioning him. But I insisted on an answer.

"No, I sat up," he finally confessed.

"Why?" I demanded.

And still again his eye tried to evade mine.

"We're a bit short of ready cash." He tried to say it indifferently, but the effort was a failure.

"Then why didn't you tell me that before?" I asked, sitting up and spurning the back-rest.

"You had worries enough of your own," proclaimed my weary-eyed lord and master. It gave me a squeezy feeling about the heart to see him looking so much like an unkempt and overworked and altogether neglected husband. And there I'd been lying in the lap of luxury, with quick-footed ladies in uniform to answer my bell and fly at my bidding.

"But I've a right, Dunkie, to know your worries, and stand my share of 'em," I promptly told him. "And that's why I want to get out of this smelly old hole and back to my home again. I may be the mother of twins, and only too often reminded that I'm one of the Mammalia, but I'm still your cave-mate and life-partner, and I don't think children ought to come between a man and wife. I don't intend to allow *my* children to do anything like that."

I said it quite bravely, but there was a little cloud of doubt drifting across the sky of my heart. Marriage is so different from what the romance-fiddlers try to make it. Even Dinky-Dunk doesn't approve of my mammalogical allusions. Yet milk, I find, is one of the most important issues of motherhood—only it's impolite to mention the fact. What makes me so impatient of life as I see it reflected in fiction is its trick of overlooking the important things and over-accentuating the trifles. It primps and tries to be genteel—for Biology doth make cowards of us all.

I was going to say, very sagely, that life isn't so mysterious after you've been the mother of three children. But that wouldn't be quite right. It's mysterious in an entirely different way. Even love itself is different, I concluded, after lying there in bed day after day and thinking the thing over. For there are so many different ways, I find, of loving a man. You are fond of him, at first, for what you consider his perfections, the same as you are fond of a brand-new traveling bag. There isn't a scratch on his polish or a flaw in his make-up. Then you live with him for a few years. You live with him and find that life is making a few dents in his loveliness of character, that the edges are worn away, that there's a weakness or two where you imagined only strength to be, and that instead of standing a saint and hero all in one, he's merely an unruly and unreliable human being with his ups and downs of patience and temper and passion. But, bless his battered old soul, you love him none the less for all that. You no longer fret about him being unco guid, and you comfortably give up trying to match his imaginary virtues with your own. You still love him, but you love him differently. There's a touch of pity in your respect for him, a mellowing compassion, a little of the eternal mother mixed up with the eternal sweetheart. And if you are wise you will no longer demand the impossible of him. Being a woman, you will still want to be loved. But being a woman of discernment, you will remember that in some way and by some means, if you want to be loved, you must remain lovable.

Thursday the Nineteenth

I had to stay in that smelly old hole of a hospital and in that bald little prairie city fully a week longer than I wanted to. I tried to rebel against being bullied, even though the hand of iron was padded with velvet. But the powers that be were too used to handling perverse and fretful women. They thwarted my purpose and broke my will and kept me in bed until I began to think I'd take root there.

But once I and my bairns were back here at Casa Grande I could see that they were right. In the first place the trip was tiring, too tiring to rehearse in detail. Then a vague feeling of neglect and desolation took possession of me, for I missed the cool-handed efficiency of that ever-dependable "special." I almost surrendered to funk, in fact, when both Poppsy and Pee-Wee started up a steady duet of crying. I sat down and began to sniffle myself, but my sense of humor, thank the Lord, came back and saved the day. There was something so utterly ridiculous in that briny circle, soon augmented and completed by the addition of Dinkie, who apparently felt as lonely and overlooked as did his spineless and sniffling mother.

So I had to tighten the girths of my soul. I took a fresh grip on myself and said: "Look here, Tabbie, this is never going to do. This is not the way Horatius held the bridge. This is not the spirit that built Rome. So, up, Guards, and at 'em! Excelsior! *Audaces fortuna juvat!*"

So I mopped my eyes, and readjusted the Twins, and did what I could to placate Dinkie, who continues to regard his little brother and sister with a somewhat hostile eye. One of my most depressing discoveries on getting back home, in fact, was to find that Dinkie has grown away from me in my absence. At first he even resented my approaches, and he still stares at me, now and then, across a gulf of perplexity. But the ice is melting. He's beginning to understand, after all, that I'm his really truly mother and that he can come to me with his troubles. He's lost a good deal of his color, and I'm beginning to suspect that his food hasn't been properly looked after during the last few weeks. It's a patent fact, at any rate, that my house hasn't been properly looked after. Iroquois Annie, that sullen-eyed breed servant of ours, will never have any medals pinned on her pinny for neatness. I'd love to ship her, but heaven only knows where we'd find any one to take her place. And I simply *must* have help, during the next few months.

Casa Grande, by the way, looked such a little dot on the wilderness, as we drove back to it, that a spear of terror pushed its way through my breast as

I realized that I had my babies to bring up away out here on the edge of this half-settled no-man's land. If only our dreams had come true! If only the plans of mice and men didn't go so aft agley! If only the railway had come through to link us up with civilization, and the once promised town had sprung up like a mushroom-bed about our still sad and solitary Casa Grande! But what's the use of repining, Tabbie McKail? You've the second-best house within thirty miles of Buckhorn, with glass door-knobs and a laundry-chute, and a brood to rear, and a hard-working husband to cook for. And as the kiddies get older, I imagine, I'll not be troubled by this terrible feeling of loneliness which has been weighing like a plumb-bob on my heart for the last few days. I wish Dinky-Dunk didn't have to be so much away from home....

Old Whinstane Sandy, our hired man, has presented me with a hand-made swing-box for Poppsy and Pee-Wee, a sort of suspended basket-bed that can be hung up in the porch as soon as my two little snoozers are able to sleep outdoors. Old Whinnie, by the way, was very funny when I showed him the Twins. He solemnly acknowledged that they were nae sae bad, conseederin'. I suppose he thought it would be treason to Dinkie to praise the newcomers who threatened to put little Dinkie's nose out of joint. And Whinnie, I imagine, will always be loyal to Dinkie. He says little about it, but I know he loves that child. He loves him in very much the same way that Bobs, our collie dog, loves me. It was really Bobs' welcome, I think, across the cold prairie air, that took the tragedy out of my homecoming. There were gladness and trust in those deep-throated howls of greetings. He even licked the snow off my overshoes and nested his head between my knees, with his bob-tail thumping the floor like a flicker's beak. He sniffed at the Twins rather disgustedly. But he'll learn to love them, I feel sure, as time goes on. He's too intelligent a dog to do otherwise....

I'll be glad when spring comes, and takes the razor-edge out of this northern air. We'll have half a month of mud first, I suppose. But "there's never anything without something," as Mrs. Teetzel very sagely announced the other day. That sour-apple philosopher, by the way, is taking her departure to-morrow. And I'm not half so sorry as I pretend to be. She's made me feel like an intruder in my own home. And she's a soured and venomous old ignoramus, for she sneered openly at my bath-thermometer and defies Poppsy and Pee-Wee to survive the winter without a "comfort." After I'd announced my intention of putting them outdoors to sleep, when they were four weeks old, she lugubriously acknowledged that there were more ways than one of murderin' infant children. *Her* ideal along this line, I've discovered, is slow asphyxiation in a sort of Dutch-oven made of an eider-down comforter, with as much air as possible shut off from their uncomfortable little bodies. But the Oracle is going, and I intend to bring up my babies in my own way. For I know a little more about the game now than I did when little Dinkie made his appearance in this vale of tears. And whatever my babies may or may not be, they are at least healthy little tikes.

Sunday the Twenty-second

I seem to be fitting into things again, here at Casa Grande. I've got my strength back, and an appetite like a Cree pony, and the day's work is no longer a terror to me. I'm back in the same old rut, I was going to say—but it is not the same. There is a spirit of unsettledness about it all which I find impossible to define, an air of something impending, of something that should be shunned as long as possible. Perhaps it's merely a flare-back from my own shaken nerves. Or perhaps it's because I haven't been able to get out in the open air as much as I used to. I am missing my riding. And Paddy, my pinto, will give us a morning of it, when we try to get a saddle on his scarred little back, for it's half a year now since he has had a bit between his teeth.

It's Dinky-Dunk that I'm really worrying over, though I don't know why. I heard him come in very quietly last night as I was tucking little Dinkie up in his crib. I went to the nursery door, half hoping to hear my lord and master sing out his old-time "Hello, Lady-Bird!" or "Are you there, Babushka?" But instead of that he climbed the stairs, rather heavily, and passed on down the hall to the little room he calls his study, his sanctum-sanctorum where he keeps his desk and papers and books—and the duck-guns, so that Dinkie can't get at them. I could hear him open the desk-top and sit down in the squeaky Bank of England chair.

When I was sure that Dinkie was off, for good, I tiptoed out and shut the nursery door. Even big houses, I began to realize as I stood there in the hall, could have their drawbacks. In the two-by-four shack where we'd lived and worked and been happy before Casa Grande was built there was no chance for one's husband to shut himself up in his private boudoir and barricade himself away from his better-half. So I decided, all of a sudden, to beard the lion in his den. There was such a thing as too much formality in a family circle. Yet I felt a bit audacious as I quietly pushed open that study door. I even weakened in my decision about pouncing on Dinky-Dunk from behind, like a leopardess on a helpless stag. Something in his pose, in fact, brought me up short.

Dinky-Dunk was sitting with his head on his hand, staring at the wall-paper. And it wasn't especially interesting wall-paper. He was sitting there in a trance, with a peculiar line of dejection about his forward-fallen shoulders. I couldn't see his face, but I felt sure it was not a happy face.

I even came to a stop, without speaking a word, and shrank rather guiltily back through the doorway. It was a relief, in fact, to find that I was able to close the door without making a sound.

When Dinky-Dunk came down-stairs, half an hour later, he seemed his same old self. He talked and laughed and inquired if Nip and Tuck—those are the names he sometimes takes from his team and pins on Poppsy and Pee-Wee—had given me a hard day of it and explained that Francois—our man on the Harris Ranch—had sent down a robe of plaited rabbit-skin for them.

I did my best, all the time, to keep my inquisitorial eye from fastening itself on Dunkie's face, for I knew that he was playing up to me, that he was acting a part which wasn't coming any too easy. But he stuck to his rôle. When I put down my sewing, because my eyes were tired, he even inquired if I hadn't done about enough for one day.

"I've done about half what I ought to do," I told him. "The trouble is, Dinky-Dunk, I'm getting old. I'm losing my bounce!"

That made him laugh a little, though it was rather a wistful laugh.

"Oh, no, Gee-Gee," he announced, momentarily like his old self, "whatever you lose, you'll never lose that undying girlishness of yours!"

It was not so much what he said, as the mere fact that he could say it, which sent a wave of happiness through my maternal old body. So I made for him with my Australian crawl-stroke, and kissed him on both sides of his stubbly old face, and rumpled him up, and went to bed with a touch of silver about the edges of the thunder-cloud still hanging away off somewhere on the sky-line.

Wednesday the Twenty-fifth

There was indeed something wrong. I knew that the moment I heard Dinky-Dunk come into the house. I knew it by the way he let the storm-door swing shut, by the way he crossed the hall as far as the living-room door and then turned back, by the way he slowly mounted the stairs and passed leaden-footed on to his study. And I knew that this time there'd be no "Are you there, Little Mother?" or "Where beest thou, *Boca Chica*?"

I'd Poppsy and Pee-Wee safe and sound asleep in the swing-box that dour old Whinstane Sandy had manufactured out of a packing-case, with Francois' robe of plaited rabbit-skin to keep their tootsies warm. I'd finished my ironing and bathed little Dinkie and buttoned him up in his sleepers and made him hold his little hands together while I said his "Now-I-lay-me" and tucked him up in his crib with his broken mouth-organ and his beloved red-topped shoes under the pillow, so that he could find them there first thing in the morning and bestow on them his customary matutinal kiss of adoration. And I was standing at the nursery window, pretty tired in body but foolishly happy and serene in spirit, staring out across the leagues of open prairie at the last of the sunset.

It was one of those wonderful sunsets of the winter-end that throw wine-stains back across this bald old earth and make you remember that although the green hasn't yet awakened into life there's release on the way. It was a sunset with an infinite depth to its opal and gold and rose and a whisper of spring in its softly prolonged afterglow. It made me glad and sad all at once, for while there was a hint of vast re-awakenings in the riotous wine-glow that merged off into pale green to the north, there was also a touch of loneliness in the flat and far-flung sky-line. It seemed to recede so bewilderingly and so oppressively into a silence and into an emptiness which the lonely plume of smoke from one lonely shack-chimney both crowned and accentuated with a wordless touch of poignancy.

That pennon of shack-smoke, dotting the northern horizon, seemed to become something valorous and fine. It seemed to me to typify the spirit of man pioneering along the fringes of desolation, adventuring into the unknown, conquering the untamed realms of his world. And it was a good old world, I suddenly felt, a patient and bountiful old world with its Browningesque old bones set out in the last of the sun—until I heard my Dinky-Dunk go lumbering up to his study and quietly yet deliberately shut himself in, as I gave one last look at Poppsy and Pee-Wee to make sure they were safely covered. Then I stood stock-still in the center of the nursery, wondering whether, at such a time, I ought to go to my husband or keep away from him.

I decided, after a minute or two of thought, to bide a wee. So I slipped quietly down-stairs and stowed Dinkie's overturned kiddie-car away in the cloak-room and warned Iroquois Annie—the meekest-looking Redskin ever togged out in the cap and apron of domestic servitude—not to burn my fricassee of frozen prairie-chicken and not to scorch the scones so beloved by my Scotch-Canadian lord and master. Then I inspected the supper table and lighted the lamp with the Ruskin-green shade and supplanted Dinky-Dunk's napkin that had a coffee-stain along its edge with a fresh one from the linen-drawer. Then, after airing the house to rid it of the fumes from Iroquois Annie's intemperate griddle and carrying Dinkie's muddied overshoes back to the kitchen and lighting the Chinese hall-lamp, I went to the bottom of the stairs to call my husband down to supper.

But still again that wordless feeling of something amiss prompted me to hesitate. So instead of calling blithely out of him, as I had intended, I went silently up the stairs. Then I slipped along the hall and just as silently opened his study door.

My husband was sitting at his desk, confronted by a litter of papers and letters, which I knew to be the mail he had just brought home and flung there. But he wasn't looking at anything on his desk. He was merely sitting there staring vacantly out of the window at the paling light. His elbows were on the arms of his Bank of England swivel-chair for which I'd made the green baize seat-pad, and as I stared in at him, half in shadow, I had an odd impression of history repeating itself. This puzzled me, for a moment, until I remembered having caught sight of him in much the same attitude, only a few days before. But this time he looked so tired and drawn and spineless that a fish-hook of sudden pity tugged at my throat. For my Dinky-Dunk sat there without moving, with the hope and the joy of life drawn utterly out of his bony big body. The heavy emptiness of his face, as rugged as a relief-map in the side-light, even made me forget the smell of the scones Iroquois Annie was vindictively scorching down in the kitchen. He didn't know, of course, that I was watching him, for he jumped as I signaled my presence by slamming the door after stepping in through it. That jump, I knew, wasn't altogether due to edgy nerves. It was also an effort at dissimulation, for his sudden struggle to get his scattered lines of manhood together still carried a touch of the heroic. But I'd caught a glimpse of his soul when it wasn't on parade. And I knew what I knew. He tried to work his poor old harried face into a smile as I crossed over to his side. But, like Topsy's kindred, it died a-borning.

"What's happened?" I asked

"What's happened?" I asked, dropping on my knees close beside him.

Instead of answering me, he swung about in the swivel-chair so that he more directly faced the window. The movement also served to pull away the hand which I had almost succeeded in capturing. Nothing, I've found, can wound a real man more than pity.

"What's happened?" I repeated. For I knew, now, that something was really and truly and tragically wrong, as plainly as though Dinky-Dunk had up and told me so by word of mouth. You can't live with a man for nearly four years without growing into a sort of clairvoyant knowledge of those subterranean little currents that feed the wells of mood and temper and character. He pushed the papers on the desk away from him without looking at me.

"Oh, it's nothing much," he said. But he said it so listlessly I knew he was merely trying to lie like a gentleman.

"If it's bad news, I want to know it, right slam-bang out," I told him. And for the first time he turned and looked at me, in a meditative and impersonal sort of way that brought the fish-hook tugging at my thorax again. He looked at me as though some inner part of him were still debating as to whether or not he was about to be confronted by a woman in tears. Then a touch of cool desperation crept up into his eyes.

"Our whole apple-cart's gone over," he slowly and quietly announced, with those coldly narrowed eyes still intent on my face, as though very little and yet a very great deal depended on just how I was going to accept that slightly enigmatic remark. And he must have noticed the quick frown of perplexity which probably came to my face, for that right hand of his resting on the table opened and then closed again, as though it were squeezing a sponge very dry. "They've got me," he said. "They've got me— to the last dollar!"

I stood up in the uncertain light, for it takes time to digest strong words, the same as it takes time to digest strong meat.

I remembered how, during the last half-year, Dinky-Dunk had been on the wing, hurrying over to Calgary, and Edmonton, flying east to Winnipeg, scurrying off to the Coast, poring over township maps and blue-prints and official-looking letters from land associations and banks and loan companies. I had been called in to sign papers, with bread-dough on my arms, and asked to witness signatures, with Dinkie on my hip, and commanded by my absent hearth-mate to send on certain documents by the next mail. I had also gathered up scattered sheets of paper covered with close-penciled rows of figures, and had felt that Dinky-Dunk for a year back had been giving more time to his speculations than to his home and his ranch. I had seen the lines deepen a little on that lean and bony face of his and the pepper-and-salt above his ears turning into almost pure salt. And I'd missed, this many a day, the old boyish note in his laughter and the old careless intimacies in his talk. And being a woman of almost ordinary intelligence—preoccupied as I was with those three precious babies of mine—I had arrived at the not unnatural conclusion that my spouse was surrendering more and more to that passion of his for wealth and power.

Wealth and power, of course, are big words in the language of any man. But I had more than an inkling that my husband had been taking a gambler's chance to reach the end in view. And now, in that twilit shadow-huddled cubby-hole of a room, it came over me, all of a heap, that having taken the gambler's chance, we had met a fate not uncommon to gamblers, and had lost.

"So we're bust!" I remarked, without any great show of emotion, feeling, I suppose, that without worldly goods we might consistently be without elegance. And in the back of my brain I was silently revising our old Kansas pioneer couplet into

In land-booms we trusted

And in land-booms we busted.

But it wasn't a joke. You can't have the bottom knocked out of your world, naturally, and find an invisible Nero blithely fiddling on your heart-strings. And I hated to see Dinky-Dunk sitting there with that dead look in his eyes. I hated to see him with his spirit broken, with that hollow and haggard misery about the jowls, which made me think of a hound-dog mourning for a dead master.

But I knew better than to show any pity for Dinky-Dunk at such a time. It would have been effective as a stage-picture, I know, my reaching out and pressing his tired head against a breast sobbing with comprehension and shaking with compassion. But pity, with real men-folks in real life, is perilous stuff to deal in. I was equally afraid to feel sorry for myself, even though my body chilled with the sudden suspicion that Casa Grande and all it held might be taken away from me, that my bairns might be turned out of their warm and comfortable beds, overnight, that the consoling sense of security which those years of labor had builded up about us might vanish in a breath. And I needed new flannelette for the Twins' nighties, and a reefer for little Dinky-Dunk, and an aluminum double-boiler that didn't leak for me maun's porritch. There were rafts of things I needed, rafts and rafts of them. But here we were bust, so far as I could tell, on the rocks, swamped, stranded and wrecked.

I held myself in, however, even if it *did* take an effort. I crossed casually over to the door, and opened it to sniff at the smell of supper.

"Whatever happens, Dinky-Dunk," I very calmly announced, "we've got to eat. And if that she-Indian scorches another scone I'll go down there and scalp her."

My husband got slowly and heavily up out of the chair, which gave out a squeak or two even when relieved of his weight. I knew by his face in the half-light that he was going to say that he didn't care to eat.

But, instead of saying that, he stood looking at me, with a tragically humble sort of contriteness. Then, without quite knowing he was doing it, he brought his hands together in a sort of clinch, with his face twisted up in an odd little grimace of revolt, as though he stood ashamed to let me see that his lip was quivering.

"It's such a rotten deal," he almost moaned, "to you and the kiddies."

"Oh, we'll survive it," I said with a grin that was plainly forced.

"But you don't seem to understand what it means," he protested. His impatience, I could see, was simply that of a man overtaxed. And I could afford to make allowance for it.

"I understand that it's almost an hour past supper-time, my Lord, and that if you don't give me a chance to stoke up I'll bite the edges off the lamp-shade!"

I was rewarded by just the ghost of a smile, a smile that was much too wan and sickly to live long.

"All right," announced Dinky-Dunk, "I'll be down in a minute or two."

There was courage in that, I saw, for all the listlessness of the tone in which it had been uttered. So I went skipping down-stairs and closed my baby grand and inspected the table and twisted the glass bowl that held my nasturtium-buds about, to the end that the telltale word of "Salt" embossed on its side would not betray the fact that it had been commandeered from the kitchen-cabinet. Then I turned up the lamp and smilingly waited until my lord and master seated himself at the other side of the table, grateful beyond words that we had at least that evening alone and were not compelled to act up to a part before the eyes of strangers.

Yet it was anything but a successful meal. Dinky-Dunk's pretense at eating was about as hollow as my pretense at light-heartedness. We each knew that the other was playing a part, and the time came when to keep it up was altogether too much of a mockery.

"Dinky-Dunk," I said after a silence that was too abysmal to be ignored, "let's look this thing squarely in the face."

"I can't!"

"Why not?"

"I haven't the courage."

"Then we've got to get it," I insisted. "I'm ready to face the music, if you are. So let's get right down to hard-pan. Have they—have they really cleaned you out?"

"To the last dollar," he replied, without looking up.

"What did it?" I asked, remaining stubbornly and persistently ox-like in my placidity.

"No one thing did it, Chaddie, except that I tried to bite off too much. And for the last two years, of course, the boom's been flattening out. If our Associated Land Corporation hadn't gone under—"

"Then it *has* gone under?" I interrupted, with a catch of the breath, for I knew just how much had been staked on that venture.

Dinky-Dunk nodded his head. "And carried me with it," he grimly announced. "But even that wouldn't have meant a knock-out, if the government had only kept its promise and taken over my Vancouver Island water-front."

That, I remembered, was to have been some sort of a shipyard. Then I remembered something else.

"When the Twins were born," I reminded Dunkie, "you put the ranch here at Casa Grande in my name. Does that mean we lose our home?"

I was able to speak quietly, but I could hear the thud of my own heart-beats.

"That's for you to decide," he none too happily acknowledged. Then he added, with sudden decisiveness: "No, they can't touch anything of *yours*! Not a thing!"

"But won't that hold good with the Harris Ranch, as well?" I further inquired. "That was actually bought in my name. It was deeded to me from the first, and always has been in my name."

"Of course it's yours," he said with a hesitation that was slightly puzzling to me.

"Then how about the cattle and things?"

"What cattle?"

"The cattle we've kept on it to escape the wild land tax? Aren't those all legally mine?"

It sounded rapacious, I suppose, under the circumstances. It must have seemed like looting on a battlefield. But I wasn't thinking entirely about myself, even though poor old Dinky-Dunk evidently assumed so, from the look of sudden questioning that came into his stricken eyes.

"Yes, they're yours," he almost listlessly responded.

"Then, as I've already said, let's look this thing fairly and squarely in the face. We've taken a gambler's chance on a big thing, and we've lost. We've lost our pile, as they phrase it out here, but if what you say is true, we haven't lost our home, and what is still more important, we haven't lost our pride."

My husband looked down at his plate.

"That's gone, too," he slowly admitted.

"It doesn't sound like my Dinky-Dunk, a thing like that," I promptly admonished. But I'd spoken before I caught sight of the tragic look in his eyes as he once more looked up at me.

"If those politicians had only kept their word, we'd have had our shipyard deal to save us," he said, more to himself than to me. Yet that, I knew, was more an excuse than a reason.

"And if the rabbit-dog hadn't stopped to scratch, he might have caught the hare!" I none too mercifully quoted. My husband's face hardened as he sat staring across the table at me.

"I'm glad you can take it lightly enough to joke over," he remarked, as he got up from his chair. There was a ponderous sort of bitterness in his voice, a bitterness that brought me up short. I had to fight back the surge of pity which was threatening to strangle my voice, pity for a man, once so proud of his power, standing stripped and naked in his weakness.

"Heaven knows I don't want to joke, Honey-Chile," I told him. "But we're not the first of these wild-catting westerners who've come a cropper. And since we haven't robbed a bank, or—"

"It's just a little worse than that," cut in Dinky-Dunk, meeting my astonished gaze with a sort of Job-like exultation in his own misery. I promptly asked him what he meant. He sat down again, before speaking.

"I mean that I've lost Allie's money along with my own," he very slowly and distinctly said to me. And we sat there, staring at each other, for all the world like a couple of penguins on a sub-Arctic shingle.

Allie, I remembered, was Dinky-Dunk's English cousin, Lady Alicia Elizabeth Newland, who'd made the Channel flight in a navy plane and the year before had figured in a Devonshire motor-car accident. Dinky-Dunk had a picture of her, from *The Queen*, up in his study somewhere, the picture of a very debonair and slender young woman on an Irish hunter. He had a still younger picture of her in a tweed skirt and spats and golf-boots, on the brick steps of a Sussex country-house, with the jaw of a bull-dog resting across her knee. It was signed and dated and in a silver frame and every time I'd found myself polishing that oblong of silver I'd done so with a wifely ruffle of temper.

"How much was it?" I finally asked, still adhering to my rôle of the imperturbable chorus.

"She sent out over seven thousand pounds. She wanted it invested out here."

"Why?"

"Because of the new English taxes, I suppose. She said she wanted a ranch, but she left everything to me."

"Then it was a trust fund!"

Dinky-Dunk bowed his head, in assent.

"It practically amounted to that," he acknowledged.

"And it's gone?"

"Every penny of it."

"But, Dinky-Dunk," I began. I didn't need to continue, for he seemed able to read my thoughts.

"I was counting on two full sections for Allie in the Simmond's Valley tract. That land is worth thirty dollars an acre, unbroken, at any time. But the bank's swept that into the bag, of course, along with the rest. The whole thing was like a stack of nine-pins—when one tumbled, it knocked the other over. I thought I could manage to save that much for her, out of the ruin. But the bank saw the land-boom was petering out. They shut off my credit, and foreclosed on the city block—and that sent the whole card-house down."

I had a great deal of thinking to do, during the next minute or two.

"Then isn't it up to us to knuckle down, Dinky-Dunk, and make good on that Lady Alicia mistake? If we get a crop this year we can—"

But Dinky-Dunk shook his head. "A thousand bushels an acre couldn't get me out of this mess," he maintained.

"Why not?"

"Because your Lady Alicia and her English maid have already arrived in Montreal," he quietly announced.

"How do you know that?"

"She wrote to me from New York. She's had influenza, and it left her with a wheezy tube and a spot on her lungs, as she put it. Her doctor told her to go to Egypt, but she says Egypt's impossible, just now, and if she doesn't like our West she says she'll amble on to Arizona, or try California for the winter." He looked away, and smiled rather wanly. "She's counting on the big game shooting we can give her!"

"Grizzly, and buffalo, and that sort of thing?"

"I suppose so!"

"And she's on her way out here?"

"She's on her way out here to inspect a ranch which doesn't exist!"

I sat for a full minute gaping into Dinky-Dunk's woebegone face. And still again I had considerable thinking to do.

"Then we'll *make* it exist," I finally announced. But Dinky-Dunk, staring gloomily off into space, wasn't even interested. They had stunned the spirit out of him. He wasn't himself. They'd put him where even a well-turned Scotch scone couldn't appeal to him.

"Listen," I solemnly admonished. "If this Cousin Allie of yours is coming out here for a ranch, she's got to be presented with one."

"It sounds easy!" he said, not without mockery.

"And apparently the only way we can see that she's given her money's worth is to hand Casa Grande over to her. Surely if she takes this, bag and baggage, she ought to be half-satisfied."

Dinky-Dunk looked up at me as though I were assailing him with the ravings of a mad-woman. He knew how proud I had always been of that prairie home of ours.

"Casa Grande is yours—yours and the kiddies," he reminded me. "You've at least got that, and God knows you'll need it now, more than ever, God knows I've at least kept my hands off *that!*"

"But don't you see it can't be ours, it can't be a home, when there's a debt of honor between us and every acre of it."

"You're in no way involved in that debt," cried out my lord and master, with a trace of the old battling light in his eyes.

"I'm so involved in it that I'm going to give up the glory of a two-story house with hardwood floors and a windmill and a laundry chute and a real bathroom, before that English cousin of yours can find out the difference between a spring-lamb and a jack-rabbit!" I resolutely informed him. "And

I'm going to do it without a whimper. Do you know what we're going to do, O lord and master? We're going to take our kiddies and our chattels and our precious selves over to that Harris Ranch, and there we're going to begin over again just as we did nearly four years ago!" Dinky-Dunk tried to stop me, but I warned him aside. "Don't think I'm doing anything romantic. I'm doing something so practical that the more I think of it the more I see it's the only thing possible."

He sat looking at me as though he had forgotten what my features were like and was, just discovering that my nose, after all, hadn't really been put on straight. Then the old battling light grew stronger than ever in his eyes.

"It's *not* going to be the only thing possible," he declared. "And I'm not going to make *you* pay for my mistakes. Not on your life! I could have swung the farm lands, all right, even though they did have me with my back to the wall, if only the city stuff hadn't gone dead—so dead that to-day you couldn't even give it away. I'm not an embezzler. Allie sent me out that money to take a chance with, and by taking a double chance I honestly thought I could get her double returns. As you say, it was a gambler's chance. But the cards broke against me. The thing that hurts is that I've probably just about cleaned the girl out."

"How do you know that?" I asked, wondering why I was finding it so hard to sympathize with that denuded and deluded English cousin.

"Because I know what's happened to about all of the older families and estates over there," retorted Dinky-Dunk. "The government has pretty well picked them clean."

"Could I see your Cousin Allie's letters?"

"What good would it do?" asked the dour man across the table from me. "The fat's in the fire, and we've got to face the consequences."

"And that's exactly what I've been trying to tell you, you foolish old calvanistic autocrat! We've got to face the consequences, and the only way to do it is to do it the way I've said."

Dinky-Dunk's face softened a little, and he seemed almost ready to smile. But he very quickly clouded up again, just as my own heart clouded up. For I knew, notwithstanding my willingness to deny it, that I was once more acting on impulse, very much as I'd acted on impulse four long years ago in that residuary old horse-hansom in Central Park when I agreed to marry Duncan Argyll McKail before I was even in love with him. But, like most women, I was willing to let Reason step down off the bridge and have Intuition pilot me through the more troubled waters of a life-crisis. For I knew that I was doing the right thing, even though it seemed absurd, even though at first sight it seemed too prodigious a sacrifice, just as I'd done the right thing when in the face of tribal reasoning and logic I'd gone kiting off to a prairie-ranch and a wickiup with a leaky roof. It was a tumble, but it was a tumble into a pansy-bed. And I was thinking that luck would surely be with me a second time, though thought skidded, like a tire on a wet pavement, every time I tried to foresee what this newer change would mean to me and mine.

"You're not going to face another three years of drudgery and shack-dirt," declared Dinky-Dunk, following, oddly enough, my own line of thought. "You went through that once, and once was enough. It's not fair. It's not reasonable. It's not even thinkable. You weren't made for that sort of thing, and—"

"Listen to me," I broke in, doing my best to speak calmly and quietly. "Those three years were really the happiest three years of all my life. I love to remember them, for they mean so much more than all the others. There were a lot of the frills and fixin's of life that we had to do without. But those three years brought us closer together, Dinky-Dunk, than we have ever been since we moved into this big house and got on bowing terms again with luxury. I don't know whether you've given it much thought or not, husband o' mine, but during the last year or two there's been a change taking place in us. You've been worried and busy and forever on the wing, and there have been days when I've felt you were almost a stranger to me, as though I'd got to be a sort of accident in your life. Remember, Honey-Chile, I'm not blaming you; I'm only pointing out certain obvious truths, now the time for a little honest talk seems to have cropped up. You were up to your ears in a fight, in a tremendously big fight, for success and money; and you were doing it more for me and Dinkie and Poppsy and Pee-Wee than for yourself. You couldn't help remembering that I'd been a city girl and imagining that prairie-life was a sort of penance I was undergoing before passing on to the joys of paradise in an apartment-hotel with a mail-chute outside the door and the sound of the Elevated outside the windows. And you were terribly wrong in all that, for there have been days and days, Dinky-Dunk, when I've been homesick for that old slabsided ranch-shack and the glory of seeing you come in ruddy and hungry and happy for the ham and eggs and bread I'd cooked with my own hands. It seemed to bring us so gloriously close together. It seemed so homy and happy-go-lucky and soul-satisfying in its completeness, and we weren't forever fretting about bank-balances and taxes and over-drafts. I was just a rancher's wife then—and I can't help feeling that all along there was something in that simple life we didn't value enough. We were just rubes and hicks and clodhoppers and hay-tossers in those days, and we weren't staying awake nights worrying about land-speculations and waterfronts and trying to make ourselves millionaires when we might have been making ourselves more at peace with our own souls. And now that our card-house of high finance has gone to smash, I realize more than ever that I've got to be at peace with my own soul and on speaking terms with my own husband. And if this strikes you as an exceptionally long-winded sermon, my beloved, it's merely to make plain to you that I haven't surrendered to any sudden wave of emotionalism when I talk about migrating over to that Harris Ranch. It's nothing more than good old hard-headed, practical self-preservation, for I wouldn't care to live without you, Dinky-Dunk, any more than I imagine you'd care to live without your own self-respect."

I sat back, after what I suppose was the longest speech I ever made in my life, and studied my lord and master's face. It was not an easy map to decipher, for man, after all, is a pretty complex animal and even in his more elemental moments is played upon by pretty complex forces. And if there was humility on that lean and rock-ribbed countenance of my soul-mate there was also antagonism, and mixed up with the antagonism was a sprinkling of startled wonder, and tangled up with the wonder was a slightly perplexed brand of contrition, and interwoven with that again was a suggestion of allegiance revived, as though he had forgotten that he possessed a wife who had a heart and mind of her own, who was even worth sticking to when the rest of the world was threatening to give him the cold shoulder. He felt abstractedly down in his coat pocket for his pipe, which is always a helpful sign.

"It's big and fine of you, Chaddie, to put it that way," he began, rather awkwardly, and with just a touch of color coming to his rather gray-looking cheek-bones. "But can't you see that now it's the children we've got to think of?"

"I *have* thought of them," I quietly announced. As though any mother, on prairie or in metropolis, didn't think of them first and last and in-between-whiles! "And that's what simplifies the situation. I want them to have a fair chance. I'd rather they—"

"It's not quite that criminal," cut in Dinky-Dunk, with almost an angry flush creeping up toward his forehead.

"I'm only taking your own word for that," I reminded him, deliberately steeling my heart against the tides of compassion that were trying to dissolve it. "And I'm only taking what is, after all, the easiest course out of the situation."

Dinky-Dunk's color receded, leaving his face even more than ever the color of old cheese, for all the tan of wind and sun which customarily tinted it, like afterglow on a stubbled hillside.

"But Lady Alicia herself still has something to say about all this," he reminded me.

"Lady Alicia had better rope in her ranch when the roping is good," I retorted, chilled a little by her repeated intrusion into the situation. For I had no intention of speaking of Lady Alicia Newland with bated breath, just because she had a title. I'd scratched dances with a duke or two myself, in my time, even though I could already see myself once more wielding a kitchen-mop and tamping a pail against a hog-trough, over at the Harris Ranch.

"You're missing the point," began Dinky-Dunk.

"Listen!" I suddenly commanded. A harried roebuck has nothing on a young mother for acuteness of hearing. And thin and faint, from above-stairs, I caught the sound of a treble wailing which was promptly augmented into a duet.

"Poppsy's got Pee-Wee awake," I announced as I rose from my chair. It seemed something suddenly remote and small, this losing of a fortune, before the more imminent problem of getting a pair of crying babies safely to sleep. I realized that as I ran upstairs and started the swing-box penduluming back and forth. I even found myself much calmer in spirit by the time I'd crooned and soothed the Twins off again. And I was smiling a little, I think, as I went down to my poor old Dinky-Dunk, for he held out a hand and barred my way as I rounded the table to resume my seat opposite him.

"You don't despise me, do you?" he demanded, holding me by the sleeve and studying me with a slightly mystified eye. It was an eye as wistful as an old hound's in winter, an eye with a hunger I'd not seen there this many a day.

"Despise you, Acushla?" I echoed, with a catch in my throat, as my arms closed about him. And as he clung to me, with a forlorn sort of desperation, a soul-Chinook seemed to sweep up the cold fogs that had gathered and swung between us for so many months. I'd worried, in secret, about that fog. I'd tried to tell myself that it was the coming of the children that had made the difference, since a big strong man, naturally, had to take second place to those helpless little mites. But my Dinky-Dunk had a place in my heart which no snoozerette could fill and no infant could usurp. He was my man, my mate, my partner in this tangled adventure called life, and so long as I had him they could take the house with the laundry-chute and the last acre of land.

"My dear, my dear," I tried to tell him, "I was never hungry for money. The one thing I've always been hungry for is love. What'd be the good of having a millionaire husband if he looked like a man in a hair-shirt on every occasion when you asked for a moment of his time? And what's the good of life if you can't crowd a little affection into it? I was just thinking we're all terribly like children in a Maypole dance. We're so impatient to get our colored bands wound neatly about a wooden stick, a wooden stick that can never be ours, that we make a mad race of what really ought to be a careless and leisurely joy. We don't remember to enjoy the dancing, and we seem to get so mixed in our ends. So *carpe diem*, say I. And perhaps you remember that sentence from Epictetus you once wrote out on a slip of paper and pinned to my bedroom door: 'Better it is that great souls should live in small habitations than that abject slaves should burrow in great houses!'"

Dinky-Dunk, as I sat brushing back his top-knot, regarded me with a sad and slightly acidulated smile.

"You'd need all that philosophy, and a good deal more, before you'd lived for a month in a place like the Harris shack," he warned me.

"Not if I knew you loved me, O Kaikobad," I very promptly informed him.

"But you do know that," he contended, man-like. I was glad to find, though, that a little of the bitterness had gone out of his eyes.

"Feather-headed women like me, Diddums, hunger to hear that sort of thing, hunger to hear it all the time. On that theme they want their husbands to be like those little Japanese wind-harps that don't even know how to be silent."

"Then why did you say, about a month ago, that marriage was like Hogan's Alley, the deeper one got into it the tougher it was?"

"Why did you go off to Edmonton for three whole days without kissing me good-by?" I countered. I tried to speak lightly, but it took an effort. For my husband's neglect, on that occasion, had seemed the first intimation that the glory was over and done with. It had given me about the same feeling that we used to have as flapperettes when the circus-manager mounted the tub and began to announce the after-concert, all for the price of ten cents, one dime!

"I wanted to, Tabbie, but you impressed me as looking rather unapproachable that day."

"When the honey is scarce, my dear, even bees are said to be cross," I reminded him. "And that's the thing that disturbs me, Dinky-Dunk. It must disturb any woman to remember that she's left her happiness in one man's hand. And it's more than one's mere happiness, for mixed up with that is one's sense of humor and one's sense of proportion. They all go, when you make me miserable. And the Lord knows, my dear, that a woman without a sense of humor is worse than a dipper without a handle."

Dinky-Dunk sat studying me.

"I guess it was my own sense of proportion that got out of kilter, Gee-Gee," he finally said. "But there's one thing I want you to remember. If I got deeper into this game than I should have, it wasn't for what money meant to me. I've never been able to forget what I took you away from. I took you away from luxury and carted you out here to the end of Nowhere and had you leave behind about everything that made life decent. And the one thing I've always wanted to do is make good on that over-draft on your bank-account of happiness. I've wanted to give back to you the things you sacrificed. I knew I owed you that, all along. And when the children came I saw that I owed it to you more than ever. I want to give Dinky-Dink and Poppsy and Pee-Wee a fair chance in life. I want to be able to start them right, just as much as you do. And you can't be dumped back into a three-roomed wickiup, with three children to bring up, and feel that you're doing the right thing by your family."

It wasn't altogether happy talk, but deep down in my heart I was glad we were having it. It seemed to clear the air, very much as a good old-fashioned thunder-storm can. It left us stumbling back to the essentials of existence. It showed us where we stood, and what we meant to each other, what we must mean to each other. And now that the chance had come, I intended to have my say out.

"The things that make life decent, Dinky-Dunk, are the things that we carry packed away in our own immortal soul, the homely old things like honesty and self-respect and contentment of mind. And if we've got to cut close to the bone before we can square up our ledger of life, let's start the carving while we have the chance. Let's get our conscience clear and know we're playing the game."

I was dreadfully afraid he was going to laugh at me, it sounded so much like pulpiteering. But I was in earnest, passionately in earnest, and my lord and master seemed to realize it.

"Have you thought about the kiddies?" he asked me, for the second time.

"I'm always thinking about the kiddies," I told him, a trifle puzzled by the wince which so simple a statement could bring to his face. His wondering eye, staring through the open French doors of the living-room, rested on my baby grand.

"How about *that*?" he demanded, with a grim head-nod toward the piano.

"That may help to amuse Lady Alicia," I just as grimly retorted.

He stared about that comfortable home which we had built up out of our toil, stared about at it as I've seen emigrants stare back at the receding shores of the land they loved. Then he sat studying my face.

"How long is it since you've seen the inside of the Harris shack?" he suddenly asked me.

"Last Friday when I took the bacon and oatmeal over to Soapy and Francois and Whinstane Sandy," I told him.

"And what did you think of that shack?"

"It impressed me as being sadly in need of soap and water," I calmly admitted. "It's like any other shack where two or three men have been batching—no better and no worse than the wickiup I came to here on my honeymoon."

Dinky-Dunk looked about at me quickly, as though in search of some touch of malice in that statement. He seemed bewildered, in fact, to find that I was able to smile at him.

"But that, Chaddie, was nearly four long years ago," he reminded me, with a morose and meditative clouding of the brow. And I knew exactly what he was thinking about.

"I'll know better how to go about it this time," I announced with my stubbornest Doctor Pangless grin.

"But there are two things you haven't taken into consideration," Dinky-Dunk reminded me.

"What are they?" I demanded.

"One is the matter of ready money."

"I've that six hundred dollars from my Chilean nitrate shares," I proudly announced. "And Uncle Carlton said that if the Company ever gets reorganized it ought to be a paying concern."

Dinky-Dunk, however, didn't seem greatly impressed with either the parade of my secret nest-egg or the promise of my solitary plunge into finance. "What's the other?" I asked as he still sat frowning over his empty pipe.

"The other is Lady Alicia herself," he finally explained.

"What can she do?"

"She may cause complications."

"What kind of complications?"

"I can't tell until I've seen her," was Dinky-Dunk's none too definite reply.

"Then we needn't cross that bridge until we come to it," I announced as I sat watching Dinky-Dunk pack the bowl of his pipe and strike a match. It seemed a trivial enough movement. Yet it was monumental in its homeliness. It was poignant with a power to transport me back to earlier and happier days, to the days when one never thought of feathering the nest of existence with the illusions of old age. A vague loneliness ate at my heart, the same as a rat eats at a cellar beam.

I crossed over to my husband's side and stood with one hand on his shoulder as he sat there smoking. I waited for him to reach out for my other hand. But the burden of his troubles seemed too heavy to let him remember. He smoked morosely on. He sat in a sort of self-immuring torpor, staring out over what he still regarded as the wreck of his career. So I stooped down and helped myself to a very smoky kiss before I went off up-stairs to bed. For the children, I knew, would have me awake early enough—and nursing mothers needs must sleep!

Thursday the Second

I have won my point. Dinky-Dunk has succumbed. The migration is under way. The great trek has begun. In plain English, we're moving.

I rather hate to think about it. We seem so like the Children of Israel bundled out of a Promised Land, or old Adam and Eve turned out of the Garden with their little Cains and Abels. "We're up against it, Gee-Gee," as Dinky-Dunk grimly observed. I could see that we were, without his telling me. But I refused to acknowledge it, even to myself. And it wasn't the first occasion. This time, thank heaven, I can at least face it with fortitude, if not with relish. I don't like poverty. And I don't intend to like it. And I'm not such a hypocrite as to make a pretense of liking it. But I do intend to show my Dinky-Dunk that I'm something more than a household ornament, just as I intend to show myself that I can be something more than a breeder of children. I have given my three "hostages to fortune"—and during the last few days when we've been living, like the infant Moses, in a series of rushes, I have awakened to the fact that they are indeed hostages. For the little tikes, no matter how you maneuver, still demand a big share of your time and energy. But one finally manages, in some way or another. Dinky-Dunk threatens to expel me from the Mothers' Union when I work over time, and Poppsy and Pee-Wee unite in letting me know when I've been foolish enough to pass my fatigue-point. Yet I've been sloughing off some of my old-time finicky ideas about child-raising and reverting to the peasant-type of conduct which I once so abhorred in my Finnish Olga. And I can't say that either I or my family seem to have suffered much in the process. I feel almost uncannily well and strong now, and am a wolf for work. If nothing else happened when our apple-cart went over, it at least broke the monotony of life. I'm able to wring, in fact, just a touch of relish out of all this migrational movement and stir, and Casa Grande itself is already beginning to remind me of a liner's stateroom about the time the pilot comes aboard and the donkey-engines start to clatter up with the trunk-nets.

For three whole days I simply ached to get at the Harris Ranch shack, just to show what I could do with it. And I realized when Dinky-Dunk and I drove over to it in the buckboard, on a rather nippy morning when it was a joy to go spanking along the prairie trail with the cold air etching rosettes on your cheek-bones, that it was a foeman well worthy of my steel. At a first inspection, indeed, it didn't look any too promising. It didn't exactly stand up on the prairie-floor and shout "Welcome" into your ears. There was an overturned windmill and a broken-down stable that needed a new roof, and a well that had a pump which wouldn't work without priming. There was an untidy-looking corral, and a reel for stringing up slaughtered beeves, and an overturned Red River cart bleached as white as a buffalo skeleton. As for the wickiup itself, it was well-enough built, but lacking in windows and quite unfinished as to the interior.

I told Dinky-Dunk I wanted two new window-frames, beaverboard for inside lining, and two gallons of paint. I have also demanded a lean-to, to serve as an extra bedroom and nursery, and a brand-new bunk-house for the hired "hands" when they happen to come along. I have also insisted on a covered veranda and sleeping porch on the south side of the shack, and fly-screens, and repairs to the chimney to stop the range from smoking. And since the cellar, which is merely timbered, will have to be both my coal-hole and my storage-room, it most assuredly will have to be cemented. I explained to Dinky-Dunk that I wanted eave-troughs on both the shack and the stable, for the sake of the soft-water, and proceeded to point out the need of a new washing-machine, and a kiddie-coop for Poppsy and Pee-Wee as soon as the weather got warm, and a fence, hog-tight and horse-high, about my half-acre of kitchen garden.

Dinky-Dunk sat staring at me with a wry though slightly woebegone face.

"Look here, Lady-Bird, all this sort of thing takes 'rhino,' which means ready money. And where's it going to come from?"

"I'll use that six hundred, as long as it lasts," I blithely retorted. "And then we'll get credit."

"But my credit is gone," Dinky-Dunk dolorously acknowledged.

"Then what's the matter with mine?" I demanded. I hadn't meant to hurt him, when I said that. But I refused to be downed. And I intended to make my ranch a success.

"It's still quite unimpaired, I suppose," he said in a thirty-below-zero sort of voice.

"Goose!" I said, with a brotherly pat on his drooping shoulder. But my lord and master refused to be cheered up.

"It's going to take more than optimism to carry us through this first season," he explained to me. "And the only way that I can see is for me to get out and rustle for work."

"What kind of work?" I demanded.

"The kind there's a famine for, at this very moment," was Dinky-Dunk's reply.

"You don't mean being somebody else's hired man?" I said, aghast.

"A hired man can get four dollars a day and board," retorted my husband. "And a man and team can get nine dollars a day. We can't keep things going without ready money. And there's only one way, out here, of getting it."

Dinky-Dunk was able to laugh at the look of dismay that came into my face. I hadn't stopped to picture myself as the wife of a hired "hand." I hadn't quite realized just what we'd descended to. I hadn't imagined just how much one needed working capital, even out here on the edge of Nowhere.

"But never that way, Diddums!" I cried out in dismay, as I pictured my husband bunking with a sweaty-smelling plowing-gang of Swedes and Finns and hoboing about the prairie with a thrashing outfit of the Great Unwashed. He'd get cooties, or rheumatism, or a sunstroke, or a knife between his ribs some fine night—and then where'd I be? I couldn't think of it. I couldn't think of Duncan Argyll McKail, the descendant of Scottish kings and second-cousin to a title, hiring out to some old skinflint of a farmer who'd have him up at four in the morning and keep him on the go until eight at night.

"Then what other way?" asked Dinky-Dunk.

"You leave it to me," I retorted. I made a bluff of saying it bravely enough, but I inwardly decided that instead of sixteen yards of fresh chintz I'd have to be satisfied with five yards. Poverty, after all, is not a picturesque thing. But I didn't intend to be poor, I protested to my troubled soul, as I went at that Harris Ranch wickiup, tooth and nail, while Iroquois Annie kept an eye on Dinkie and the Twins.

These same Twins, I can more than ever see, are going to be somewhat of a brake on the wheels of industry. I have even been feeding on "slops," of late, to the end that Poppsy and Pee-Wee may thrive. And already I see sex-differences asserting themselves. Pee-Wee is a bit of a stoic, while his sister shows a tendency to prove a bit of a squealer. But Poppsy is much the daintier feeder of the two. I'll probably have to wean them both, however, before many more weeks slip by. As soon as we get settled in our new shack and I can be sure of a one-cow supply of milk I'll begin a bottle-feed once in every twenty-four hours. Dinky-Dunk says I ought to take a tip from the Indian mother, who sometimes nurses her babe until he's two and three years old. I asked Ikkie—as Dinkie calls Iroquois Annie—about this and Ikkie says the teepee squaw has no cow's milk and has to keep on the move, so she feeds him breast-milk until he's able to eat meat. Ikkie informs me that she has seen a papoose turn away from its mother's breast to take a puff or two at a pipe. From which I assume that the noble Red Man learns to smoke quite early in life.

Ikkie has also been enlightening me on other baby-customs of her ancestors, explaining that it was once the habit for a mother to name her baby for the first thing seen after its birth. That, I told Dinky-Dunk, was probably why there were so many "Running Rabbits," and "White Pups" and "Black Calfs" over on the Reservation. And that started me maun enlarging on the names of Indians he'd known, the most elongated of which, he acknowledged, was probably "The-Man-Who-Gets-Up-In-The-Middle-Of-The-Night-To-Feed-Oats-To-His-Pony," while the most descriptive was "Slow-To-Come-Over-The-Hill," though "Shot-At-Many-Times" was not without value, and "Long-Time-No-See-Him," as the appellative for a disconsolate young squaw, carried a slight hint of the Indian's genius for nomenclature. Another thing mentioned by Dunkie, which has stuck in my memory, was his running across a papoose's grave in an Indian burying-ground at Pincer Creek, when he was surveying, where the Indian baby had been buried—above-ground, of course—*in an old Saratoga trunk*. That served to remind me of Francois' story about "Old Sun," who preceded "Running Rabbit"—note the name—as chief of the Alberta Blackfoot tribe, and always carried among his souvenirs of conquest a beautiful white scalp, with hair of the purest gold, very long and fine, but would never reveal how or where he got it. Many a night, when I couldn't sleep, I've worried about that white scalp, and dramatized the circumstances of its gathering. Who was the girl with the long and lovely tresses of purest gold? And did she die bravely? And did she meet death honorably and decently, or after the manner of certain of the Jesuits' *Relations?*...

I have had a talk with Whinnie, otherwise Whinstane Sandy, who has been ditching at the far end of our half-section. I explained the situation to him quite openly, acknowledging that we were on the rocks but not yet wrecked, and pointing out that there might be a few months before the ghost could walk again. And Whinstane Sandy has promised to stick. Poor old Whinnie not only promised to stick, but volunteered that if he could get over to Seattle or 'Frisco and raise some money on his Klondike claim our troubles would be a thing of the past. For Whinnie, who is an old-time miner and stampeder, is, I'm afraid, a wee bit gone in the upper story. He dreams he has a claim up North where there's millions and millions in gold to be dug out. On his moose-hide watch-guard he wears a nugget almost half as big as a praline, a nugget he found himself in ninety-nine, and he'd part with his life, I believe, before he'd part with that bangle of shiny yellow metal. In his chest of black-oak, too, he keeps a package of greasy and dog-eared documents, and some day, he proclaims, those papers will bring him into millions of money.

I asked Dinky-Dunk about the nugget, and he says it's genuine gold, without a doubt. He also says there's one chance in a hundred of Whinnie actually having a claim up in the gold country, but doubts if the poor old fellow will ever get up to it again. It's about on the same footing, apparently, as Uncle Carlton's Chilean nitrate mines. For Whinnie had a foot frozen, his third winter on the Yukon, and this, of course, has left him lame. It means that he's not a great deal of good when it comes to working the land, but he's a clever carpenter, and a good cement-worker, and can chore about milking the cows and looking after the stock and repairing the farm implements. Many a night, after supper, he tells us about the Klondike in the old days, about the stampedes of ninety-eight and ninety-nine, and the dance-halls and hardships and gamblers and claim-jumpers. I have always had a weakness for him because of his blind and unshakable love for my little Dinkie, for whom he whittles out ships and windmills and decoy-ducks. But when I explained things to simple-minded old Whinnie, and he offered to hand over the last of his ready money—the money he was hoarding dollar by dollar to get back to his hidden *El Dorado*—it brought a lump up into my throat.

I couldn't accept his offer, of course, but I loved him for making it. And whatever happens, I'm going to see that Whinnie has patches on his panties and no holes in his socks as long as he abides beneath our humble roof-tree. I intend to make the new bunk-house just as homy and comfortable as I can, so that Whinnie, under that new roof, won't feel that he's been thrust out in the cold. But I must have my own house for myself and my babes. Soapy Stennet, by the way, has been paid off by Dinky-Dunk and is moving on to the Knee-Hill country, where he says he can get good wages breaking and seeding. Soapy, of course, was a good man on the land, but I never took a shine to that hard-eyed Canuck, and we'll get along, in some way or other, without him. For, in the language of the noble Horatius, "I'll find a way, or make it!"

On the way back to Casa Grande to-night, after a hard day's work, I asked Dinky-Dunk if we wouldn't need some sort of garage over at the Harris Ranch, to house our automobile. He said he'd probably put doors on the end of one of the portable granaries and use that. When I questioned if a car of that size would ever fit into a granary he informed me that we couldn't keep our big car.

"I can get seventeen hundred dollars for that boat," he explained. "We'll have to be satisfied with a tin Lizzie, and squander less on gasoline."

So once again am I reminded that the unpardonable crime of poverty is not always picturesque. But I wrestled with my soul then and there, and put my pride in my pocket and told Dinky-Dunk I didn't give a rip what kind of a car I rode in so long as I had such a handsome *chauffeur*. And I reached out and patted him on the knee, but he was too deep in his worries about business matters, I suppose, to pay any attention to that unseemly advance.

To-night after supper, when the bairns were safely in bed, I opened up the baby grand, intent on dying game, whatever happened or was to happen. But my concert wasn't much of a success. When you do a thing for the last time, and know it's to be the last time, it gives you a graveyardy sort of feeling, no matter how you may struggle against it. And the blither the tune the heavier it seemed to make my heart. So I swung back to the statelier things that have come down to us out of the cool and quiet of Time. I eased my soul with the *Sonata Appassionata* and lost myself in the *Moonlight* and pounded out the *Eroica*. But my fingers were stiff and my touch was wooden—so it was small wonder my poor lord and master tried to bury himself in his four-day-old newspaper. Then I tried Schubert's *Rosamonde*, though that wasn't much of a success. So I wandered on through Liszt to Chopin. And even Chopin struck me as too soft and sugary and far-away for a homesteader's wife, so I sang

"In the dead av the night, acushla,

When the new big house is still,"—

to see if it would shake any sign of recognition out of my harried old Dinky-Dunk.

As I beheld nothing more than an abstracted frown over the tip-top edge of his paper, I defiantly swung into *The Humming Coon*, which apparently had no more effect than Herman Lohr. So with malice aforethought I slowly and deliberately pounded out the Beethoven Funeral March. I lost myself, in fact, in that glorious and melodic wail of sorrow, merged my own puny troubles in its god-like immensities, and was brought down to earth by a sudden movement from Dinky-Dunk.

"Why rub it in?" he almost angrily demanded as he got up and left the room....

But that stammering little soul-flight has done me good. It has given me back my perspective. I refuse to be downed. I'm still the captain of my soul. I'm still at the wheel, no matter if we are rolling a bit. And life, in some way, is still going to be good, still well worth the living!

Wednesday the Eighth

Dinky-Dunk has had word that Lady Alicia is on her way west. He seems to regard that event as something very solemn, but I refuse to take seriously either her ladyship or her arrival. To-night, I'm more worried about Dinkie, who got at the floor-shellac with which I'd been furbishing up the bathroom at Casa Grande. He succeeded in giving his face and hair a very generous coat of it—and I'm hoping against hope he didn't get too much of it in his little stomach. He seems normal enough, and in fairly good spirits, but I had to scrub his face with coal-oil, to get it clean, and his poor little baby-skin is burnt rather pink.

The winter has broken, the frost is coming out of the ground and the mud is not adding to our joy in life. Our last load over to the Harris shack was ferried and tooled through a batter. On the top of it (the *load*, and not the batter!) I placed Olie's old banjo, for whatever happens, we mustn't be entirely without music.

Yesterday Dinky-Dunk got Paddy saddled and bridled for me. Paddy bucked and bit and bolted and sulked and tried to brush his rider off against the corral posts. But Dinky-Dunk fought it out with him, and winded him, and mastered him, and made him meek enough for me to slip up into the saddle. My riding muscles, however, have gone flabby, and two or three miles, for the first venture, was all I cared to stand. But I'm glad to know that Paddy can be pressed into service again, whenever the occasion arises. Poor old Bobs, by the way, keeps looking at me with a troubled and questioning eye. He seems to know that some unsettling and untoward event is on the way. When a coyote howled last night, far off on the sky-line, Bobs poured out his soul in an answering solo of misery. This morning, when I was pretty busy, he poked his head between my knees. I had a dozen things calling me, but I took the time to rub his nose and brush back his ears and tell him he was the grandest old dog on all God's green earth. And he repaid me with a look of adoration that put springs under my heels for the rest of the morning, and came and licked Pee-Wee's bare heels, and later Poppsy's, when I was giving them their bath.

Friday the Tenth

Lady Alicia has arrived. So have her trunks, eleven in number—count 'em!—trunks of queer sizes and shapes, of pigskin and patent leather and canvas, with gigantic buckles and straps, and all gaudily initialed and plastered with foreign labels. Her ladyship had to come, of course, at the very worst time of year, when the mud was at its muckiest and the prairie was at its worst. The trails were simply awful, with the last of the frost coming out of the ground and mother earth a foot-deep sponge of engulfing stickiness. All the world seemed turned to mud. I couldn't go along, of course, when Dinky-Dunk started off in the Teetzels' borrowed spring "democrat" to meet his English cousin at the Buckhorn station, with Whinstane Sandy and the wagon trailing behind for the luggage.

We expected a lady in somewhat delicate health, so I sent along plenty of rugs and a foot-warmer, and saw that the house was well heated, and the west room bed turned down. Even a hot-water bottle stood ready and waiting to be filled.

But Lady Alicia, when she arrived with Dinky-Dunk just before nightfall, didn't impress me as very much of an invalid. She struck me more as a very vital and audacious woman, neither young nor old, with an odd quietness of manner to give a saber-edge to her audacity. I could hear her laughing, musically and not unpleasantly, at the mud-coated "democrat," which on its return looked a good deal like a 'dobe hut mounted on four chariot wheels. But *everything*, for that matter, was covered with mud, horses and harness and robes and even the blanket in which Lady Alicia had wrapped herself. She had done this, I could see, to give decent protection to a Redfern coat of plucked beaver with immense reveres, though there was mud enough on her stout tan shoes, so unmistakably English in their common-sense solidity, and some on her fur turban and even a splash or two on her face. That face, by the way, has an apple-blossom skin of which I can see she is justly proud. And she has tourmaline eyes, with reddish hazel specks in an iris of opaque blue, and small white teeth and lips with a telltale curve of wilfulness about them. She isn't exactly girlish, but with all her worldly wisdom she has a touch of the clinging-ivy type which must make her inordinately appealing to men. Her voice is soft and full-voweled, with that habitual rising inflection characteristic of the English, and that rather insolent drawl which in her native land seems the final flower of unchallenged privilege. Her hands are very white and fastidious looking, and most carefully manicured. She is, in fact, wonderful in many ways, but I haven't yet decided whether I'm going to like her or not. Her smile strikes me as having more glitter than warmth, and although she is neither tall nor full-bodied, she seems to have the power of making point take the place of weight. Yet, oddly enough, there is an occasional air of masculine loose-jointedness about her movements, a half-defiant sort of slouch and swagger which would probably carry much farther in her Old World than in our easier-moving New World, where disdain of decorum can not be regarded as quite such a novelty.

It wasn't until she was within the protecting door of Casa Grande that I woke up to the fact of how incongruous she stood on a northwest ranch. She struck me, then, as distinctly an urban product, as one of those lazy and silk-lined and limousiny sort of women who could face an upholstery endurance-test without any apparent signs of heart-failure, but might be apt to fall down on engine-performance. Yet I was determined to suspend all judgment, even after I could see that she was making no particular effort to meet me half-way, though she did acknowledge that Dinkie, in his best bib and tucker, was a "dawling" and even proclaimed that his complexion— due, of course, to the floor-shellac and coal-oil—reminded her very much of the higher-colored English children. She also dutifully asked about Poppsy and Pee-Wee, after announcing that she found the house uncomfortably hot, and seemed surprised that Dinky-Dunk should descend to the stabling and feeding and watering of his own horses.

She appeared rather constrained and ill-at-ease, in fact, until Dinky-Dunk had washed up and joined us. Yet I saw, when we sat down to our belated supper, that the fair Allie had the abundant and honest appetite of a healthy boy. She also asked if she might smoke between courses—which same worried the unhappy Dinky-Dunk much more than it did me. My risibilities remained untouched until she languidly remarked that any woman who had twins on the prairie ought to get a V.C.

But she automatically became, I retorted, a K.C.B. This seemed to puzzle the cool-eyed Lady Alicia.

"That means a Knight Commander of the Bath," she said with her English literalness.

"Exactly," I agreed. And Dinky-Dunk had to come to her rescue and explain the joke, like a court-interpreter translating Cree to the circuit judge, so that by the time he got through it didn't seem a joke at all and his eyes were flashing me a code-signal not to be too hard on a tenderfoot. When, later on, Lady Alicia looked about Casa Grande, which we'd toiled and moiled and slaved to make like the homestead prints in the immigration pamphlets, she languidly acknowledged that it was rather ducky, whatever that may mean, and asked Dinky-Dunk if there'd be any deer-shooting this spring. I notice, by the way, that she calls him "Dooncan" and sometimes

"Cousin Doonk," which strikes me as being over-intimate, seeing he's really her second cousin. It seems suggestive of some hidden joke between them. And Duncan addresses her quite openly as "Allie."

This same Allie has brought a lady's maid with her whom she addresses, *more Anglico*, simply by her surname of "Struthers." Struthers is a submerged and self-obliterating and patient-eyed woman of nearly forty, I should say, with a face that would be both intelligent and attractive, if it weren't so subservient. But I've a floaty sort of feeling that this same maid knows a little more than she lets on to know, and I'm wondering what western life will do to her. In one year's time, I'll wager a plugged nickel against an English sovereign, she'll not be sedately and patiently dining at second-table and murmuring "Yes, me Lady" in that meek and obedient manner. But it fairly took my breath, the adroit and expeditious manner in which Struthers had that welter of luggage unstrapped and unbuckled and warped into place and things stowed away, even down to her ladyship's rather ridiculous folding canvas bathtub. In little more than two shakes she had a shimmering litter of toilet things out on the dresser tops, and even a nickel alcohol-lamp set up for brewing the apparently essential cup of tea. It made me wish that I had a Struthers or two of my own on the string. And that made my thoughts go hurtling back to my old Hortense and how we had parted at the Hotel de L'Athenee, and to Theobald Gustav and his aunt the Baroness, and the old lost life that seemed such years and years away....

But I promptly put the lid down on those over-disturbing reminiscences. There should be no *post-mortems* in this family circle, no jeremiads over what has gone before. This is the New World and the new age where life is too crowded for regrets. I am a woman twenty-seven years old, married and the mother of three children. I am the wife of a rancher who went bust in a land-boom and is compelled to start life over again. I must stand beside him, and start from the bottom. I must also carry along with me all the hopes and prospects of three small lives. This, however, is something which I refuse to accept as a burden and a handicap. It is a weight attached to me, of course, but it's only the stabilizing weight which the tail contributes to the kite, allowing it, in the end, to fly higher and keep steadier. It won't seem hard to do without things, when I think of those kiddies of mine, and hard work should be a great and glorious gift, if it is to give them the start in life which they deserve. We'll no longer quarrel, Diddums and I, about whether Dinkie shall go to Harvard or McGill. There'll be much closer problems than that, I imagine, before Dinkie is out of his knickers. Fate has shaken us down to realities—and my present perplexity is to get possession of six new milk-pans and that new barrel-churn, not to mention the flannelette I simply must have for the Twins' new nighties!...

Saturday the Eleventh

These imperturbable English! I didn't know whether I should take off my hat to 'em or despise 'em. They seem to come out of a different mold to what we Americans do. Lady Alicia takes everything as a matter of course. She seems to have accepted one of the finest ranches west of the Peg as impassively as an old work-horse accepts a new shoe. Even the immensity of our western prairie-land hasn't quite stumped her. She acknowledged that Casa Grande was "quaint," and is obviously much more interested in Iroquois Annie, the latter being partly a Redskin, than in my humble self. I went up in her estimation a little, however, when I coolly accepted one of her cigarettes, of which she has brought enough to asphyxiate an army. I managed it all right, though it was nearly four long years since I'd flicked the ash off the end of one—in Chinkie's yacht going up to Monte Carlo. But I was glad enough to drop the bigger half of it quietly into my nasturtium window-box, when the lady wasn't looking.

The lady in question, by the way, seems rather disappointed to find that Casa Grande has what she called "central heating." About the middle of next February, when the thermometer is flirting with the forty-below mark, she may change her mind. I suppose the lady expected to get a lodge and a deer-park along with her new home, to say nothing of a picture 'all—open to the public on Fridays, admission one shilling—and a family ghost, and, of course, a terrace for the aforesaid ghost to ambulate along on moonlight nights.

But the thing that's been troubling me, all day long, is: Now that Lady Alicia has got her hand-made ranch, what's she going to do with it? I scarcely expect her to take me into her confidence on the matter, since she seems intent on regarding me as merely a bit of the landscape. The disturbing part of it all is that her aloofness is so unstudied, so indifferent in its lack of deliberation. It makes me feel like a bump on a log. I shouldn't so much mind being actively and martially snubbed, for that would give me something definite and tangible to grow combative over. But you can't cross swords with a Scotch mist.

With Dinky-Dunk her ladyship is quite different. I never see that look of mild impatience in her opaque blue eyes when he is talking. She flatters him openly, in fact, and a man takes to flattery, of course, as a kitten takes to cream. Yet with all her outspokenness I am conscious of a tremendous sense of reservation. Already, more than once, she has given me a feeling which I'd find it very hard to describe, a feeling as though we were being suspended over peril by something very fragile. It's the feeling you have when you stand on one of those frail little Alpine bridges that can sway so forebodingly with your own weight and remind you that nothing but a rustic paling or two separates you from the thousand-footed abysses below your heels.

But I mustn't paint the new mistress of Casa Grande all in dark colors. She has her good points, and a mind of her own, and a thought or two of her own. Dinky-Dunk was asking her about Egypt. That country, she retorted, was too dead for her. She couldn't wipe out of her heart the memory of what man had suffered along the banks of the Nile, during the last four thousand years, what millions of men had suffered there because of religion and war and caste.

"I could never be happy in a country of dead races and dead creeds and dead cities," protested Lady Alicia, with more emotion than I had expected. "And those are the things that always stare me in the face out there."

This brought the talk around to the New World.

"I rather fancy that a climate like yours up here," she coolly observed, "would make luxuries of furniture and dress, and convert what should be the accidents of life into essentials. You will always have to fight against nature, you know, and that makes man attach more importance to the quest of comfort. But when he lives in the tropics, in a surrounding that leaves him with few desires, he has time to sit down and think about his soul. That's why you can never have a great musician or a great poet in your land of blizzards, Cousin Dooncan. You are all kept too busy laying up nuts for the winter. You can't afford to turn gipsy and go off star-gazing."

"You can if you join the I. W. W.," I retorted. But the allusion was lost on her.

"I can't imagine a Shelley or a Theocritus up here on your prairie," she went on, "or a Marcus Aurelius in the real-estate business in Winnipeg."

Dinky-Dunk was able to smile at this, though I wasn't.

"But we have the glory of doing things," I contended, "and somebody, I believe, has summed up your Marcus Aurelius by saying he left behind him a couple of beautiful books, an execrable son, and a decaying nation. And we don't intend to decay! We don't live for the moment, it's true. But we live for To-morrow. We write epics in railway lines, and instead of working out sonnets we build new cities, and instead of sitting down under a palm-tree and twiddling our thumbs we turn a wilderness into a new nation, and grow grain and give bread to the hungry world where the gipsies don't seem quite able to make both ends meet!"

I had my say out, and Lady Alicia sat looking at me with a sort of mild and impersonal surprise. But she declined to argue about it all. And it was just as well she didn't, I suppose, for I had my Irish up and didn't intend to sit back and see my country maligned.

But on the way home to the Harris Ranch last night, with Dinky-Dunk silent and thoughtful, and a cold star or two in the high-arching heavens over us, I found that my little fire of enthusiasm had burnt itself out and those crazy lines of John Davidson kept returning to my mind:

"After the end of all things,

After the years are spent,

After the loom is broken,

After the robe is rent,

Will there be hearts a-beating,

Will friend converse with friend,

Will men and women be lovers,

After the end?"

I felt very much alone in the world, and about as cheerful as a moonstruck coyote, after those lines had rattled in my empty brain like a skeleton in the wind. It wasn't until I saw the light in our wickiup window and heard Bobs' bay of welcome through the crystal-clear twilight that the leaden weight of desolation slipped off the ledge of my heart. But as I heard that deep-noted bark of gladness, that friendly intimation of guardianship unrelaxed and untiring, I remembered that I had one faithful and unexacting friend, even though it was nothing better than a dog.

Sunday the Twelfth

Dinky-Dunk rather surprised me to-day by asking why I was so stand-offish with his Cousin Allie. I told him that I wasn't in the habit of curling up like a kitten on a slab of Polar ice.

"But she really likes you, Tabbie," my husband protested. "She wants to know you and understand you. Only you keep intimidating her, and placing her at a disadvantage."

This was news to me. Lady Alicia, I'd imagined, stood in awe of nothing on the earth beneath nor the heavens above. She can speak very sharply, I've already noticed, to Struthers, when the occasion arises. And she's been very calm and deliberate, as I've already observed, in her manner of taking over Casa Grande. For she *has* formally taken it over, Dinky-Dunk tells me, and in a day or two we all have to trek to town for the signing of the papers. She is, apparently, going to run the ranch on her own hook, and in her own way. It will be well worth watching.

I was rather anxious to hear the particulars of the transfer to Lady Allie, but Dinky-Dunk seemed a little reluctant to go into details, and I didn't intend to make a parade of my curiosity. I can bide my time.... Yesterday I put on my old riding-suit, saddled Paddy, fed the Twins to their last mouthful, and went galloping off through the mud to help bring the cattle over to the Harris Ranch. I was a sight, in that weather-stained old suit and ragged toppers, even before I got freckled and splashed with prairie-mud. I was standing up in the stirrups laughing at Francois, who'd had a bad slip and fallen in a puddle just back of our old corral, when her Ladyship came out. She must have taken me for a drunken cowboy who'd rolled into a sheep-dip, for my nose was red and my old Stetson sombrero was crooked on the back of my head and even my hair was caked with mud. She called to me, rather imperiously, so I went stampeding up to her, and let Paddy indulge in that theatrical stop-slide of his, on his haunches, so that it wasn't until his nose was within two feet of her own that she could be quite sure she wasn't about to be run down.

Her eyes popped a little when she saw it was a woman on Paddy, though she'd refused to show a trace of fear when we went avalanching down on her. Then she studied my get-up.

"I should rather like to ride that way," she coolly announced.

"It's the only way," I told her, making Paddy pirouette by pressing a heel against his short-ribs. She meant, of course, riding astride, which must have struck her as the final word in audacity.

"I like your pony," next remarked Lady Alicia, with a somewhat wistful intonation in her voice.

"He's a brick," I acknowledged. Then I swung about to help Francois head off a bunch of rampaging steers. "Come and see us," I called back over my shoulder. If Lady Alicia answered, I didn't have time to catch what she said.

But that romp on Paddy has done me good. It shook the solemnity out of me. I've just decided that I'm not going to surrender to this middle-aged Alice-Sit-by-the-Fire stuff before my time. I'm going to refuse to grow old and poky. I'm going to keep the spark alive, the sacred spark of youth, even though folks write me down as the biggest loon west of the Dirt Hills. So dear Lord—this is my prayer—whatever You do to me, keep me *alive*. O God, don't let me, in Thy divine mercy, be a Dead One. Don't let me be a soured woman with a self-murdered soul. Keep the wine of youth in my body and the hope of happiness in my heart. Yea, permit me deeply to live and love and laugh, so that youth may abide in my bones, even as it did in that once-renowned Duchess of Lienster,

Who lived to the age of a hundred and ten,

To die of a fall from a cherry-tree then!

My poor old Dinky-Dunk, by the way, meanders about these days so moody and morose it's beginning to disturb me. He's at the end of his string, and picked clean to the bone, and I'm beginning to see that it's my duty to buoy that man up, to nurse him back into a respectable belief in himself. His nerves are a bit raw, and he's not always responsible for his manners. The other night he came in tired, and tried to read, when Poppsy and Pee-Wee were both going it like the Russian Balalaika. To tell the truth, their little tummies were a bit upset, because the food purveyor had had too strenuous a day to be regular in her rounds.

"Can't you keep those squalling brats quiet?" Dinky-Dunk called out to me. It came like a thunder clap. It left me gasping, to think that he could call his own flesh and blood "squalling brats." And I was shocked and hurt, but I decided not to show it.

"Will somebody kindly page Lord Chesterfield?" I quietly remarked as I went to the Twins and wheeled them out to the kitchen, where I gave them hot peppermint and rubbed their backs and quieted them down again.

I suppose there's no such thing as a perfect husband. That's a lesson we've all got to learn, the same as all children, apparently, have to find out that acorns and horse-chestnuts aren't edible. For the nap wears off men the same as it does off clothes. I dread to have to write it down, but I begin to detect thinnesses in Dinky-Dunk, and a disturbing little run or two in the even web of his character. But he knows when he's played Indian and attempts oblique and rather shamefaced efforts to make amends, later on, when it won't be too noticeable. Last night, as I sat sewing, our little Dinkie must have had a bad dream, for he wakened from a sound sleep with a scream of terror. Dinky-Dunk went to him first, and took him up and sang to him, and when I glanced in I saw a rumply and tumbly and sleepy-eyed tot with his kinky head against his father's shoulder. As I took up my sewing again and heard Dinky-Dunk singing to his son, it seemed a proud and happy and contented sort of voice. It rose and fell in that next room, in a sort of droning bass, and for the life of me I can't tell why, but as I stopped in my sewing and sat listening to that father singing to his sleepy-eyed first-born, it brought the sudden tears to my eyes. It has been a considerable length of time, *en passant*, since I found myself sitting down and pumping the brine. I must be getting hardened in my old age.

Tuesday the Fourteenth

Lady Allie sent over for Dinky-Dunk yesterday morning, to fix the windmill at Casa Grande. They'd put it out of commission in the first week, and emptied the pressure-tank, and were without water, and were as helpless as a couple of canaries. We have a broken windmill of our own, right here at home, but Diddums went meekly enough, although he was in the midst of his morning work—and work is about to loom big over this ranch, for we're at last able to get on the land. And the sooner you get on the land, in this latitude, the surer you are of your crop. We daren't shave down any margins of chance. We need that crop....

I am really beginning to despair of Iroquois Annie. She is the only thing I can get in the way of hired help out here, and yet she is hopeless. She is sullen and wasteful, and she has never yet learned to be patient with the children. I try to soften and placate her with the gift of trinkets, for there is enough Redskin in her to make her inordinately proud of anything with a bit of flash and glitter to it. But she is about as responsive to actual kindness as a diamond-back rattler would be, and some day, if she drives me too far, I'm going off at half-cock and blow that breed into mince-meat.

By the way, I can see myself writ small in little Dinkie, my moods and waywardnesses and wicked impulses, and sudden chinooks of tenderness alternating with a perverse sort of shrinking away from love itself, even when I'm hungering for it. I can also catch signs of his pater's masterfulness cropping out in him. Small as he is, he disturbs me by that combative stare of his. It's almost a silent challenge I see in his eyes as he coolly studies me, after a proclamation that he will be spanked if he repeats a given misdeed.

I'm beginning to understand the meaning of that very old phrase about one's chickens coming home to roost. I can even detect sudden impulses of cruelty in little Dinkie, when, young and tender as he appears to the casual eye, a quick and wilful passion to hurt something takes possession of him. Yesterday I watched him catch up his one-eyed Teddy Bear, which he loves, and beat its head against the shack-floor. Sometimes, too, he'll take possession of a plate and fling it to the floor with all his force, even though he knows such an act is surely followed by punishment. It's the same with Poppsy and Pee-Wee, with whom he is apt to be over-rough, though his offenses in that direction may still be touched with just a coloring of childish jealousy, long and arduously as I struggle to implant some trace of fraternal feeling in his anarchistic little breast. There are even times, after he's been hugging my knees or perhaps stroking my cheek with his little velvet hands and murmuring "Maaa-maa!" in his small and bird-like coo, when he will suddenly turn savage and try to bite my patella or pull my ear out by the root.

Most of this cruelty, I think, is born of a sheer excess of animal spirits. But not all of it. Some of it is based on downright wilfulness. I have seen him do without things he really wanted, rather than unbend and say the necessary "Ta-ta" which stands for both "please" and "thanks" in his still limited vocabulary. The little Hun will also fall on his picture-books, at times, and do his best to tear the linen pages apart, flailing them about in the air with genuine Berserker madness. But along with this, as I've already said, he has his equally sudden impulses of affection, especially when he first wakens in the morning and his little body seems to be singing with the pure joy of living. He'll smooth my hair, after I've lifted him from the crib into my bed, and bury his face in the hollow of my neck and kiss my cheek and pat my forehead and coo over me until I squeeze him so hard he has to grunt. Then he'll probably do his best to pick my eyes out, if I pretend to be asleep, or experiment with the end of my nose, to see why it doesn't lift up like a door-knocker. Then he'll snuggle down in the crook of my arm, perfectly still except for the wriggling of his toes against my hip, and croon there with happiness and contentment, like a ring-neck dove.

Friday the Seventeenth

Lady Allie couldn't have been picked quite clean to the bone by the McKails, for she's announced her intention of buying a touring-car and a gasoline-engine and has had a conference with Dinky-Dunk on the matter. She also sent to Montreal for the niftiest little English sailor suit, for Dinkie, together with a sailor hat that has "Agamemnon" printed in gold letters on its band.

I ought to be enthusiastic about it, but I can't. Dinkie himself, however, who calls it his "new nailor nuit"—not being yet able to manage the sibilants—struts about in it proud as a peacock, and refuses to sit down in his supper-chair until Ikkie has carefully wiped off the seat of the same, to the end that the beloved nailor nuit might remain immaculate. He'll lose his reverence for it, of course, when he knows it better. It's a habit men have, big or little.

Lady Allie has confessed that she is succumbing to the charm of prairie life. It ought to make her more of a woman and less of a silk-lined idler. Dinky-Dunk still nurses the illusion that she is delicate, and manages to get a lot of glory out of that clinging-vine pose of hers, big oak that he is! But it is simply absurd, the way he falls for her flattery. She's making him believe that he's a twentieth-century St. Augustine and a Saint Christopher all rolled into one. Poor old Dinky-Dunk, I'll have to keep an eye on him or they'll be turning his head, for all its gray hairs. He is wax in the hand of designing beauty, as are most of the race of man. And the fair Allie, I must acknowledge, is dangerously appealing to the eye. It's no wonder poor old Dinky-Dunk nearly broke his neck trying to teach her to ride astride. But I intend to give her ladyship an inkling, before long, that I'm not quite so stupid as I seem to be. She mustn't imagine she can "vamp" my Kaikobad with impunity. It's a case of any port in a storm, I suppose, for she has to practise on somebody. But I must say she looks well on horseback and can lay claim to a poise that always exacts its toll of respect. She rides hard, though I imagine she would be unwittingly cruel to her mount. Yet she has been more offhanded and friendly, the last two or three times she has dropped over to the shack, and she is kind to the kiddies, especially Dinkie. She seems genuinely and unaffectedly fond of him. As for me, she thinks I'm hard, I feel sure, and is secretly studying me—trying to decipher, I suppose, what her sainted cousin could ever see in me to kick up a dust about!

Lady Allie's London togs, by the way, make me feel rather shoddy and slattern. I intend to swing in a little stronger for personal adornment, as soon as we get things going again. When a woman gives up, in that respect, she's surely a goner. And I may be a hard-handed and slabsided prairie huzzy, but there was a time when I stood beside the big palms by the fountain in the conservatory of Prince Ernest de Ligne's Brussels house in the *Rue Montoyer* and the Marquis of What-Ever-His-Name-Was bowed and set all the orders on his chest shaking when he kissed my hand and proclaimed that I was the most beautiful woman in Belgium!

Yes, there was such a time. But it was a long, long time ago, and I never thought then I'd be a rancher's wife with a barrel-churn to scald out once a week and a wheezy old pump to prime in the morning and a little hanging garden of Babylon full of babies to keep warm and to keep fed and to keep from falling on their boneless little cocos! I might even have married Theobald Gustav von Brockdorff and turned into an embassy ball lizard and ascended into the old family landau of his aunt the baroness, to disport along the boulevards therein very much like an oyster on the half-shell. I might have done all that, and I might not. But it's all for the best, as the greatest pessimist who ever drew the breath of life once tried to teach in his *Candide*. And in my career, as I have already written, there shall be no jeremiads.

Sunday the Nineteenth

I've been trying to keep tab on the Twins' weight, for it's important that they should gain according to schedule. But I've only Dinky-Dunk's bulky grain-scales, and it's impossible to figure down to anything as fine as ounces or even quarter-pounds on such a balancer. Yet my babies, I'm afraid, are not gaining as they ought. Poppsy is especially fretful of late. Why can't somebody invent children without colic, anyway? I have a feeling that I ought to run on low gear for a while. But that's a luxury I can't quite afford.

Last night, when I was dead-tired and trying to give the last licks to my day's work without doing a Keystone fall over the kitchen table, Dinky-Dunk said: "Why haven't you ever given a name to this new place? They tell me you have a genius for naming things—and here we are still dubbing our home the Harris shack."

"I suppose it ought to be an Indian name, in honor of Ikkie?" I suggested, doing my best to maintain an unruffled front. And Duncan Argyll absently agreed that it might just as well.

"Then what's the matter with calling it Alabama?" I mordantly suggested. "For as I remember it, that means 'Here we rest.' And I can imagine nothing more appropriate."

I was half-sorry I said it, for the Lord deliver me always from a sarcastic woman. But I've a feeling that the name is going to stick, whether we want it or not. At any rate, Alabama Ranch has rather a musical turn to it....

I wonder if there are any really perfect children in the world? Or do the good little boys and girls only belong to that sentimentalized mid-Victorian fiction which tried so hard to make the world like a cross between an old maid's herb-garden and a Sunday afternoon in a London suburb? I have tried talking with little Dinkie, and reasoning with him. I have striven long and patiently to blow his little spark of conscience into the active flame of self-judgment. And averse as I am to cruelty and hardness, much as I hate the humiliation of physical punishment, my poor kiddie and I can't get along without the slipper. I have to spank him, and spank him soundly, about once a week. I'm driven to this, or there'd be no sleep nor rest nor roof about our heads at Alabama Ranch. I don't give a rip what Barrie may have written about the bringing up of children—for he never had any of his own! He never had an imperious young autocrat to democratize. He never had a family to de-barbarize, even though he did write very pretty books about the subject. It's just another case, I suppose, where fiction is too cowardly or too finicky to be truthful. I had theories about this child-business myself, at one time, but my pipe of illusion has plumb gone out. It wasn't so many years ago that I imagined about all a mother had to do was to dress in clinging *negligees*, such as you see in the toilet-soap advertisements, and hold a spotless little saint on her knee, or have a miraculously docile nurse in cap and apron carry in a little paragon all done up in dotted Swiss and rose-pink, and pose for family groups, not unlike popular prints of the royal family in full evening dress, on *Louis Quinze* settees. And later on, of course, one could ride out with a row of sedate little princelings at one's side, so that one could murmur, when the world marveled at their manners, "It's blood, my dears, merely blood!"

But fled, and fled forever, are all such dreams. Dinkie prefers treading on his bread-and-butter before consuming it, and does his best to consume the workings of my sewing-machine, and pokes the spoons down through the crack in the kitchen floor, and betrays a weakness for yard-mud and dust in preference to the well-scrubbed boards of the sleeping porch, which I've tried to turn into a sort of nursery by day. Most fiction, I find, glides lightly over this eternal Waterloo between dirt and water—for no active and healthy child is easy to keep clean. That is something which you never, never, really succeed at. All that you can do is to keep up the struggle, consoling yourself with the memory that cleanness, even surgical cleanness, is only an approximation. The plain everyday sort of cleanness promptly resolves itself into a sort of neck and neck race with dirt and disorder, a neck and neck race with the soap-bar habitually running second. Sometimes it seems hopeless. For it's incredible what can happen to an active-bodied boy of two or three years in one brief but crowded afternoon. It's equally amazing what can happen to a respectably furnished room after a healthy and high-spirited young Turk has been turned loose in it for an hour or two.

It's a battle, all right. But it has its compensations. It *has* to, or the race would wither up like an unwatered cucumber-vine. Who doesn't really love to tub a plump and dimpled little body like my Dinkie's? I'm no petticoated Paul Peel, but I can see enough beauty in the curves of that velvety body to lift it up and bite it on its promptly protesting little flank. And there's unclouded glory in occasionally togging him out in spotless white, and beholding him as immaculate as a cherub, if only for one brief half-hour. It's the transiency of that spotlessness, I suppose, which crowns it with glory. If he was forever in that condition, we'd be as indifferent to it as we are to immortelles and wax flowers. If he was always cherubic and perfect, I suppose, we'd never appreciate that perfection or know the joy of triumphing over the mother earth that has an affinity for the finest of us.

But I *do* miss a real nursery, in more ways than one. The absence of one gives Dinkie the range of the whole shack, and when on the range he's a timber-wolf for trouble, and can annoy his father even more than he can me by his depredations. Last night after supper I heard an icy voice speaking from the end of the dining-room where Dinky-Dunk has installed his desk.

"Will you kindly come and see what your son has done?" my husband demanded, with a sort of in-this-way-madness-lies tone.

I stepped in through the kitchen door, ignoring the quite unconscious humor of "*my* son" under the circumstances, and found that Dinkie had provided a novel flavor for his dad by emptying the bottle of ink into his brand-new tin of pipe-tobacco. There was nothing to be done, of course, except to wash as much of the ink as I could off Dinkie's face. Nor did I reveal to his father that three days before I had carefully compiled a list of his son and heir's misdeeds, for one round of the clock. They were, I find, as follows:

Overturning a newly opened tin of raspberries, putting bread-dough in his ears; breaking my nail-buffer, which, however, I haven't used for a month and more; paring the bark, with the bread-knife, off the lonely little scrub poplar near the kitchen door, our one and only shade; breaking a drinking-glass, which was accident; cutting holes with the scissors in Ikkie's new service-apron; removing the covers from two of his father's engineering books; severing the wire joint in my sewing-machine belt (expeditiously and secretly mended by Whinnie, however, when he came in with the milk-pails); emptying what was left of my bottle of vanilla into the bread mixer; and last but not least, trying to swallow and nearly choking on my silver thimble, in which he seems to find never-ending disappointment because it will not remain fixed on the point of his nose.

It may sound like a busy day, but it was, on the whole, merely an average one. Yet I'll wager a bushel of number one Northern winter wheat to a doughnut ring that if Ibsen had written an epilogue for *The Doll's House*, Nora would have come crawling back to her home and her kiddies, in the end.

Wednesday the Twenty-second

Lady Allie is either dunderheaded or designing. She has calmly suggested that her rural phone-line be extended from Casa Grande to Alabama Ranch so that she can get in touch with Dinky-Dunk when she needs his help and guidance. Even as it is, he's called on about five times a week, to run to the help of that she-remittance-man in corduroy and dog-skin gauntlets and leggings.

She seems thunderstruck to find that she can't get the hired help she wants, at a moment's notice. Dinky-Dunk says she's sure to be imposed on, and that although she's as green as grass, she's really anxious to learn. He feels that it's his duty to stand between her and the outsiders who'd be only too ready to impose on her ignorance.

She rode over to see the Twins yesterday, who were sleeping out under the fly-netting I'd draped over them, the pink-tinted kind they put over fruit-baskets in the city markets and shops. Poppsy and Pee-Wee looked exactly like two peaches, rosy and warm and round.

Lady Allie stared at them with rather an abstracted eye, and then, idiot that she is, announced that she'd like to have twelve. But talk is cheap. The modern woman who's had even half that number has pretty well given up her life to her family. It's remarkable, by the way, the silent and fathomless pity I've come to have for childless women. The thought of a fat spinster fussing over a French poodle or a faded blond forlornly mothering a Pekinese chow gives me a feeling that is at least first cousin to sea-sickness.

Lady Allie, I find, has very fixed and definite theories as to the rearing of children. They should never be rocked or patted, or be given a "comfort," and they should be in bed for the night at sundown. There was a time I had a few theories of my own, but I've pretty well abandoned them. I've been taught, in this respect, to travel light, as the overland voyageurs of this country would express it, to travel light and leave the final resort to instinct.

Friday the Twenty-fourth

I was lazy last night, so both the ink-pot and its owner had a rest. Or perhaps it wasn't so much laziness as wilful revolt against the monotony of work, for, after all, it's not the 'unting as 'urts the 'osses, but the 'ammer, 'ammer, 'ammer on the 'ard old road! I loafed for a long time in a sort of sit-easy torpor, with Bobs' head between my knees while Dinky-Dunk pored over descriptive catalogues about farm-tractors, for by hook or by crook we've got to have a tractor for Alabama Ranch.

"Bobs," I said after studying my collie's eyes for a good many minutes, "you are surely one grand old dog!"

Whereupon Bobs wagged his tail-stump with sleepy content. As I bent lower and stared closer into those humid eyes of his, it seemed as though I were staring down into a bottomless well, through a peep-hole into Infinity, so deep and wonderful was that eye, that dusky pool of love and trust. It was like seeing into the velvet-soft recesses of a soul. And I could stare into them without fear, just as Bobs could stare back without shame. That's where dogs are slightly different from men. If I looked into a man's eye like that he'd either rudely inquire just what the devil I was gaping at or he'd want to ask me out to supper in one of those Pompeian places where a bald-headed waiter serves lobsters in a *chambre particulière*.

But all I could see in the eye of my sedate old Bobs was love, love infinite and inarticulate, love too big ever to be put into words.

"Dinky-Dunk," I said, interrupting my lord and master at his reading, "if God is really love, as the Good Book says, I don't see why they ever started talking about the Lamb of God."

"Why shouldn't they?" asked Diddums, not much interested.

"Because lambs may be artless and innocent little things, but when you've got their innocence you've got about everything. They're not the least bit intelligent, and they're self-centered and self-immured. Now, with dogs it's different. Dogs love you and guard you and ache to serve you." And I couldn't help stopping to think about the dogs I'd known and loved, the dogs who once meant so much in my life: Chinkie's Bingo, with his big baptizing tongue and his momentary rainbow as he emerged from the water and shook himself with my stick still in his mouth; Timmie with his ineradicable hatred for cats; Maxie with all his tricks and his singsong of howls when the piano played; Schnider, with his mania for my slippers and undies, which he carried into most unexpected quarters; and Gyp, God bless him, who was so homely of face and form but so true blue in temper and trust.

"Life, to a dog," I went on, "really means devotion to man, doesn't it?"

"What are you driving at, anyway?" asked Dinky-Dunk.

"I was just wondering," I said as I sat staring into Bobs' eyes, "how strange it would be if, after all, God was really a dog, the loving and faithful Watch-Dog of His universe!"

"Please don't be blasphemous," Dinky-Dunk coldly remarked.

"But I'm not blasphemous," I tried to tell him. "And I was never more serious in my life. There's even something sacred about it, once you look at it in the right way. Just think of the Shepherd-Dog of the Stars, the vigilant and affectionate Watcher who keeps the wandering worlds in their folds! That's not one bit worse than the lamb idea, only we've got so used to the lamb it doesn't shock us into attention any more. Why, just look at these eyes of Bobs right now. There's more nobility and devotion and trust and love in them than was ever in all the eyes of all the lambs that ever frisked about the fields and sheep-folds from Dan to Beersheba!"

"Your theory, I believe, is entertained by the Igorrotes," remarked Dinky-Dunk as he made a pretense of turning back to his tractor-pamphlet. "The Igorrotes and other barbarians," he repeated, so as to be sure the screw was being turned in the proper direction.

"And now I know why she said the more she knew about men the better she liked dogs," I just as coldly remarked, remembering Madame de Stael. "And I believe you're jealous of poor old Bobs just because he loves me more than you do."

Dinky-Dunk put down his pamphlet. Then he called Bobs over to his side of the table. But Bobs, I noticed, didn't go until I'd nodded approval. So Dinky-Dunk took his turn at sitting with Bobs' nose in his hand and staring down into the fathomless orbs that stared up at him.

"You'll never get a lady, me lud, to look up at you like that," I told him.

"Perhaps they have," retorted Dinky-Dunk, with his face slightly averted.

"And having done so in the past, there's the natural chance that they'll do so in the future," I retorted, making it half a question and half a statement. But he seemed none too pleased at that thrust, and he didn't even answer me when I told him I supposed I was his Airedale, because they say an Airedale is a one-man dog.

"Then don't at least get distemper," observed my Kaikobad, very quietly, over the top of his tractor-catalogue.

I made no sign that I had heard him. But Dinky-Dunk would never have spoken to me that way, three short years ago. And I imagine he knows it. For, after all, a change has been taking place, insubstantial and unseen and subterranean, a settling of the foundations of life which comes not only to a building as it grows older but also to the heart as it grows older. And I'm worried about the future.

Monday the—Monday the I-forget-what

It's Monday, blue Monday, that's all I remember, except that there's a rift in the lute of life at Alabama Ranch. Yesterday of course was Sunday. And out of that day of rest Dinky-Dunk spent just five hours over at Casa Grande. When he showed up, rather silent and constrained and an hour and a half late for dinner, I asked him what had happened.

He explained that he'd been adjusting the carbureter on Lady Alicia's new car.

"Don't you think, Duncan," I said, trying to speak calmly, though I was by no means calm inside, "that it's rather a sacrifice of dignity, holding yourself at that woman's beck and call?"

"We happen to be under a slight debt of obligation to *that woman*," my husband retorted, clearly more upset than I imagined he could be.

"But, Dinky-Dunk, you're not her hired man," I protested, wondering how, without hurting him, I could make him see the thing from my standpoint.

"No, but that's about what I'm going to become," was his altogether unexpected answer.

"I can't say that I quite understand you," I told him, with a sick feeling which I found it hard to keep under. Yet he must have noticed something amusingly tragic in my attitude, for he laughed, though it wasn't without a touch of bitterness. And laughter, under the circumstances, didn't altogether add to my happiness.

"I simply mean that Allie's made me an offer of a hundred and fifty dollars a month to become her ranch-manager," Dinky-Dunk announced with a casualness that was patently forced. "And as I can't wring that much out of this half-section, and as I'd only be four-flushing if I let outsiders come in and take everything away from a tenderfoot, I don't see—"

"And such a lovely tenderfoot," I interrupted.

"—I don't see why it isn't the decent and reasonable thing," concluded my husband, without stooping to acknowledge the interruption, "to accept that offer."

I understood, in a way, every word he was saying; yet it seemed several minutes before the real meaning of a somewhat startling situation seeped through to my brain.

"But surely, if we get a crop," I began. It was, however, a lame beginning. And like most lame beginnings, it didn't go far.

"How are we going to get a crop when we can't even raise money enough to get a tractor?" was Dinky-Dunk's challenge. "When we haven't help, and we're short of seed-grain, and we can't even get a gang-plow on credit?"

It didn't sound like my Dinky-Dunk of old, for I knew that he was equivocating and making excuses, that he was engineering our ill luck into an apology for worse conduct. But I was afraid of myself, even more than I was afraid of Dinky-Dunk. And the voice of Instinct kept whispering to me to be patient.

"Why couldn't we sell off some of the steers?" I valiantly suggested.

"It's the wrong season for selling steers," Dinky-Dunk replied with a ponderous sort of patience. "And besides, those cattle don't belong to me."

"Then whose are they?" I demanded.

"They're yours," retorted Dinky-Dunk, and I found his hair-splitting, at such a time, singularly exasperating.

"I rather imagine they belonged to the family, if you intend it to remain a family."

He winced at that, as I had proposed that he should.

"It seems to be getting a dangerously divided one," he flung back, with a quick and hostile glance in my direction.

I was ready to fly to pieces, like a barrel that's lost its hoops. But a thin and quavery and over-disturbing sound from the swing-box out on the sleeping-porch brought me up short. It was a pizzicato note which I promptly recognized as the gentle Pee-Wee's advertisement of wakefulness. So I beat a quick and involuntary retreat, knowing only too well what I'd have ahead of me if Poppsy joined in to make that solo a duet.

But Pee-Wee refused to be silenced, and what Dinky-Dunk had just said felt more and more like a branding-iron against my breast. So I carried my wailing infant back to the dinner-table where my husband still stood beside his empty chair. The hostile eye with which he regarded the belcantoing Pee-Wee reminded me of the time he'd spoken of his own off-spring as "squalling brats." And the memory wasn't a tranquillizing one. It was still another spur roweling me back to the ring of combat.

"Then you've decided to take that position?" I demanded as I surveyed the cooling roast-beef and the fallen Yorkshire pudding.

"As soon as they can fix up my sleeping-quarters in the bunk-house over at Casa Grande," was Dinky-Dunk's reply. He tried to say it casually, but didn't quite succeed, for I could see his color deepen a little. And this, in turn, led to a second only too obvious gesture of self-defense.

"My monthly check, of course, will be delivered to you," he announced, with an averted eye.

"Why to me?" I coldly inquired.

"It wouldn't be of much use to me," he retorted. And I resented his basking thus openly in the fires of martyrdom.

"In that case," I asked, "what satisfaction are you getting out of your new position?"

That sent the color ebbing from his face again, and he looked at me as I'd never seen him look at me before. We'd both been mauled by the paw of Destiny, and we were both nursing ragged nerves and oversensitized spirits, facing each other as irritable as teased rattlers, ready to thump rocks with our head. More than once I'd heard Dinky-Dunk proclaim that the right sort of people never bickered and quarreled. And I remembered Theobald Gustav's pet aphorism to the effect that *Hassen machts nichts*. But life had its limits. And I wasn't one of those pink-eared shivery little white mice who could be intimidated into tears by a frown of disapproval from my imperial mate. And married life, after all, is only a sort of *guerre d'usure*.

"And you think you're doing the right thing?" I demanded of my husband, not without derision, confronting him with a challenge on my face and a bawling Pee-Wee on my hip.

Dinky-Dunk sniffed.

"That child seems to have its mother's disposition," he murmured, ignoring my question.

"The prospects of its acquiring anything better from its father seem rather remote," I retorted, striking blindly. For that over-deft adding of insult to injury had awakened every last one of my seven sleeping devils. It was an evidence of cruelty, cold and calculated cruelty. And by this time little waves of liquid fire were running through my tingling body.

"Then I can't be of much service to this family," announced Dinky-Dunk, with his maddening note of mockery.

"I fail to see how you can be a retriever for a flabby-minded idler and the head of this household at one and the same time," I said out of the seething crater-fogs of my indignation.

"She's never impressed me as being flabby," he ventured, with a quietness which only a person who knew him would or could recognize as dangerous.

"Well, I don't share your admiration for her," I retorted, letting the tide of vitriol carry me along in its sweep.

Dinky-Dunk's face hardened.

"Then what do you intend doing about it?" he demanded.

That was a poser, all right. That was a poser which, I suppose, many a woman at some time in her life has been called on to face. What did I intend doing about it? I didn't care much. But I at least intended to save the bruised and broken hulk of my pride from utter annihilation.

"I intend," I cried out with a quaver in my voice, "since you're not able to fill the bill, to be head of this household myself."

"That sounds like an ultimatum," said Dinky-Dunk very slowly, his face the sickly color of a meerschaum-pipe bowl.

"You can take it any way you want to," I passionately proclaimed, compelled to raise my voice to the end that it might surmount Pee-Wee's swelling cries. "And while you're being lackey for Lady Alicia Newland I'll run this ranch. I'll run it in my own way, and I'll run it without hanging on to a woman's skirt!"

Dinky-Dunk stared at me as though he were looking at me through a leper-squint. But he had been brutal, was being brutal. And it was a case of fighting fire with fire.

"Then you're welcome to the job," I heard him proclaiming out of his blind white heat of rage. "After *that*, I'm through!"

"It won't be much of a loss," I shot back at him, feeling that he'd soured a bright and sunny life into eternal blight.

"I'll remember that," he said with his jaw squared and his head down. I saw him push his chair aside and wheel about and stride away from the Yorkshire pudding with the caved-in roof, and the roast-beef that was as cold as my own heart, and the indignantly protesting Pee-Wee who in some vague way kept reminding me that I wasn't quite as free-handed as I had been so airily imagining myself. For I mistily remembered that the Twins, before the day was over, were going to find it a very flatulent world. But I wasn't crushed. For there are times when even wives and worms will turn. And this was one of them.

Thursday the Thirtieth

It's a busy three days I've been having, and if I'm a bit tuckered out in body I'm still invincible in spirit. For I've already triumphed over a tangle or two and now I'm going to see this thing through. I'm going to see Alabama Ranch make good.

I teamed in to Buckhorn, with Dinkie and the Twins and Ikkie bedded down in the wagon-box on fresh wheat-straw, and had a talk with Syd Woodward, the dealer there. It took me just about ten minutes to get down to hard-pan with him, once he was convinced that I meant business. He's going to take over my one heavy team, Tumble-Weed and Cloud-Maker, though it still gives my heart a wrench to think of parting with those faithful animals. I'm also going to sell off fifteen or eighteen of the heaviest steers and turn back the tin Lizzie, which can be done without for a few months at least.

But, on the other hand, I'm going to have an 8-16 tractor that'll turn over an acre of land in little more than an hour's time, and turn it over a trifle better than the hired hand's usual "cut and cover" method, and at a cost of less than fifty cents an acre. Later on, I can use my tractor for hauling, or turn it to practically any other form of farm-power there may be a call for. I'm also getting a special grade of seed-wheat. There was a time when I thought that wheat was just merely wheat. It rather opened my eyes to be told that in one season the Shippers' Clearance Association definitely specified and duly handled exactly four hundred and twenty-eight grades of this particular grain. Even straight Northern wheat, without the taint of weed-seed, may be classified in any of the different numbers up to six, and also assorted into "tough," "wet," "damp," "musty," "binburnt" and half a dozen other grades and conditions, according to the season. But since I'm to be a wheat-grower, it's my duty to find out all I can about the subject.

I am also the possessor of three barrels of gasoline, and a new disk-drill, together with the needed repairs for the old drill which worked so badly last season. I've got Whinstane Sandy patching up the heavy sets of harness, and at daybreak to-morrow I'm going to have him out on the land, and also Francois, who has promised to stay with us another two weeks. It may be that I'll put Ikkie in overalls and get her out there too, for there's not a day, not an hour, to be lost. I want my crop in. I want my seed planted, and the sooner the better.

Whinstane Sandy, on account of his lame foot, can't follow a plow. But there's no reason he shouldn't run a tractor. If it wasn't for my bairns, of course, I'd take that tractor in hand myself. But my two little hostages to fortune cut off that chance. I've decided, however, to have Whinnie build a canopy-top over the old buckboard, and fit two strong frames, just behind the dashboard, that will hold a couple of willow-baskets, end to end. Then I can nest Poppsy and Pee-Wee in these two baskets, right under my nose, with little Dinkie beside me in the seat, and drive from one end of the ranch to the other and see that the work is being done, and done right. The Lord knows how I'll get back to the shack in time to rustle the grub—but we'll manage, in some way.

The Twins have been doing better, the last week or two. And I rather dread the idea of weaning them. If I had somebody to look after them I could, I suppose, get a breast-pump and leave their mid-morning and mid-afternoon luncheons in cold-storage for them, and so ride my tractor without interruption. I remember a New York woman who did that, left the drawn milk of her breast on ice, so that she might gad and shop for a half-day at a time. But the more I think it over the more unnatural and inhuman it seems. Yet to hunt for help, in this busy land, is like searching for a needle in a hay-stack. Already, in the clear morning air, one can hear the stutter and skip and cough of the tractors along the opalescent sky-line, accosting the morning sun with their rattle and tattle of harvests to be. And I intend to be in on the game.

Sunday the Second

I'm too busy to puddle in spilt milk or worry over things that are past. I can't even take time to rhapsodize over the kitchen-cabinet to which Whinnie put the finishing touches to-day at noon, though I know it will save me many a step. Poor old Whinnie, I'm afraid, is more a putterer than a plowman. He's had a good deal of trouble with the tractor, and his lame foot seems to bother him, on account of the long hours, but he proclaims he'll see me through.

Tractor-plowing, I'm beginning to discover, isn't the simple operation it sounds, for your land, in the first place, has to be staked off and marked with guidons, since you must know your measurements and have your headlands uniform and your furrows straight or there'll be a woeful mix-up before you come to the end of your job. The great trouble is that a tractor can't turn in its own length, as a team of horses can. Hence this deploying space must be wasted, or plowed later with horses, and your headlands themselves must be wide enough for the turning radius of your tractor. Some of the ranchers out here, I understand, even do their tractor-plowing in the form of a series of elongated figure-eights, beginning at one corner of their tract, claiming this reduces the time spent with plows out of the ground. But that looked too complex for me to tackle.

Then, too, machinery has one thing in common with man: they occasionally get out of kilter at the very time you expect most from them. So this morning I had to bend, if I did not actually break, the Sabbath by working on my tractor-engine. I put on Ikkie's overalls—for I *have* succeeded in coercing Ikkie into a jumper and the riding-seat of the old gang-plow—and went out and studied that tractor. I was determined to understand just what was giving the trouble.

It was two hours before I located the same, which was caused by the timer. But I've conquered the doggoned thing, and got her to spark right, and I went a couple of rounds, Sunday and all, just to make sure she was in working order. And neither my actions nor my language, I know, are those of a perfect lady. But any one who'd lamped me in that get-up, covered with oil and dust and dirt, would know that never again could I be a perfect lady. I'm a wiper, a greaser, a clodhopper, and, according to the sullen and brooding-eyed Ikkie, a bit of a slave-driver. And the odd part of it all is that I'm wringing a perverse sort of enjoyment out of the excitement and the novelty of the thing. I'm being something more than a mere mollusk. I'm making my power felt, and producing results. And self-expression, I find, is the breath of life to my soul. But I've scarcely time to do my hair, and my complexion is gone, and I've got cracks in my cheek-skin. I'm getting old and ugly, and no human being will ever again love me. Even my own babies gape at me kind of round-eyed when I take them in my arms.

But I'm wrong there, and I know I'm wrong. My little Dinkie will always love me. I know that by the way his little brown arms cling about my wind-roughened neck, by the way he burrows in against my breast and hangs on to me and hollers for his Mummsy when she's out of sight. He's not a model youngster, I know. I'm afraid I love him too much to demand perfection from him. It's the hard and selfish women, after all, who make the ideal mothers—at least from the standpoint of the disciplinarian. For the selfish woman refuses to be blinded by love, just as she refuses to be imposed upon and declines to be troubled by the thought of inflicting pain on those perverse little toddlers who grow so slowly into the knowledge of what is right and wrong. It hurts me like Sam-Hill, sometimes, to have to hurt my little man-child. When the inevitable and slow-accumulating spanking *does* come, I try to be cool-headed and strictly just about it—for one look out of a child's eyes has the trick of bringing you suddenly to the judgment-bar. Dinkie, young as he is, can already appraise and arraign me and flash back his recognition of injustice. More than once he's made me think of those lines of Frances Lyman's:

"Just a look of swift surprise

From the depths of childish eyes,

Yet my soul to judgment came,

Cowering, as before a flame.

Not a word, a lisp of blame:

Just a look of swift surprise

In the quietly lifted eyes!"

Saturday the Twenty-second

I've got my seed in, glory be! The deed is done; the mad scramble is over. And Mother Earth, as tired as a child of being mauled, lies sleeping in the sun.

If, as some one has said, to plow is to pray, we've been doing a heap of mouth-worship on Alabama Ranch this last few weeks. But the final acre has been turned over, the final long sea of furrows disked and plank-dragged and seeded down, and after the heavy rains of Thursday night there's just the faintest tinge of green, here and there, along my billiard-table of a granary-to-be.

But the mud is back, and to save my kitchen floor, last night, I trimmed down a worn-out broom, cut off most of the handle, and fastened it upside down in a hole I'd bored at one end of the lower door-step.

All this talk of mine about wheat sounds as though I were what they call out here a Soil Robber, or a Land Miner, a get-rich-quick squatter who doesn't bother about mixed farming or the rotation of crops, with no true love for the land which he impoverishes and leaves behind him when he's made his pile. I want to make my pile, it's true, but we'll soon have other things to think about. There's my home garden to be made ready, and the cattle and pigs to be looked after, and a run to be built for my chickens. The latter, for all their neglect, have been laying like mad and I've three full crates of eggs in the cellar, all dipped in water-glass and ready for barter at Buckhorn. If the output keeps up I'll store away five or six crates of the treated eggs for Christmas-season sale, for in midwinter they easily bring eighty cents a dozen.

And speaking of barter reminds me that both Dinkie and the Twins are growing out of their duds, and heaven knows when I'll find time to make more for them. They'll probably have to promenade around like Ikkie's ancestors. I've even run out of safety-pins. And since the enduring necessity for the safety-pin is evidenced by the fact that it's even found on the baby-mummies of ancient Egypt, and must be a good four thousand years old, I've had Whinnie supply me with some home-made ones, manufactured out of hair-pins.... My little Dinkie, I notice, is going to love animals. He seems especially fond of horses, and is fearless when beside them, or on them, or even under them—for he walked calmly in under the belly of Jail-Bird, who could have brained him with one pound of his wicked big hoof. But the beast seemed to know that it was a friend in that forbidden quarter, and never so much as moved until Dinkie had been rescued. It won't be long now before Dinkie has a pinto of his own and will go bobbing off across the prairie-floor, I suppose, like a monkey on a circus-horse. Even now he likes nothing better than coming with his mother while she gathers her "clutch" of eggs. He can scramble into a manger—where my unruly hens persist in making an occasional nest—like a marmoset. The delight on his face at the discovery of even two or three "cackle-berries," as Whinnie calls them, is worth the occasional breakage and yolk-stained rompers. For I share in that delight myself, since egg-gathering always gives me the feeling that I'm partaking of the bounty of Nature, that I'm getting something for next-to-nothing. It's the same impulse, really, which drives city women to the bargain-counter and the auction-room, the sublimated passion to adorn the home teepee-pole with the fruits of their cunning!

Tuesday the Twenty-fifth

Yesterday I teamed in to Buckhorn, for supplies. And as I drove down the main street of that squalid little western town I must have looked like something the crows had been roosting on. But just as I was swinging out of Syd Woodward's store-yard I caught sight of Lady Allie in her big new car, drawn up in front of the modestly denominated "New York Emporium." What made me stare, however, was the unexpected vision of Duncan Argyll McKail, emerging from the aforesaid "Emporium" laden down with parcels. These he carried out to the car and was dutifully stowing away somewhere down in the back seat, when he happened to look up and catch sight of me as I swung by in my wagon-box. He turned a sort of dull brick-red, and pretended to be having a lot of trouble with getting those parcels where they ought to be. But he looked exactly like a groom. And he knew it. And he knew that I knew he knew it. And if he was miserable, which I hope he was, I'm pretty sure he wasn't one-half so miserable as I was—and as I am. *"Damn that woman!"* I caught myself saying, out loud, after staring at my mottled old map in my dressing-table mirror.

I've been watching the sunset to-night, for a long time, and thinking about things. It was one of those quiet and beautiful prairie sunsets which now and then flood you with wonder, in spite of yourself, and give you an achey little feeling in the heart. It was a riot of orange and Roman gold fading out into pale green, with misty opal and pearl-dust along the nearer sky-line, then a big star or two, and then silence, the silence of utter peace and beauty. But it didn't bring peace to my soul. I could remember watching just such a sunset with my lord and master beside me, and turning to say: "Don't you sometimes feel, Lover, that you were simply made for joy and rapture in moments like this? Don't you feel as though your body were a harp that could throb and sing with the happiness of life?"

And I remembered the way my Dunkie had lifted up my chin and kissed me.

But that seemed a long, long time ago. And I wasn't in tune with the Infinite. And I felt lonely and old and neglected, with callouses on my hands and the cords showing in my neck, and my nerves not exactly what they ought to be. For Sunday, which is reckoned as a day of rest, had been a long and busy day for me. Dinkie had been obstreperous and had eaten most of the paint off his Noah's Ark, and had later burnt his fingers pulling my unbaked loaf-cake out of the oven, after eventually tiring of breaking the teeth out of my comb, one by one. Poppsy and Pee-Wee had been peevish and disdainful of each other's society, and Iroquois Annie had gruntingly intimated that she was about fed up on trekking the floor with wailing infants. But I'd had my week's mending to do, and what was left of the ironing to get through and Whinnie's work-pants to veneer with a generous new patch, and thirteen missing buttons to restore to the kiddies' different garments. My back ached, my finger-bones were tired, and there was a jumpy little nerve in my left temple going for all the world like a telegraph-key. And then I gave up.

I sat down and stared at that neatly folded pile of baby-clothes two feet high, a layer-cake of whites and faded blues and pinks. I stared at it, and began to gulp tragically, wallowing in a wave of self-pity. I felt so sorry for myself that I let my flat-iron burn a hole clean through the ironing-sheet, without even smelling it. That, I told myself, was all that life could be to me, just a round of washing and ironing and meal-getting and mending, fetch and carry, work and worry, from sun-up until sun-down, and many a time until midnight.

And what, I demanded of the frying-pan on its nail above the stove-shelf, was I getting out of it? What was it leading to? And what would it eventually bring me? It would eventually bring me crabbed and crow-footed old age, and fallen arches and a slabsided figure that a range-pinto would shy at. It would bring me empty year after year out here on the edge of Nowhere. It would bring me drab and spiritless drudgery, and faded eyes, and the heart under my ribs slowly but surely growing as dead as a door-nail, and the joy of living just as slowly but surely going out of my life, the same as the royal blue had faded out of Dinkie's little denim jumpers.

At that very moment, I remembered, there were women listening to symphony music in Carnegie Hall, and women sitting in willow-rockers at Long Beach contentedly listening to the sea-waves. There were women driving through Central Park, soft and lovely with early spring, or motoring up to the Clairemont for supper and watching the searchlights from the war-ships along the Hudson, and listening to the music on the roof-gardens and dancing their feet off at that green-topped heaven of youth which overlooks the Plaza where Sherman's bronze horse forever treads its spray of pine. There were happy-go-lucky girls crowding the soda-fountains and regaling themselves on fizzy water and fruit sirups, and dropping in at first nights or motoring out for sea-food dinners along lamp-pearled and moonlit boulevards of smooth asphalt. And here I was planted half-way up to the North Pole, with coyotes for company, with a husband who didn't love me, and not a jar of decent face-cream within fifteen miles of the shack! I was lost there in a sea of flat desolation, without companionable neighbors, without an idea, without a chance for any exchange of thought. I had no time for reading, and what was even worse, I had no desire for reading, but plodded on, like the stunned ox, kindred to the range animals and sister to the cow.

Then, as I sat luxuriating before my crowded banquet-table of misery, as I sat mopping my nose—which was getting most unmistakably rough with prairie-winds and alkali-water—and thinking what a fine mess I'd made of a promising young life, I fancied I heard an altogether too familiar C-sharp cry. So I got wearily up and went tiptoeing in to see if either Poppsy or Pee-Wee were awake.

But they were there, safe and sound and fast asleep, curled up like two plump little kittens, with their long lashes on their cheeks of peach-blow pink and their dewy little lips slightly parted and four little dimples in the back of each of the four little hands. And as I stood looking down at them, with a shake still under my breastbone, I couldn't keep from saying: "God bless your sleepy old bones!" Something melted and fell from the dripping eaves of my heart, and I felt that it was a sacred and God-given and joyous life, this life of being a mother, and any old maid who wants to pirouette around the Plaza roof with a lounge-lizard breathing winy breaths into her false hair was welcome to her choice. I was at least in the battle of life— and life is a battle which scars you more when you try to keep out of it than when you wade into it. I was a mother and a home-maker and the hope and buttress of the future. And all I wanted was a good night's sleep and some candid friend to tell me not to be a feather-headed idiot, but a sensible woman with a sensible perspective on things!

Friday the Twenty-seventh—Or Should It Be the Twenty-eighth

It has turned quite cold again, with frosts sharp enough at night to freeze a half-inch of ice on the tub of soft-water I've been so carefully saving for future shampoos. It's just as well I didn't try to rush the season by getting too much of my truck-garden planted. We're glad of a good fire in the shack-stove after sun-down. I've rented thirty acres from the Land Association that owns the half-section next to mine and am going to get them into oats. If they don't ripen up before the autumn frosts come and blight them, I can still use the stuff for green feed. And I've bargained for the hay-rights from the upper end of the section, but heaven only knows how I'll ever get it cut and stacked.

Whinnie had to kill a calf yesterday, for we'd run out of meat. As we're in a district that's too sparsely settled for a Beef Ring, we have to depend on ourselves for our roasts. But whatever happens, I believe in feeding my workers. I wonder, by the way, how the fair Lady Allie is getting along with her *cuisine*. Is she giving Dinky-Dunk a Beautiful Thought for breakfast, instead of a generous plate of ham and eggs? If she is, I imagine she's going to blight Romance in the bud.

I've just had a circular letter from the Women Grain Growers' Association explaining their fight for community medical service and a system of itinerant rural nurses. They're organized, and they're in earnest, and I'm with them to the last ditch. They're fighting for the things that this raw new country is most in need of. It will take us some time to catch up with the East. But the westerner's a scrambler, once he's started.

I can't get away from the fact, since I know them both, that there's a big gulf between the East and the West. It shouldn't be there, of course, but that doesn't seem to affect the issue. It's the opposition of the New to the Old, of the Want-To-Bes to the Always-Has-Beens, of the young and unruly to the settled and sedate. We seem to want freedom, and they seem to prefer order. We want movement, and they want repose. We look more feverishly to the future, and they dwell more fondly on the past. They call us rough, and we try to get even by terming them *effete*. They accentuate form, and we remain satisfied with performance. We're jealous of what they have and they're jealous of what we intend to be. We're even secretly envious of certain things peculiarly theirs which we openly deride. We're jealous, at heart, of their leisure and their air of permanence, of their accomplishments and arts and books and music, of their buildings and parks and towns with the mellowing tone of time over them. And as soon as we make money enough, I notice, we slip into their neighborhood for a gulp or two at their fountains of culture. Some day, naturally, we'll be more alike, and have more in common. The stronger colors will fade out of the newer fabric and we'll merge into a more inoffensive monotone of respectability. Our Navajo-blanket audacities will tone down to wall-tapestry sedateness—but not too, too soon, I pray the gods!

Speaking of Navajo reminds me of Redskins, and Redskins take my thoughts straight back to Iroquois Annie, who day by day becomes sullener and stupider and more impossible. I can see positive dislike for my Dinkie in her eyes, and I'm at present applying zinc ointment to Pee-Wee's chafed and scalded little body because of her neglect. I'll ring-welt and quarter that breed yet, mark my words! As it is, there's a constant cloud of worry over my heart when I'm away from the shack and my bairns are left behind. This same Ikkie, apparently, tried to scald poor old Bobs the other day, but Bobs dodged most of that steaming potato-water and decided to even up the ledger of ill-usage by giving her a well-placed nip on the hip. Ikkie now sits down with difficulty, and Bobs shows the white of his eye when she comes near him, which isn't more often than Ikkie can help—And of such, in these troublous Ides of March, and April and May, is the kingdom of Chaddie McKail!

Tuesday the Second

I may as well begin at the beginning, I suppose, so as to get the whole thing straight. And it started with Whinstane Sandy, who broke the wheel off the spring-wagon and the third commandment at one and the same time. So I harnessed Slip-Along up to the buckboard, and put the Twins in their two little crow's-nests and started out to help get my load out of that bogged trail, leaving Dinkie behind with Iroquois Annie.

There was a chill in the air and I was glad of my old coonskin coat. It was almost two hours before Whinnie and I got the spring-wagon out of its mud-bath, and the load on again, and a willow fence-post lashed under the drooping axle-end to sustain it on its journey back to Alabama Ranch. The sun was low, by this time, so I couldn't wait for Whinnie and the team, but drove on ahead with the Twins.

I was glad to see the smoke going up from my lonely little shack-chimney, for I was mud-splashed and tired and hungry, and the thought of fire and home and supper gave me a comfy feeling just under the tip of the left ventricle. I suppose it was the long evening shadows and the chill of the air that made the shack look so unutterably lonely as I drove up to it. Or perhaps it was because I stared in vain for some sign of life. At any rate, I didn't stop to unhitch Slip-Along, but gathered up my Twins and made for the door, and nearly stumbled on my nose over the broom-end boot-wiper which hadn't proved such a boon as I'd expected.

I found Iroquois Annie in front of my home-made dressing-table mirror, with my last year's summer hat on her head and a look of placid admiration on her face. The shack seemed very quiet. It seemed so disturbingly quiet that I even forgot about the hat.

"Where's Dinkie?" I demanded, as I deposited the Twins in their swing-box.

"He play somew'ere roun'," announced Ikkie, secreting the purloined head-gear and circling away from the forbidden dressing-table.

"But where?" I asked, with exceptional sharpness, for my eye had already traversed the most of that shack and had encountered no sign of him.

That sloe-eyed breed didn't know just where, and apparently didn't care. He was playing somewhere outside, with three or four old wooden decoy-ducks. That was all she seemed to know. But I didn't stop to question her. I ran to the door and looked out. Then my heart began going down like an elevator, for I could see nothing of the child. So I made the rounds of the shack again, calling "Dinkie!" as I went.

Then I looked through the bunk-house, and even tried the cellar. Then I went to the rainwater tub, with my heart up in my throat. He wasn't there, of course. So I made a flying circle of the out-buildings. But still I got no trace of him.

I was panting when I got back to the shack, where Iroquois Annie was fussing stolidly over the stove-fire. I caught her by the snake-like braid of her hair, though I didn't know I was doing it, at the moment, and swung her about so that my face confronted hers.

"Where's my boy?" I demanded in a sort of shout of mingled terror and rage and dread. "Where is he, you empty-eyed idiot? *Where is he?*"

But that half-breed, of course, couldn't tell me. And a wave of sick fear swept over me. My Dinkie was not there. He was nowhere to be found. He was lost—lost on the prairie. And I was shouting all this at Ikkie, without being quite conscious of what I was doing.

"And remember," I hissed out at her, in a voice that didn't sound like my own as I swung her about by her suddenly parting waist, "if anything has happened to that child, *I'll kill you!* Do you understand, I'll kill you as surely as you're standing in those shoes!"

I went over the shack, room by room, for still the third time. Then I went over the bunk-house and the other buildings, and every corner of the truck-garden, calling as I went.

But still there was no answer to my calls. And I had to face the steel-cold knowledge that my child was lost. That little toddler, scarcely more than a baby, had wandered away on the open prairie.

For one moment of warming relief I thought of Bobs. I remembered what a dog is sometimes able to do in such predicaments. But I also remembered that Bobs was still out on the trail with Whinnie. So I circled off on the undulating floor of the prairie, calling "Dinkie" every minute or two and staring into the distance until my eyes ached, hoping to see some moving dot in the midst of all that silence and stillness.

"My boy is lost," I kept saying to myself, in sobbing little whimpers, with my heart getting more and more like a ball of lead. And there could only be an hour or two of daylight left. If he wasn't found before night came on—I shut the thought out of my heart, and started back for the shack, in a white heat of desperation.

"If you want to live," I said to the now craven and shrinking Ikkie, "you get in that buckboard and make for Casa Grande. Drive there as fast as you can. Tell my husband that our boy, that my boy, is lost on the prairie. Tell him to get help, and come, come quick. And stop at the Teetzel ranch on your way. Tell them to send men on horses, and lanterns! But move, woman, move!"

Ikkie went, with Slip-Along making the buckboard skid on the uneven trail as though he were playing a game of crack-the-whip with that frightened Indian. And I just as promptly took up my search again, forgetting about the Twins, forgetting about being tired, forgetting everything.

Half-way between the fenced-in hay-stacks and the corral-gate I found a battered decoy-duck with a string tied to its neck. It was one of a set that Francois and Whinstane Sandy had whittled out over a year ago. It was at least a clue. Dinkie must have dropped it there.

It sent me scuttling back among the hay-stacks, going over the ground there, foot by foot and calling as I went, until my voice had an eerie sound in the cold air that took on more and more of a razor-edge as the sun and the last of its warmth went over the rim of the world. It seemed an empty world, a plain of ugly desolation, unfriendly and pitiless in its vastness. Even the soft green of the wheatlands took on a look like verdigris, as though it were something malignant and poisonous. And farther out there were muskegs, and beyond the three-wire fence, which would stand no bar to a wandering child, there were range-cattle, half-wild cattle that resented the approach of anything but a man on horseback. And somewhere in those darkening regions of peril my Dinky-Dink was lost.

I took up the search again, with the barometer of hope falling lower and lower. But I told myself that I must be systematic, that I must not keep covering the same ground, that I must make the most of what was left of the daylight. So I blocked out imaginary squares and kept running and calling until I was out of breath, then resting with my hand against my heart, and running on again. But I could find no trace of him.

He was such a little tot, I kept telling myself. He was not warmly dressed, and night was coming on. It would be a cold night, with several degrees of frost. He would be alone, on that wide and empty prairie, with terror in his heart, chilled to the bone, wailing for his mother, wailing until he was able to wail no more. Already the light was going, I realized with mounting waves of desperation, and no child, dressed as Dinkie was dressed, could live through the night. Even the coyotes would realize his helplessness and come and pick his bones clean.

I kept thinking of Bobs, more than of anything else, and wondering why Whinnie was so slow in getting back with his broken wagon, and worrying over when the men would come. I told myself to be calm, to be brave, and the next moment was busy picturing a little dead body with a tear-washed face. But I went on, calling as I went. Then suddenly I thought of praying.

"O God, it wouldn't be fair, to take that little mite away from me," I kept saying aloud. "O God, be good to me in this, be merciful, and lead me to him! Bring him back before it is too late! Bring him back, and do with me what You wish, but have pity on that poor little toddler! What You want of me, I will do, but don't, O God, don't take my boy away from me!"

I made promises to God, foolish, desperate, infantile promises; trying to placate Him in His might with my resolutions for better things, trying to strike bargains, at the last moment, with the Master of Life and Death—even protesting that I'd forgive Dinky-Dunk for anything and everything he might have done, and that it was the Evil One speaking through my lips when I said I'd surely kill Iroquois Annie.

Then I heard the signal-shots of a gun, and turned back toward the shack, which looked small and squat on the floor of the paling prairie. I couldn't run, for running was beyond me now. I heard Bobs barking, and the Twins crying, and I saw Whinnie. I thought for one fond and foolish moment, as I hurried toward the house, that they'd found my Dinkie. But it was a false hope. Whinnie had been frightened at the empty shack and the wailing babies, and had thought something might have happened to me. So he had taken my duck-gun and fired those signal-shots.

He leaned against the muddy wagon-wheel and said "Guid God! Guid God!" over and over again, when I told him Dinkie was lost. Then he flung down the gun and drew his twisted old body up, peering through the twilight at my face.

I suppose it frightened him a little.

"Dinna fear, lassie, dinna fear," he said. He said it in such a deep and placid voice that it carried consolation to my spirit, and brought a shadow of conviction trailing along behind it. "We'll find him. I say it before the livin' God, *we'll find him!*"

But that little candle of hope went out in the cold air, for I could see that night was coming closer, cold and dark and silent. I forgot about Whinnie, and didn't even notice which direction he took when he strode off on his lame foot. But I called Bobs to me, and tried to quiet his whimpering, and talked to him, and told him Dinkie was lost, the little Dinkie we all loved, and implored him to go and find my boy for me.

But the poor dumb creature didn't seem to understand me, for he cringed and trembled and showed a tendency to creep off to the stable and hide there, as though the weight of this great evil which had befallen his house lay on him and him alone. And I was trying to coax the whimpering Bobs back to the shack-steps when Dinky-Dunk himself came galloping up through the uncertain light, with Lady Alicia a few hundred yards behind him.

"Have you found him?" my husband asked, quick and curt. But there was a pale greenish-yellow tint to his face that made me think of Rocquefort cheese.

"No," I told him. I tried to speak calmly, determined not to break down and make a scene there before Lady Alicia, who'd reined up, stock-still, and sat staring in front of her, without a spoken word.

I could see Dinky-Dunk's mouth harden.

"Have you any clue—any hint?" he asked, and I could catch the quaver in his voice as he spoke.

"Not a thing," I told him, remembering that we were losing time. "He simply wandered off, when that Indian girl wasn't looking. He didn't even have a cap or a coat on."

I heard Lady Alicia, who had slipped down out of the saddle, make a little sound as I said this. It was half a gasp and half a groan of protest. For one brief moment Dinky-Dunk stared at her, almost accusingly, I thought. Then he swung his horse savagely about, and called out over our heads. Other horsemen, I found, had come loping up in the ghostly twilight where we stood. I could see the breath from their mounts' nostrils, white in the frosty air.

"You, Teetzel, and you, O'Malley," called my husband, in an oddly authoritative and barking voice, "and you on the roan there, swing twenty paces out from one another and circle the shack. Then widen the circle, each turn. There's no use calling, for the boy'll be down. He'll be done out. But don't speak until you see something. And for the love of God, watch close. He's not three yet, remember. He couldn't have got far away!"

I should have found something reassuring in those quick and purposeful words of command, but they only served to bring the horror of the situation closer home to me. They brought before me more graphically than ever the thought that I'd been trying to get out of my head, the picture of a huddled small body, with a tear-washed face, growing colder and colder, until the solitary little flame of life went completely out in the midst of that star-strewn darkness. Only too willingly, I knew, I would have covered that chilling body with the warmth of my own, though wild horses rode over me until the end of time. I tried to picture life without Dinkie. I tried to imagine my home without that bright and friendly little face, without the patter of those restless little feet, without the sound of those beleaguering little coos of child-love with which he used to burrow his head into the hollow of my shoulder.

It was too much for me. I had to lean against the wagon-wheel and gulp. It was Lady Alicia, emerging from the shack, who brought me back to the world about me. I could just see her as she stood beside me, for night had fallen by this time, night nearly as black as the blackness of my own heart.

"Look here," she said almost gruffly. "Whatever happens, you've got to have something to drink. I've got a kettle on, and I'm going back to make tea, or a pot of coffee, or whatever I can find."

"Tea?" I echoed, as the engines of indignation raced in my shaken body. "Tea? It sounds pretty, doesn't it, sitting down to a pink tea, when there's a human being dying somewhere out in that darkness!"

My bitterness, however, had no visible effect on Lady Alicia.

"Perhaps coffee would be better," she coolly amended. "And those babies of yours are crying their heads off in there, and I don't seem to be able to do anything to stop them. I rather fancy they're in need of feeding, aren't they?"

It was then and then only that I remembered about my poor neglected Twins. I groped my way in through the darkness, quite calm again, and sat down and unbuttoned my waist and nursed Poppsy, and then took up the indignant and wailing Pee-Wee, vaguely wondering if the milk in my breast wouldn't prove poison to them and if all my blood hadn't turned to acid.

I was still nursing Pee-Wee when Bud Teetzel came into the shack and asked how many lanterns we had about the place. There was a sullen look on his face, and his eyes refused to meet mine. So I knew his search had not succeeded.

Then young O'Malley came in and asked for matches, and I knew even before he spoke, that he too had failed. They had all failed.

I could hear Dinky-Dunk's voice outside, a little hoarse and throaty. I felt very tired, as I put Pee-Wee back in his cradle. It seemed as though an invisible hand were squeezing the life out of my body and making it hard for me to breathe. I could hear the cows bawling, reminding the world that they had not yet been milked. I could smell the strong coffee that Lady Alicia was pouring out into a cup. She stepped on something as she carried it to me. She stopped to pick it up—and it was one of Dinkie's little stub-toed button shoes.

"Let me see it," I commanded, as she made a foolish effort to get it out of sight. I took it from her and turned it over in my hand. That was the way, I remembered, mothers turned over the shoes of the children they had lost, the children who could never, never, so long as they worked and waited and listened in this wide world, come back to them again.

Then I put down the shoe, for I could hear one of the men outside say that the upper muskeg ought to be dragged.

"Try that cup of coffee now," suggested Lady Alicia. I liked her quietness. I admired her calmness, under the circumstances. And I remembered that I ought to give some evidence of this by accepting the hot drink she had made for me. So I took the coffee and drank it. The bawling of my milk-cows, across the cold night air, began to annoy me.

"My cows haven't been milked," I complained. It was foolish, but I couldn't help it. Then I reached out for Dinkie's broken-toed shoe, and studied it for a long time. Lady Alicia crossed to the shack door, and stood staring out through it....

She was still standing there when Whinnie came in, with the stable lantern in his hand, and brushed her aside. He came to where I was sitting and knelt down in front of me, on the shack-floor, with his heavy rough hand on my knee. I could smell the stable-manure that clung to his shoes.

"God has been guid to ye, ma'am!" he said in a rapt voice, which was little more than an awed whisper. But it was more his eyes, with the uncanny light in them making them shine like a dog's, that brought me to my feet. For I had a sudden feeling that there was Something just outside the door which he hadn't dared to bring in to me, a little dead body with pinched face and trailing arms.

I tried to speak, but I couldn't. I merely gulped. And Whinnie's rough hand pushed me back into my chair.

"Dinna greet," he said, with two tears creeping crookedly down his own seamed and wind-roughened face.

But I continued to gulp.

"Dinna greet, for *your laddie's safe and sound!*" I heard the rapt voice saying.

I could hear what he'd said, quite distinctly, yet his words seemed without color, without meaning, without sense.

"Have you found him?" called out Lady Alicia sharply.

"Aye, he's found," said Whinnie, with an exultant gulp of his own, but without so much as turning to look at that other woman, who, apparently, was of small concern to him. His eyes were on me, and he was very intimately patting my leg, without quite knowing it.

"He says that the child's been found," interpreted Lady Alicia, obviously disturbed by the expression on my face.

"He's just yon, as warm and safe as a bird in a nest," further expounded Whinstane Sandy.

"Where?" demanded Lady Alicia. But Whinnie ignored her.

"It was Bobs, ma'am," were the blessed words I heard the old lips saying to me, "who kept whimper-in' and grievin' about the upper stable door, which had been swung shut. It was Bobs who led me back yon, fair against my will. And there I found our laddie, asleep in the manger of Slip-Along, nested deep in the hay, as safe and warm as if in his own bed."

I didn't speak or move for what must have been a full minute. I couldn't. I felt as though my soul had been inverted and emptied of all feeling, like a wine-glass that's turned over. For a full minute I sat looking straight ahead of me. Then I got up, and went to where I remembered Dinky-Dunk kept his revolver. I took it up and started to cross to the open door. But Lady Alicia caught me sharply by the arm.

"What are you doing?" she gasped, imagining, I suppose, that I'd gone mad and was about to blow my brains out. She even took the firearm from my hand.

"It's the men," I tried to explain. "They should be told. Give them three signal-shots to bring them in." Then I turned to Whinnie. He nodded and took me by the hand.

"Now take me to my boy," I said very quietly.

I was still quite calm, I think. But deep down inside of me I could feel a faint glow. It wasn't altogether joy, and it wasn't altogether relief. It was something which left me just a little bewildered, a good deal like a school-girl after her first glass of champagne at Christmas dinner. It left me oddly self-immured, miles and miles from the figures so close to me, remote even from the kindly old man who hobbled a little and went with a decided list to starboard as he led me out toward what he always spoke of as the upper stable.

He was warm and breathing, and safe and sound

Yet at the back of my brain, all the while, was some shadow of doubt, of skepticism, of reiterated self-warning that it was all too good to be true. It wasn't until I looked over the well-gnawed top rail of Slip-Along's broken manger and saw that blessed boy there, by the light of Whinnie's lantern, saw that blessed boy of mine half buried in that soft and cushioning prairie-grass, saw that he was warm and breathing, and safe and sound, that I fully realized how he had been saved for me.

"The laddie'd been after a clutch of eggs, I'm thinkin'," whispered Whinnie to me, pointing to a yellow stain on his waist, which was clearly caused by the yolk of a broken egg. And Whinnie stooped over to take Dinkie up in his arms, but I pushed him aside.

"No, I'll take him," I announced.

He'd be the hungry boy when he awakened, I remembered as I gathered him up in my arms. My knees were a bit shaky, as I carried him back to the shack, but I did my best to disguise that fact. I could have carried him, I believe, right on to Buckhorn, he seemed such a precious burden. And I was glad of that demand for physical expenditure. It seemed to bring me down to earth again, to get things back into perspective. But for the life of me I couldn't find a word to say to Lady Allie as I walked into my home with Dinky-Dink in my arms. She stood watching me for a moment or two as I started to undress him, still heavy with slumber. Then she seemed to realize that she was, after all, an outsider, and slipped out through the door. I was glad she did, for a minute later Dinkie began to whimper and cry, as any child would with an empty stomach and an over-draft of sleep. It developed into a good lusty bawl, which would surely have spoilt the picture to an outsider. But it did a good turn in keeping me too busy to pump any more brine on my own part.

When Dinky-Dunk came in I was feeding little Dinkie a bowl of hot tapioca well drowned in cream and sugar. My lord and master took off his hat—which struck me as funny—and stood regarding us from just inside the door. He stood there by the door for quite a long while.

"Hadn't I better stay here with you to-night?" he finally asked, in a voice that didn't sound a bit like his own.

I looked up at him. But he stood well back from the range of the lamplight and I found it hard to decipher his expression. The one feeling I was certain of was a vague feeling of disappointment. What caused it, I could not say. But it was there.

"After what's happened," I told him as quietly as I could, "I think I'd rather be alone!"

He stood for another moment or two, apparently letting this sink in. It wasn't until he'd turned and walked out of the door that I realized the ambiguity of that retort of mine. I was almost prompted to go after him. But I checked myself by saying: "Well, if the shoe fits, put it on!" But in my heart of hearts I didn't mean it. I wanted him to come back, I wanted him to share my happiness with me, to sit and talk the thing over, to exploit it to the full in a sweet retrospect of relief, as people seem to want to do after they've safely passed through great peril.

It wasn't until half an hour later, when Dinkie was sound asleep again and tucked away in his crib, that I remembered my frantic promises to God to forgive Dinky-Dunk everything, if He'd only bring my boy back to me. And there'd been other promises, equally foolish and frantic. I've been thinking them over, in fact, and I *am* going to make an effort to keep them. I'm so happy that it hurts. And when you're happy, you want other people to be that way, too.

Wednesday the Third

Humor is the salt of life. The older I grow the more I realize that truth. And I'm going to keep more of it, if I can, in the work-room of my soul. Last night, when Dinky-Dunk and I were so uppish with each other, one single clap of humor might have shaken the solemnity out of the situation and shown us up for the poseurs we really were. But Pride is the mother of all contention. If Dinky-Dunk, when I was so imperially dismissing him from his own home, had only up and said: "Look here, Lady-bird, this is as much my house as it is yours, you feather-headed little idiot, and I'll put a June-bug down your neck if you don't let me stay here!" If he'd only said that, and sat down and been the safety-valve to my emotions which all husbands ought to be to all wives, the igloo would have melted about my heart and left me nothing to do but crawl over to him and tell him that I missed him more than tongue could tell, and that getting Dinkie's daddy back was almost as good as getting Dinkie himself back to me.

But we missed our chance. And I suppose Lady Allie sat up until all hours of the night, over at Casa Grande, consoling my Diddums and talking things over. It gives me a sort of bruised feeling, for I've nobody but Whinstane Sandy to unbosom my soul to....

Iroquois Annie has flown the coop. She has gone for good. I must have struck terror deeper into the heart of that Redskin than I imagined, for rather than face death and torture at my hands she left Slip-Along and the buckboard at the Teetzel Ranch and vamoosed off into the great unknown. I have done up her valuables in an old sugar-sack, and if they're not sent for in a week's time I'll make a bonfire of the truck. Whinnie, by the way, is to help me with the house-work. He is much better at washing dishes than I ever thought he could be. And he announces he can make a fair brand of bannock, if we run out of bread.

Tuesday the Ninth

I've got a hired man. He dropped like manna, out of the skies, or, rather, he emerged like a tadpole out of the mud. But there's something odd about him and I've a floaty idea he's a refugee from justice and that some day one of the Mounties will come riding up to my shack-door and lead my farm-help away in handcuffs.

Whatever he is, I can't quite make him out. But I have my suspicions, and I'm leaving everything in abeyance until they're confirmed.

I was on Paddy the other morning, in my old shooting-jacket and Stetson, going like the wind for the Dixon Ranch, after hearing they had a Barnado boy they wanted to unload on anybody who'd undertake to keep him under control. The trail was heavy from the night rain that had swept the prairie like a new broom, but the sun was shining again and the air was like champagne. The ozone and the exercise and Paddy's *legato* stride all tended to key up my spirits, and I went along humming:

"Bake me a bannock,

And cut me a callop,

For I've stole me a grey mare

And I'm off at a gallop!"

It wasn't until I saw Paddy's ear prick up like a rabbit's that I noticed the gun-boat on the trail ahead. At least I thought it was a gun-boat, for a minute or two, until I cantered closer and saw that it was a huge gray touring-car half foundered in the prairie-mud. Beside it sat a long lean man in very muddy clothes and a rather disreputable-looking hat. He sat with a ridiculously contented look on his face, smoking a small briar pipe, and he laughed outright as I circled his mud-hole and came to a stop opposite the car with its nose poked deep down in the mire, for all the world like a rooting shote.

"Good morning, Diana," he said, quite coolly, as he removed his battered-looking cap.

His salutation struck me as impertinent, so I returned it in the curtest of nods.

"Are you in trouble?" I asked.

"None whatever," he airily replied, still eying me. "But my car seems to be, doesn't it?"

"What's wrong?" I demanded, determined that he shouldn't elbow me out of my matter-of-factness.

He turned to his automobile and inspected it with an indifferent eye.

"I turned this old tub into a steam-engine, racing her until the water boiled, and she got even with me by blowing up an intake hose. But I'm perfectly satisfied."

"With what?" I coldly inquired.

"With being stuck here," he replied; He had rather a bright gray eye with greenish lights in it, and he looked rational enough. But there was something fundamentally wrong with him.

"What makes you feel that way?" I asked, though for a moment I'd been prompted to inquire if they hadn't let him out a little too soon.

"Because I wouldn't have seen you, who should be wearing a crescent moon on your brow, if my good friend Hyacinthe hadn't mired herself in this mud-hole," he had the effrontery to tell me.

"Is there anything so remarkably consolatory in that vision?" I asked, deciding that I might as well convince him he wasn't confronting an untutored she-coolie of the prairie. Whereupon he studied me more pointedly and more impersonally than ever.

"It's more than consolatory," he said with an accentuating flourish of the little briar pipe. "It's quite compensatory."

It was rather ponderously clever, I suppose; but I was tired of both verbal quibbling and roadside gallantry.

"Do you want to get out of that hole?" I demanded. For it's a law of the prairie-land, of course, never to side-step a stranger in distress.

"Not if it means an ending to this interview," he told me.

It was my turn to eye him. But there wasn't much warmth in the inspection.

"What are you trying to do?" I calmly inquired, for prairie life hadn't exactly left me a shy and timorous gazelle in the haunts of that stalker known as Man.

"I'm trying to figure out," he just as calmly retorted, apparently quite unimpressed by my uppity tone, "how anything as radiant and lovely as you ever got landed up here in this heaven of chilblains and coyotes."

The hare-brained idiot was actually trying to make love to me. And I then and there decided to put a brake on his wheel of eloquence.

"And I'm still trying to figure out," I told him, "how what impresses me as rather a third-class type of man is able to ride around in what looks like a first-class car! Unless," and the thought came to me out of a clear sky, and when they come that way they're inspirations and are usually true, "unless you stole it!"

He turned a solemn eye on the dejected-looking vehicle and studied it from end to end.

"If I'm that far behind Hyacinthe," he indifferently acknowledged, "I begin to fathom the secret of my life failure. So my morning hasn't been altogether wasted."

"But you did steal the car?" I persisted.

"That must be a secret between us," he said, with a distinctly guilty look about the sky-line, as though to make sure there were no sheriffs and bloodhounds on his track.

"What are you doing here?" I demanded, determined to thrash the thing out, now that it had been thrust upon me.

"Talking to the most charming woman I've encountered west of the Great Lakes," he said with an ironic and yet a singularly engaging smile. But I didn't intend him to draw a herring across the trail.

"I'd be obliged if you'd be sincere," I told him, sitting up a little straighter on Paddy.

"I am sincere," he protested, putting away his pipe.

"But the things you're saying are the things the right sort of person refrains from expressing, even when he happens to be the victim of their operation."

"Yes, that's quite true, in drawing-rooms," he airily amended. "But this is God's open and untrammeled prairie."

"Where crudeness is king," I added.

"Where candor is worth more than convention," he corrected, with rather a wistful look in his eye. "And where we mortals ought to be at least as urbane as that really wonderful robin-egg sky up there with the chinook arch across it."

He wasn't flippant any more, and I had a sense of triumph in forcing his return to sobriety. I wanted to ask him what his name was, once we were back to earth again. But as that seemed a little too direct, I merely inquired where his home happened to be.

"I've just come from up North!" he said. And that, I promptly realized, was an evasive way of answering an honest question, especially as there was a California license-number on the front of his car.

"And what's your business?" I inquired, deciding to try him out with still one more honest question.

"I'm a windmill man," he told me, as he waded in toward his dejected-looking automobile and lifted up its hood. I took him literally, for there wasn't anything, at the time, to make me think of Cervantes. But I'd already noticed his hands, and I felt sure they weren't the hands of a laboring man. They were long and lean and finicky-fingered hands, the sort that could span an octave much better than they could hold a hayfork. And I decided to see him hoisted by his own petard.

"Then you're just the man I'm looking for," I told him. He stopped for a moment to look up from the bit of heavy rubber-hose he was winding with a stretch of rubber that looked as though it had been cut from an inner tube.

"Words such as those are honey to my ears," he said as he went on with his work. And I saw it was necessary to yank him down to earth again.

"I've a broken-down windmill over on my ranch," I told him. "And if you're what you say you are, you ought to be able to put it in running order for me."

"Then you've a ranch?" he observed, stopping in his work.

"A ranch and a husband and three children," I told him with the well-paraded air of a tabby-cat who's dragged her last mouse into the drawing-room. But my announcement didn't produce the effect I'd counted on. All I could see on the face of the windmill man was a sort of mild perplexity.

"That only deepens the mystery," he observed, apparently as much to himself as to me.

"What mystery?" I asked.

"You!" he retorted.

"What's wrong with me?" I demanded.

"You're so absurdly alive and audacious and sensitive and youthful-hearted, dear madam! For the life of me I can't quite fit you into the narrow little frame you mention."

"Is it so narrow?" I inquired, wondering why I wasn't much more indignant at him. But instead of answering that question, he asked me another.

"Why hasn't this husband of yours fixed the windmill?" he casually asked over his shoulder, as he resumed his tinkering on the car-engine.

"My husband's work keeps him away from home," I explained, promptly on the defensive.

"I thought so," he announced, with the expression of a man who's had a pet hypothesis unexpectedly confirmed.

"Then what made you think so?" I demanded, with a feeling that he was in some way being subtler than I could quite comprehend.

"Instinct—if you care to call it that," he said as he stooped low over his engine. He seemed offensively busy there for a considerable length of time. I could see that he was not what in the old days I'd have called a window-dresser. And I rather liked that pretense of candor in his make-up, just as I cottoned to that melodious drawl of his, not altogether unlike Lady Alicia's, with its untoward suggestion of power and privilege. He was a man with a mind of his own; there was no denying that. I was even compelled to remind myself that with all his coolness and suavity he was still a car-thief, or perhaps something worse. And I had no intention of sitting there and watching him pitch shut-out ball.

"What are you going to do about it?" I asked, after he'd finished his job of bailing ditch-water into his car-radiator with a little collapsible canvas bucket.

He climbed into his driving-seat, mud to the knees, before he answered me.

"I'm going to get Hyacinthe out of this hole," was what he said. "And then I'm going to fix that windmill!"

"On what terms?" I inquired.

"What's the matter with a month's board and keep?" he suggested.

It rather took my breath away, but I tried not to betray the fact. He *was* a refugee, after all, and only too anxious to go into hiding for a few weeks.

"Can you milk?" I demanded, deciding to keep him in his place, from the start. And he sadly acknowledged that he wasn't able to milk. Windmill men seldom were, he casually asserted.

"Then you'll have to make yourself handy, in other ways," I proclaimed as he sat appraising me from his deep-padded car-seat.

"All right," he said, as though the whole thing were settled, on the spot. But it wasn't so simple as it seemed.

"How about this car?" I demanded. His eye met mine; and I made note of the fact that he was compelled to look away.

"I suppose we'll have to hide it somewhere," he finally acknowledged.

"And how'll you hide a car of that size on the open prairie?" I inquired.

"Couldn't we bury it?" he asked with child-like simplicity.

"It's pretty well that way now, isn't it? But I saw it three miles off," I reminded him.

"Couldn't we pile a load of prairie-hay over it?" he suggested next, with the natural cunning of the criminal. "Then they'd never suspect."

"Suspect what?" I asked.

"Suspect where we got it," he explained.

"Kindly do not include me in any of your activities of this nature," I said with all the dignity that Paddy would permit of, for he was getting restless by this time.

"But you've included yourself in the secret," he tried to argue, with a show of injured feelings. "And surely, after you've wormed that out of me, you're not going to deliver a poor devil over to—"

"You can have perfect confidence in me," I interrupted, trying to be stately but only succeeding, I'm afraid, in being stiff. And he nodded and laughed in a companionable and *laisser-faire* sort of way as he started his engine and took command of the wheel.

Then began a battle which I had to watch from a distance because Paddy evinced no love for that purring and whining thing of steel as it rumbled and roared and thrashed and churned up the mud at its flying heels. It made the muskeg look like a gargantuan cake-batter, in which it seemed to float as dignified and imperturbable as a schooner in a canal-lock. But the man at the wheel kept his temper, and reversed, and writhed forward, and reversed again. He even waved at me, in a grim sort of gaiety, as he rested his engine and then went back to the struggle. He kept engaging and releasing his clutch until he was able to impart a slight rocking movement to the car. And again the big motor roared and churned up the mud and again Paddy took to prancing and pirouetting like a two-year-old. But this time the spinning rear wheels appeared to get a trace of traction, flimsy as it was, for the throbbing gray mass moved forward a little, subsided again, and once more nosed a few inches ahead. Then the engine whined in a still higher key, and slowly but surely that mud-covered mass emerged from the swale that had sought to engulf and possess it, emerged slowly and awkwardly, like a dinosauros emerging from its primeval ooze.

The man in the car stepped down from his driving-seat, once he was sure of firm ground under his wheels again, and walked slowly and wistfully about his resurrected devil-wagon.

"The wages of sin is mud," he said as I trotted up to him. "And how much better it would have been, O Singing Pine-Tree, if I'd never taken that car!"

The poor chap was undoubtedly a little wrong in the head, but likable withal, and not ill-favored in appearance, and a man that one should try to make allowances for.

"It would have been much better," I agreed, wondering how long it would be before the Mounted Police would be tracking him down and turning him to making brooms in the prison-factory at Welrina.

"Now, if you'll kindly trot ahead," he announced as he relighted his little briar pipe, "and show me the trail to the ranch of the blighted windmill, I'll idle along behind you."

I resented the placidity with which he was accepting a situation that should have called for considerable meekness on his part. And I sat there for a silent moment or two on Paddy, to make that resentment quite obvious to him.

"What's your name?" I asked, the same as I'd ask the name of any new help that arrived at Alabama Ranch.

"Peter Ketley," he said, for once both direct and sober-eyed.

"All right, Peter," I said, as condescendingly as I was able. "Just follow along, and I'll show you where the bunk-house is."

It was his grin, I suppose, that irritated me. So I started off on Paddy and went like the wind. I don't know whether he called it idling or not, but once or twice when I glanced back at him that touring-car was bounding like a reindeer over some of the rougher places in the trail, and I rather fancy it got some of the mud shaken off its running-gear before it pulled up behind the upper stable at Alabama Ranch.

"You ride like a *ritt-meister*," he said, with an approvingly good-natured wag of the head, as he came up as close as Paddy would permit.

"*Danke-schön!*" I rather listlessly retorted, "And if you leave the car here, close beside this hay-stack, it'll probably not be seen until after dinner.

Then some time this afternoon, if the coast is clear, you can get it covered up."

I was a little sorry, the next moment, that I'd harped still again on an act which must have become painful for him to remember, since I could see his face work and his eye betray a tendency to evade mine. But he thanked me, and explained that he was entirely in my hands.

Such being the case, I was more excited than I'd have been willing to admit when I led him into the shack. Frontier life had long since taught me not to depend too much on appearances, but the right sort of people, the people who out here are called "good leather," would remain the right sort of people in even the roughest wickiup. We may have been merely ranchers, but I didn't want Peter, whatever his morals, to think that we ate our food raw off the bone and made fire by rubbing sticks together.

Yet he must have come pretty close to believing that, unimpeachable as his manners remained, for Whinnie had burned the roast of veal to a charry mass, the Twins were crying like mad, and Dinkie had painted himself and most of the dining-room table with Worcestershire sauce. I showed Peter where he could wash up and where he could find a whisk to remove the dried mud from his person. Then I hurriedly appeased my complaining bairns, opened a can of beans to take the place of Whinnie's boiled potatoes, which most unmistakably tasted of yellow soap, and supplemented what looked dishearteningly like a Dixon dinner with my last carefully treasured jar of raspberry preserve.

Whinstane Sandy, it is true, remained as glum and silent as a glacier through all that meal. But my new man, Peter, talked easily and uninterruptedly. And he talked amazingly well. He talked about mountain goats, and the Morgan rose-jars in the Metropolitan, and why he disliked George Moore, and the difference between English and American slang, and why English women always wear the wrong sort of hats, and the poetry in Indian names if we only had the brains to understand 'em, and how the wheat I'd manufactured my home-made bread out of was made up of cellulose and germ and endosperm, and how the alcohol and carbonic acid gas of the fermented yeast affected the gluten, and how the woman who could make bread like that ought to have a specially designed decoration pinned on her apron-front. Then he played "Paddy-cake, paddy-cake, Baker's man," with Dinkie, who took to him at once, and when I came back from getting the extra cot ready in the bunk-house, my infant prodigy was on the new hired man's back, circling the dinner-table and shouting "Gid-dap, 'ossie, gid-dap!" as he went, a proceeding which left the seamed old face of Whinstane Sandy about as blithe as a coffin-lid. So I coldly informed the newcomer that I'd show him where he could put his things, if he had any, before we went out to look over the windmill. And Peter rather astonished me by lugging back from the motor-car so discreetly left in the rear a huge suit-case of pliable pigskin that looked like a steamer-trunk with carrying-handles attached to it, a laprobe lined with beaver, a llama-wool sweater made like a Norfolk-jacket, a chamois-lined ulster, a couple of plaid woolen rugs, and a lunch-kit in a neatly embossed leather case.

"Quite a bit of loot, isn't it?" he said, a little red in the face from the effort of portaging so pretentious a load.

That word "loot" stuck in my craw. It was a painful reminder of something that I'd been trying very hard to forget.

"Did it come with the car?" I demanded.

"Yes, it came with the car," he was compelled to acknowledge. "But it would be exhausting, don't you see, to have to tunnel through a hay-stack every time I wanted a hair-brush!"

I icily agreed that it would, scenting tacit reproof in that mildly-put observation of his. But I didn't propose to be trifled with. I calmly led Mr. Peter Ketley out to where the overturned windmill tower lay like a museum skeleton along its bed of weeds and asked him just what tools he'd need. It was a simple question, predicating a simple answer. Yet he didn't seem able to reply to it. He scratched his close-clipped pate and said he'd have to look things over and study it out. Windmills were tricky things, one kind demanding this sort of treatment and another kind demanding that.

"You'll have no trouble, of course, in raising the tower?" I asked, looking him square in the eye. More than once I'd seen these windmill towers of galvanized steel girders put up on the prairie, and I had a very good idea of how the thing was done. They were assembled lying on the ground, and then a heavy plank was bolted to the bottom side of the tower base. This plank was held in place by two big stakes. Then a block and tackle was attached to the upper part of the tower, with the running-rope looped over a tripod of poles, to act as a fulcrum, so that when a team of horses was attached to the tackle the tower pivoted on its base and slowly rose in the air, steadied by a couple of guy-ropes held out at right angles to it.

"Oh, no trouble at all," replied the expert quite airily. But I noticed that his eye held an especially abstracted and preoccupied expression.

"Just how is it done?" I innocently inquired.

"Well, that all depends," he sapiently observed. Then, apparently nettled by my obviously superior smile, he straightened up and said: "I want you to leave this entirely to me. It's my problem, and you've no right to be worried over it. It'll take study, of course, and it'll take time. Rome wasn't built in a day. But before I leave you, madam, your tower will be up."

"I hope you're not giving yourself a life sentence," I remarked as I turned and left him.

I knew that he was looking after me as I went, but I gave no outer sign of that inner knowledge. I was equally conscious of his movements, through the shack window, when he possessed himself of a hay-fork and with more than one backward look over his shoulder circled out to where his car still stood. He tooled it still closer up beside the hay-stack, which he mounted, and then calmly and cold-bloodedly buried under a huge mound of sun-cured prairie-grass that relic of a past crime which he seemed only too willing to obliterate.

But he was callous, I could see, for once that telltale car was out of sight, he appeared much more interested in the water-blisters on his hands than the stain on his character. I could even see him inspect his fingers, from time to time, as he tried to round off the top of his very badly made stack, and test the joints by opening and closing them, as though not quite sure they were still in working order. And when the stack-making was finished and he returned to the windmill, circling about the fallen tower and examining its mechanism and stepping off its dimensions, I noticed that he kept feeling the small of his back and glancing toward the stack in what seemed an attitude of resentment.

When Whinnie came in with one of the teams, after his day a-field, I noticed that Peter approached him blithely and attempted to draw him into secret consultation. But Whinnie, as far as I could see, had no palate for converse with suspicious-looking strangers. He walked several times, in fact, about that mysterious new hay-stack, and moved shackward more dour and silent than ever. So that evening the worthy Peter was a bit silent and self-contained, retiring early, though I strongly suspected, and still suspect, that he'd locked himself in the bunk-house to remove unobserved all the labels from his underwear.

In the morning his appearance was not that of a man at peace with his own soul. He even asked me if he might have a horse and rig to go in to the nearest town for some new parts which he'd need for the windmill. And he further inquired if I'd mind him bringing back a tent to sleep in.

"Did you find the bunk-house uncomfortable?" I asked, noticing again the heavy look about his eyes.

"It's not the bunk-house," he admitted. "It's that old Caledonian saw-mill with the rock-ribbed face."

"What's the matter with Whinnie?" I demanded, with a quick touch of resentment. And Peter looked up in astonishment.

"Do you mean you've never heard him—and your shack not sixty paces away?"

"Heard him what?" I asked.

"*Heard him snore*," explained Peter, with a sigh.

"Are you sure?" I inquired, remembering the mornings when I'd had occasion to waken Whinnie, always to find him sleeping as silent and placid as one of my own babies.

"I had eight hours of it in which to dissipate any doubts," he pointedly explained.

This mystified me, but to object to the tent, of course, would have been picayune. I had just the faintest of suspicions, however, that the fair Peter might never return from Buckhorn, though I tried to solace myself with the thought that the motor-car and the beaver-lined lap-robe would at least remain with me. But my fears were groundless. Before supper-time Peter was back in high spirits, with the needed new parts for the windmill, and an outfit of blue denim apparel for himself, and a little red sweater for Dinkie, and an armful of magazines for myself.

Whinnie, as he stood watching Peter's return, clearly betrayed the disappointment which that return involved. He said nothing, but when he saw my eye upon him he gazed dourly toward his approaching rival and tapped a weather-beaten brow with one stubby finger. He meant, of course, that Peter was a little locoed.

But Peter is not. He is remarkably clear-headed and quick-thoughted, and if there's any madness about him it's a madness with a deep-laid method. The one thing that annoys me is that he keeps me so continuously and yet so obliquely under observation. He pretends to be studying out my windmill, but he is really trying to study out its owner. Whinnie, I know, won't help him much. And I refuse to rise to his gaudiest flies. So he's still puzzling over what he regards as an anomaly, a farmerette who knows the difference between De Bussey and a side-delivery horse-rake, a mother of three children who can ride a pinto and play a banjo, a clodhopper in petticoats who can talk about Ragusa and Toarmina and the summer races at Piping Rock. But it's a relief to converse about something besides summer-fallowing and breaking and seed-wheat and tractor-oil and cows' teats. And it's a stroke of luck to capture a farm-hand who can freshen you up on foreign opera at the same time that he campaigns against the domestic weed!

Thursday the Eleventh

We are a peaceful and humdrum family, very different from the westerners of the romantic movies. If we were the cinema kind of ranchers Pee-Wee would be cutting his teeth on a six-shooter, little Dinkie would be off rustling cattle, Poppsy would be away holding up the Transcontinental Limited, and Mummsie would be wearing chaps, toting a gun, and pretending to the sheriff that her jail-breaking brother was *not* hidden in the cellar!

Whereas, we are a good deal like the easterners who till the soil and try to make a home for themselves and their children, only we are without a great many of their conveniences, even though we do beat them out in the matter of soil. But breaking sod isn't so picturesque as breaking laws, and a plow-handle isn't so thrilling to the eye as a shooting-iron, so it's mostly the blood-and-thunder type of westerners, from the ranch with the cow-brand name, who goes ki-yi-ing through picture and story, advertising us as an aggregation of train-robbers and road-agents and sheriff-rabbits. And it's a type that makes me tired.

The open range, let it be remembered, is gone, and the cowboy is going after it. Even the broncho, they tell me, is destined to disappear. It seems hard to think that the mustang will be no more, the mustang which Dinky-Dunk once told me was the descendant of the three hundred Arab and Spanish horses which Cortez first carried across the Atlantic to Mexico. For we, the newcomers, mesh the open range with our barb-wire, and bring in what Mrs. Eagle-Moccasin called our "stink-wagon" to turn the grass upside down and grow wheat-berries where the buffalo once wallowed. But sometimes, even in this newfangled work-a-day world, I find a fresh spirit of romance, quite as glamorous, if one has only the eye to see it, as the romance of the past. In one generation, almost, we are making a home-land out of a wilderness, we are conjuring up cities and threading the continent with steel, we are feeding the world on the best and cleanest wheat known to hungry man. And on these clear and opaline mornings when I see the prairie-floor waving with its harvest to be, and hear the clack and stutter of the tractor breaking sod on the outer quarter and leaving behind it the serried furrows of umber, I feel there is something primal and poetic in the picture, something mysteriously moving and epic....

The weather has turned quite warm again, with glorious spring days of winy and heart-tugging sunlight and cool and starry nights. In my spare time I've been helping Whinnie get in my "truck" garden, and Peter, who has reluctantly forsaken the windmill and learned to run the tractor, is breaking sod and summer-fallowing for me. For there is always another season to think of, and I don't want the tin-can of failure tied to my spirit's tail. As I say, the days slip by. Morning comes, fresh as a new-minted nickel, we mount the treadmill, and somebody rolls the big red ball off the table and it's night again. But open-air work leaves me healthy, my children grow a-pace, and I should be most happy.

But I'm not.

I'm so homesick for something which I can't quite define that it gives me a misty sort of ache just under the fifth rib. It's just three weeks now since Dinky-Dunk has ventured over from Casa Grande. If this aloofness continues, he'll soon need to be formally introduced to his own offspring when he sees them.

Now that I have Peter out working on the land, I can safely give a little more time to my household. But meals are still more or less a scramble. Peter has ventured the opinion that he might get a Chinaman for me, if he could have a week off to root out the right sort of Chink. But I prefer that Peter sticks to his tractor, much as I need help in the house.

My new hired man is still a good deal of a mystery to me, just as I seem to remain a good deal of a mystery to him. I've been asking myself just why it is that Peter is so easy to get along with, and why, in some indescribable way, he has added to the color of life since coming to Alabama Ranch. It's mostly, I think, because he's supplied me with the one thing I had sorely missed, without being quite conscious of it. He has been able to give me mental companionship, at a time when my mind was starving for an idea or two beyond the daily drudgery of farm-work. He has given a fillip to existence, loath as I am to acknowledge it. He's served to knock the moss off my soul by more or less indirectly reminding me that all work and no play could make Chaddie McKail a very dull girl indeed.

I was rather afraid, at one time, that he was going to spoil it all by making love to me, after the manner of young Bud Dyruff, from the Cowen Ranch, who, because I waded bare-kneed into a warm little slough-end when the horses were having their noonday meal, assumed that I could be persuaded to wade with equal celerity into indiscriminate affection. That rudimentary and ingenuous youth, in fact, became more and more offensive in his approaches, until finally I turned on him. "Are you trying to make love to me?" I demanded. "The surest thing you know," he said with a rather moonish smile. "Then let me tell you something," I hissed out at him, with my nose within six inches of his, "I'm a high-strung hell-cat, I am. I'm a bob-cat, and I'm not aching to be pawed by you or any other hare-brained he-mutt. So now, right from this minute, keep your distance! Is that clear? Keep your distance, or I'll break your head in with this neck-yoke!"

Poor Bud! That rather blighted the flower of Bud's tender young romance, and to this day he effects a wide detour when he happens to meet me on the trail or in the byways of Buckhorn.

But Peter Ketley is not of the Bud Dyruff type. He is more complex, and, accordingly, more disturbing. For I can see admiration in his eye, even though he no longer expresses it by word of mouth. And there is something tonic to any woman in knowing that a man admires her. In my case, in fact, it's so tonic that I've ordered some benzoin and cucumber-cream, and think a little more about how I'm doing my hair, and argue with myself that it's a woman's own fault if she runs to seed before she's seen thirty. I may be the mother of three children, but I still have a hankering after personal power—and that comes to women through personal attractiveness, disquieting as it may be to have to admit it. We can't be big strong men and conquer through force, but our frivolous little bodies can house the triumphant weaknesses which make men forget their strength.

Sunday the Fourteenth

I've had a talk with Peter. It simply *had* to come, for we couldn't continue to play-act and evade realities. The time arrived for getting down to brass tacks. And even now the brass tacks aren't as clear-cut as I'd like them to be.

But Peter is not and never was a car-thief. That beetle-headed suspicion has passed slowly but surely away, like a snow-man confronted by a too affectionate sun. It slipped away from me little by little, and began losing its lines, not so much when I found that Peter carried a bill-fold and a well-thumbed copy of *Marius The Epicurean* and walked about in undergarments that were expensive enough for a *prima donna*, but more because I found myself face to face with a Peter-Panish sort of honorableness that was not to be dissembled. So I cornered Peter and put him through his paces.

I began by telling him that I didn't seem to know a great deal about him.

"The closed makimono," he cryptically retorted, "is the symbol of wisdom."

I was ashamed to ask just what that meant, so I tried another tack.

"Folks are thrown pretty intimately together, in this frontier life, like worms in a bait-tin. So they naturally need to know what they're tangled up with."

Peter, at that, began to look unhappy.

"Would you mind telling me what brought you to this part of the country?" I asked.

"Would you mind telling me what brought *you* to this part of the country?" countered Peter.

"My husband," I curtly retorted. And that chilled him perceptibly. But he saw that I was not to be shuttled aside.

"I was interested," he explained with a shrug of finality, "in the nesting-ground of the Canada goose!"

"Then you came to the right point," I promptly retorted. "For *I* am it!"

But he didn't smile, as I'd expected him to do. He seemed to feel that something approaching seriousness was expected of that talk.

"I really came because I was more interested in one of your earliest settlers," he went on. "This settler, I might add, came to your province some three million years ago and is now being exhumed from one of the cut-banks of the Red Deer River. He belongs to the Mesozoic order of archisaurian gentlemen known as *Dinosauria*, and there's about a car-load of him. This interest in one of your cretaceous dinosaur skeletons would imply, of course, that I'm wedded to science. And I *am*, though to nothing else. I'm as free as the wind, dear lady, or I wouldn't be holidaying here with a tractor-plow that makes my legs ache and a prairie Penelope, who, for some reason or other, has the power of making my heart ache."

"*Verboten!*" I promptly interjected.

Peter saluted and then sighed.

"There are things up here even more interesting than your Edmonton formation," he remarked. "But I was born a Quaker, you see, and I can't get rid of my self-control!"

"I like you for that," I rather depressed him by saying. "For I find that one accepts you, Peter, as one accepts a climate. You're intimate in your very remoteness."

Peter looked at me out of a rueful yet ruminative eye. But Whinnie came forth and grimly announced that the Twins were going it. So I had to turn shackward.

"You really ought to get that car out," I called over my shoulder to him, with a head-nod toward the hay-stack. And he nodded absently back at me.

Thursday the—I Can't Remember

Dinky-Dunk rode over to-day when Peter was bolting some new wire stuts on the windmill tower and I was busy dry-picking two polygamous old roosters which Whinnie had beheaded for me. My husband attempted an offhand and happy-go-lucky air which, I very soon saw, was merely a mask to hide his embarrassment. He even flushed up to the ears when little Dinkie drew back for a moment or two, as any child might who didn't recognize his own father, though he later solicitously tiptoed to the sleeping-porch where the Twins were having their nap, and remarked that they were growing prodigiously.

It was all rather absurd. But when one member of this life-partnership business is stiff with constraint, you can't expect the other member to fall on his neck and weep. And Dinky-Dunk, for all his nonchalance, looked worried and hollow-eyed. He was in the saddle again, and headed back for Casa Grande, when he caught sight of Peter at work on the windmill. So he loped over to my hired man and had a talk with him. What they talked about I couldn't tell, of course, but it seemed a casual and friendly enough conversation. Peter, in his blue-jeans, dirt-marked and oil-stained, and with a wrench in his hand, looked like an I. W. W. agitator who'd fallen on evil days.

I felt tempted to sally forth and reprove Dinky-Dunk for wasting the time of my hired help. But that, I remembered in time, might be treading on rather thin ice, or, what would be even worse, might seem like snooping. And speaking of snooping, reminds me that a few nights ago I listened carefully at the open window of the bunk-house where Whinstane Sandy was deep in repose. Not a sound, not a trace of a snore, arose from Whinnie's cot.

So my suspicions were confirmed. That old sourdough had deliberately lain awake and tried to trumpet my second man from the precincts which Whinnie felt he'd already preempted. He had attempted to snore poor Peter off the map and away from Alabama Ranch!

Saturday the Thirtieth

The sedatest lives, I suppose, have their occasional Big Surprises. Life, at any rate, has just treated me to one. Lady Alicia Newland's English maid, known as Struthers, arrived at Alabama Ranch yesterday afternoon and asked if I'd take her in. She'd had some words, she said, with her mistress, and didn't propose to be treated like the scum of the earth by anybody.

So the inevitable has come about. America, the liberalizer, has touched the worthy Struthers with her wand of democracy and transformed her from a silent machine of service into a Vesuvian female with a mind and a voice of her own.

I told Struthers, who was still a bit quavery and excited, to sit down and we'd talk the matter over, for rustling maids, in a land where they're as scarce as hen's teeth, is a much graver crime than rustling cattle. Yet if Lady Allie had taken my husband away from me, I didn't see why, in the name of poetic justice, I shouldn't appropriate her hand-maid.

And Struthers, I found, was quite definite as to her intentions. She is an expert needle-woman, can do plain cooking, and having been a nurse-maid in her younger days, is quite capable of looking after children, even American children. I winced at that, naturally, and winced still harder when she stipulated that she must have four o'clock tea every afternoon, and every alternate Sunday morning off for the purpose of "saging" her hair, which was a new one on me. But I weighed the pros and cons, very deliberately, and discussed her predicament very candidly, and the result is that Struthers is now duly installed at Alabama Ranch. Already, in fact, that efficient hand of hers has left its mark on the shack. Her muffins this morning were above reproach and to-morrow we're to have Spotted Dog pudding. But already, I notice, she is casting sidelong glances in the direction of poor Peter, to whom, this evening at supper, she deliberately and unquestionably donated the fairest and fluffiest quarter of the lemon pie. I have no intention of pumping the lady, but I can see that there are certain matters pertaining to Casa Grande which she is not averse to easing her mind of. I am not quite sure, in fact, that I could find it possible to lend an ear to the gossipings of a servant. And yet—and yet, there are a few things I'd like to find out. And dignity may still be slaughtered on the altar of curiosity.

Sunday the Sixth

Now that I've had a breathing-spell, I've been sitting back and mentally taking stock. The showers of last week have brought the needed moisture for our wheat, which is looking splendid. Our oats are not quite so promising, but everything will depend upon the season. The season, in fact, holds our fate and our fortune in its lap. Those ninety days that include June and July and August are the days when the northwest farmer is forever on tiptoe watching the weather. It's his time of trial, his period of crisis, when our triple foes of Drought and Hail and Fire may at any moment creep upon him. It keeps one on the *qui vive*, making life a gamble, giving the zest of the uncertain to existence, and leaving no room for boredom. It's the big drama which even dwarfs the once momentous emotions of love and hate and jealousy. For when the Big Rush is on, I've noticed, husbands are apt to neglect their wives, and lovers forget their sweethearts, and neighbors their enmities. Let the world go hang, but before and above everything else, *save your crop!*

Yet, as I was saying, I've been taking stock. It's clear that I should have more cattle. And if all goes well, I want a bank-barn, the same as they have in the East, with cement flooring and modern stalling. And I've got to comb over my herd, and get rid of the boarders and hatracks, and acquire a blooded bull for Alabama Ranch, to improve the strain. Two of my milkers must go for beef, as well as several scrub springers which it would be false economy to hold. I've also got to do something about my hogs. They are neither "easy feeders" nor good bacon types. With them, too, I want a good sire, a pure-bred Yorkshire or Berkshire. And I must have cement troughs and some movable fencing, so that my young shoats may have pasture-crop. For there is money in pigs, and no undue labor, provided you have them properly fenced.

My chickens, which have been pretty well caring for themselves, have done as well as could be expected. I've tried to get early hatchings from my brooders, for pullets help out with winter eggs when prices are high, laying double what a yearling does during the cold months. My yellow-beaks and two-year-olds I shall kill off as we're able to eat them, for an old hen is a useless and profitless possession and I begin to understand why lordly man has appropriated that phrase as a term of contempt for certain of my sex. I'm trading in my eggs—and likewise my butter—at Buckhorn, selling the Number One grade and holding back the Number Twos for home consumption. There is an amazing quantity of Number Twos, because of "stolen nests" and the lack of proper coops and runs. But we seem to get away with them all. Dinkie now loves them and would eat more than one at a time if I'd let him.

The gluttony of the normal healthy three-year-old child, by the way, is something incredible. Dinkie reminds me more and more of a robin in cherry-time. He stuffs sometimes, until his little tummy is as tight as a drum, and I verily believe he could eat his own weight in chocolate blanc-mange, if I'd let him. Eating, with him, is now a serious business, demanding no interruptions or distractions. Once he's decently filled, however, his greediness takes the form of exterior application. He then rejoices to plaster as much as he can in his hair and ears and on his face, until he looks like a cross between a hod-carrier and a Fiji-Islander. And grown men, I've concluded, are very much the same with their appetite of love. They come to you with a brave showing of hunger, but when you've given until no more remains to be given, they become finicky and capricious, and lose their interest in the homely old porridge-bowl which looked all loveliness to them before they had made it theirs....

This afternoon, tired of scheming and conceiting for the future, I had a longing to be frivolous and care-free. So I got out the old rusty-rimmed banjo, tuned her up, and sat on an overturned milk-bucket, with Dinkie and Bobs and Poppsy and Pee-Wee for an audience.

I was leaning back with my knees crossed, strumming out *Turkey in the Straw* when Peter walked up and sat down between Bobs and Dinkie. So I gave him *The Whistling Coon*, while the Twins lay there positively pop-eyed with delight, and he joined in with me on *Dixie*, singing in a light and somewhat throaty baritone. Then we swung on to *There's a Hole in the Bottom of the Sea*, which must always be sung to a church-tune, and still later to that dolorous ballad, *Oh, Bury Me Not on the Lone Prair-hee!* Then we tried a whistling duet with banjo accompaniment, pretty well murdering the Tinker's Song from *Robin Hood* until Whinstane Sandy, who was taking his Sabbath bath in the bunk-house, loudly opened the window and stared out with a dourly reproving countenance, which said as plain as words: "This is nae the day for whustlin', folks!"

But little Dinkie, obviously excited by the music, shouted "A-more! A-more!" so we went on, disregarding Whinnie and the bunk-house window and Struthers' acrid stare from the shack-door. I was in the middle of Fay Templeton's lovely old *Rosie, You Are My Posey*, when Lady Alicia rode up, as spick and span as though she'd just pranced off Rotten Row. And as I'd no intention of showing the white feather to her ladyship, I kept right on to the end. Then I looked up and waved the banjo at her where she sat stock-still on her mount. There was an enigmatic look on her face, but she laughed and waved back, whereupon Peter got up, and helped her dismount as she threw her reins over the pony's head.

I noticed that her eye rested very intently on Peter's face as I introduced him, and he in turn seemed to size the stately newcomer up in one of those lightning-flash appraisals of his. Then Lady Allie joined our circle, and confessed that she'd been homesick for a sight of the kiddies, especially Dinkie, whom she took on her knee and regarded with an oddly wistful and abstracted manner.

My hired man, I noticed, was in no way intimidated by a title in our midst, but wagered that Lady Allie's voice would be a contralto and suggested that we all try *On the Road to Mandalay* together. But Lady Allie acknowledged that she had neither a voice nor an ear, and would prefer listening. We couldn't remember the words, however, and the song wasn't much of a success. I think the damper came when Struthers stepped out into full view, encased in my big bungalow-apron of butcher's linen. Lady Alicia, after the manner of the English, saw her without seeing her. There wasn't the flicker of an eyelash, or a moment's loss of poise. But it seemed too much like a Banquo at the feast to go on with our banjo-strumming, and I attempted to bridge the hiatus by none too gracefully inquiring how things were getting along over at Casa Grande. Lady Allie's contemplative eye, I noticed, searched my face to see if there were any secondary significances to that bland inquiry.

"Everything seems to be going nicely," she acknowledged. Then she rather took the wind out of my sails by adding: "But I really came over to see if you wouldn't dine with me to-morrow at seven. Bring the children, of course. And if Mr.—er—Ketley can come along, it will be even more delightful."

Still again I didn't intend to be stumped by her ladyship, so I said that I'd be charmed, without one second of hesitation, and Peter, with an assumption of vast gravity, agreed to come along if he didn't have to wear a stiff collar and a boiled shirt. And he continued to rag Lady Allie in a manner which seemed to leave her a little bewildered. But she didn't altogether dislike it, I could see, for Peter has the power of getting away with that sort of thing.

Tuesday the Eighth

Lady Alicia's dinner is over and done with. I can't say that it was a howling success. And I'm still very much in doubt as to its *raison d'être*, as the youthful society reporters express it. At first I thought it might possibly be to flaunt my lost grandeur in my face. And then I argued with myself that it might possibly be to exhibit Sing Lo, the new Chink man-servant disinterred from one of the Buckhorn laundries. And still later I suspected that it might be a sort of demonstration of preparedness, like those carefully timed naval parades on the part of one of the great powers disquieted by the activities of a restive neighbor. And then came still another suspicion that it might possibly be a move to precipitate the impalpable, as it were, to put certain family relationships to the touch, and make finally certain as to how things stood.

But that, audacious as I felt Lady Alicia to be, didn't quite hold water. It didn't seem any more reasonable than my earlier theories. And all I'm really certain of is that the dinner was badly cooked and badly served, rather reminding me of a chow-house meal on the occasion of a Celestial New Year. We all wore our every-day clothes (with Peter's most carefully pressed and sponged by the intriguing Struthers) and the Twins were put asleep up-stairs in their old nursery and Dinkie was given a place at the table with two sofa-cushions to prop him up in his armchair (and acted like a little barbarian) and Peter nearly broke his neck to make himself as pleasant as possible, chattering like a magpie and reminding me of a circus-band trying to make the crowd forget the bareback rider who's just been carried out on a stretcher. But Constraint was there, all the while, first in the form of Dinky-Dunk's unoccupied chair, which remained that way until dinner was two-thirds through, and then in the form of Dinky-Dunk himself, whose explanation about some tractor-work keeping him late didn't quite ring true. His harried look, I must acknowledge, wore away with the evening, but to me at least it was only too plain that he was there under protest.

I did my utmost to stick to the hale-fellow-well-met rôle, but it struck me as uncommonly like dancing on a coffin. And for all his garrulity, I know, Peter was really watching us with the eye of a hawk.

"I'm too old a dog," I overheard him telling Lady Alicia, "ever to be surprised at the crumbling of an ideal or the disclosure of a skeleton."

I don't know what prompted that statement, but it had the effect of making Lady Allie go off into one of her purl-two knit-two trances.

"I think you English people," I heard him telling her a little later, "have a tendency to carry moderation to excess."

"I don't quite understand that," she said, lighting what must have been about her seventeenth cigarette.

"I mean you're all so abnormally normal," retorted Peter—which impressed me as being both clever and true. And when Lady Allie, worrying over that epigram, became as self-immured as a Belgian milk-dog, Peter cocked an eye at me as a robin cocks an eye at a fish-worm, and I had the audacity to murmur across the table at him, "Lady Barbarina." Whereupon he said back, without batting an eye: "Yes, I happen to have read a bit of Henry James."

But dinner came to an end and we had coffee in what Lady Alicia had rechristened the Lounge, and then made doleful efforts to be light and airy over a game of bridge, whereat Dinky-Dunk lost fourteen dollars of his hard-earned salary and twice I had to borrow six bits from Peter to even up with Lady Allie, who was inhospitable enough to remain the winner of the evening. And I wasn't sorry when those devastating Twins of mine made their voices heard and thrust before me an undebatable excuse for trekking homeward. And another theatricality presented itself when Dinky-Dunk announced that he'd take us back in the car. But we had White-Face and Tumble-Weed and our sea-going spring-wagon, with plenty of rugs, and there was no way, of course, of putting a team and rig in the tonneau. So I made my adieux and planted Peter meekly in the back seat with little Dinkie to hold and took the reins myself.

I started home with a lump in my throat and a weight in my heart, feeling it really wasn't a home that I was driving toward. But it was one of those crystal-clear prairie nights when the stars were like electric-lights shining through cut-glass and the air was like a razor-blade wrapped in panne-velvet. It took you out of yourself. It reminded you that you were only an infinitely small atom in the immensity of a crowded big world, and that even your big world was merely a microscopic little mote lost amid its uncounted millions of sister-motes in the infinitudes of time and space.

"*Nitchevo!*" I said out loud, as I stopped on the trail to readjust and wrap the Twins in their rug-lined laundry-basket.

"In that case," Peter unexpectedly remarked, "I'd like to climb into that front seat with you."

"Why?" I asked, not greatly interested.

"Because I want to talk to you," was Peter's answer.

"But I think I'd rather not talk," I told him.

"Why?" it was his turn to inquire.

"Isn't it a rum enough situation as it is?" I demanded. For Peter, naturally, had not used his eyes for nothing that night.

But Peter didn't wait for my permission to climb into the front seat. He plumped himself down beside me and sat there with my first-born in his arms and one-half of the mangy old buffalo-robe pulled up over his knees.

"I think I'm beginning to see light," he said, after a rather long silence, as we went spanking along the prairie-trail with the cold air fanning our faces.

"I wish *I* did," I acknowledged.

"You're not very happy, are you?" he ventured, in a voice with just the slightest trace of *vibrato* in it.

But I didn't see that anything was to be gained by parading my troubles before others. And life, of late, had been teaching me to consume my own smoke. So I kept silent.

"Do you like me, Peter?" I suddenly asked. For I felt absurdly safe with Peter. He has a heart, I know, as clean as an Alpine village, and the very sense of his remoteness, as I'd already told him, gives birth to a sort of intimacy, like the factory girl who throws a kiss to the brakeman on the through freight and remains Artemis-on-ice to the delicatessen-youth from whom she buys her supper "weenies."

"What do you suppose I've been hanging around for?" demanded Peter, with what impressed me as an absence of finesse.

"To fix the windmill, of course," I told him. "Unless you have improper designs on Struthers!"

He laughed a little and looked up at the Great Bear.

"If it's true, as they say, that Fate weaves in the dark, I suppose that's why she weaves so badly," he observed, after a short silence.

"She undoubtedly drops a stitch now and then," I agreed, wondering if he was thinking of me or Struthers when he spoke. "But you do like me, don't you?"

"I adore you," admitted Peter quite simply.

"In the face of all these?" I said with a contented little laugh, nodding toward my three children.

"In the face of everything," asserted Peter.

"Then I wish you'd do something for me," I told him.

"What?"

"Break that woman's heart," I announced, with a backward nod of my head toward Casa Grande.

"I'd much rather break *yours*," he coolly contended. "Or I'd prefer knowing I had the power of doing it."

I shook my head. "It can't be done, Peter. And it can't even be pretended. Imagine the mother of twins trying to flirt with a man even as nice as you are! It would be as bad as an elephant trying to be kittenish and about as absurd as one of your dinosauria getting up and trying to do a two-step. And I'm getting old and prosy, Peter, and if I pretend to be skittish now and then it's only to mask the fact that I'm on the shelf, that I've eaten my pie and that before long I'll be dyeing my hair every other Sunday, the same as Struthers, and———"

"Rot!" interrupted Peter. "All rot!"

"Why rot?" I demanded.

"Because to me you're the embodiment of undying youth," asserted the troubadour beside me. It was untrue, and it was improper, but for a moment or two at least my hungry heart closed about that speech the same as a child's hand closes about a chocolate-drop. Women are made that way. But I had to keep to the trail.

"Supposing we get back to earth," I suggested.

"What's the matter with the way we were heading?" countered the quiet-eyed Peter.

"It doesn't seem quite right," I argued. And he laughed a little wistfully.

"What difference does it make, so long as we're happy?" he inquired. And I tried to reprove him with a look, but I don't think it quite carried in the misty starlight.

"I can't say," I told him, "that I approve of your reasoning."

"That's just the point," he said with a slightly more reckless note in his laughter. "It doesn't pretend to be reasoning. It's more like that abandoning of all reasoning which brings us our few earthly glories."

"*Cogito, ergo sum,*" I announced, remembering my Descartes.

"Well, I'm going to keep on just the same," protested Peter.

"Keep on at what?" I asked.

"At thinking you're adorable," was his reply.

"Well, the caterpillars have been known to stop the train, but you must remember that it's rather hard on the caterpillars," I proclaimed as we swung off the trail and headed in for Alabama Ranch.

Sunday the Thirteenth

On Friday night there were heavy showers again, and now Whinnie reports that our Marquis wheat couldn't look better and ought to run well over forty bushels to the acre. We are assured of sufficient moisture, but our two enemies yclept Fire and Hail remain. I should like to have taken out hail insurance, but I haven't the money on hand.

I can at least make sure of my fire-guards. Turning those essential furrows will be good training for Peter. That individual, by the way, has been quieter and more ruminative of late, and, if I'm not mistaken, a little gentler in his attitude toward me. Yet there's not a trace of pose about him, and I feel sure he wouldn't harm the morals of a lady-bug. He's kind and considerate, and doing his best to be a good pal. Whinnie, by the way, regards me with a mildly reproving eye, and having apparently concluded that I am a renegade, is concentrating his affection on Dinkie, for whom he is whittling out a new Noah's Ark in his spare time. He is also teaching Dinkie to ride horseback, lifting him up to the back of either Nip or Tuck when they come for water and letting him ride as far as the stable. He looks very small up on that big animal.

At night, now that the evenings are so long, Whinnie takes my laddie on his knee and tells him stories, stories which he can't possibly understand, I'm sure, but Dinkie likes the drone of Whinnie's voice and the feel of those rough old arms about his little body. We all hunger for affection. The idiot who said that love was the bitters in the cocktail of life wasn't either a good liver or a good philosopher. For love is really the whole cocktail. Take that away, and nothing is left....

I seem to be getting moodier, as summer advances. Alternating waves of sourness and tenderness sweep through me, and if I wasn't a busy woman I'd possibly make a fine patient for one of those fashionable nerve-specialists who don't flourish on the prairie.

But I can't quite succeed in making myself as miserable as I feel I ought to be. There seems to be a great deal happening all about us, and yet nothing ever happens. My children are hale and hearty, my ranch is fat with its promise of harvest, and I am surrounded by people who love and respect me. But it doesn't seem enough. Coiled in my heart is one small disturbing viper which I can neither scotch nor kill. Yet I decline to be the victim of anything as ugly as jealousy. For jealousy is both poisonous and pathetic. But I'd like to choke that woman!

Yesterday Lady Alicia, who is now driving her own car, picked up Peter from his fire-guard work and carried him off on an experimental ride to see what was wrong with her carbureter—the same old carbureter! She let him out at the shack, on her way home, and Struthers witnessed the tail end of that *enlèvement*. It spoilt her day for her. She fumed and fretted and made things fly—for Struthers always works hardest, I've noticed, when in a temper—and surrendering to the corroding tides which were turning her gentle nature into gall and wormwood, obliquely and tremulously warned the somewhat startled Peter against ungodly and frivolous females who 'ave no right to be corrupting simple-minded colonials and who 'ave no scruples against playing with men the same as a cat would play with a mouse.

"So be warned in time," I sternly exclaimed to Peter, when I accidentally overheard the latter end of Struthers' exhortation.

"And there are others as ought to be warned in time!" was Struthers' Parthian arrow as she flounced off to turn the omelette which she'd left to scorch on the cook-stove.

Peter's eye met mine, but neither of us said anything. It reminded me of cowboy honor, which prompts a rider never to "touch leather," no matter how his bronco may be bucking. And *omelette*, I was later reminded, comes from the French *alumelle*, which means ship's plating, a bit of etymology well authenticated by Struthers' skillet.

Wednesday the Twenty-third

Summer is here, here in earnest, and already we've had a few scorching days. Haying will soon be upon us, and there is no slackening in the wheels of industry about Alabama Ranch. My Little Alarm-Clocks have me up bright and early, and the morning prairie is a joy that never grows old to the eye. Life is good, and I intend to be happy, for

I'm going alone,

    Though Hell forefend,

By a way of my own

    To the bitter end!

And our miseries, after all, are mostly in our own minds. Yesterday I came across little Dinkie lamenting audibly over a scratch on his hand at least seven days old. He insisted that I should kiss it, and, after witnessing that healing touch, was perfectly satisfied. And there's no reason why grown-ups should be more childish than children themselves.

One thing that I've been missing this year, more than ever before, is fresh fruit. During the last few days I've nursed a craving for a tart Northern-Spy apple, or a Golden Pippin with a water-core, or a juicy and buttery Bartlett pear fresh from the tree. Those longings come over me occasionally, like my periodic hunger for the Great Lakes and the Atlantic, a vague ache for just one vision of tumbling beryl water, for the plunge of cool green waves and the race of foam. And Peter overheard me lamenting our lack of fruit and proclaiming I could eat my way right across the Niagara Peninsula in peach time. So when he came back from Buckhorn this afternoon with the farm supplies, he brought on his own hook two small boxes of California plums and a whole crate of oranges.

It was very kind of him, and also very foolish, for the oranges will never keep in this hot weather, and the only way that I can see to save them is to make them up into marmalade. It was pathetic to see little Dinkie with his first orange. It was hard to persuade him that it wasn't a new kind of ball. But once the flavor of its interior juices was made known to him, he took to it like a cat to cream.

It brought home to me how many things there are my kiddies have had to do without, how much that is a commonplace to the city child must remain beyond the reach of the prairie tot. But I'm not complaining. I am resolved to be happy, and in my prophetic bones is a feeling that things are about to take a turn for the better, something better than the humble stewed prune for Dinkie's little tummy and something better than the companionship of the hired help for his mother. Not that both Peter and Whinnie haven't a warm place in my heart! They couldn't be better to me. But I'm one of those neck-or-nothing women, I suppose, who are silly enough to bank all on a single throw, who have to put all their eggs of affection in one basket. I can't be indiscriminate, like Dinkie, for instance, whom I found the other day kissing every picture of a man in the Mail-Order Catalogue and murmuring "Da-da!" and doing the same to every woman-picture and saying "Mummy." To be lavish with love is, I suppose, the prerogative of youth. Age teaches us to treasure it and sustain it, to guard it as we'd guard a lonely flame against the winds of the world. But the flame goes out, and we grope on through the darkness wondering why there can never be another....

I wonder if Lady Alicia is as cold as she seems? For she has the appearance of keeping her emotions in an ice-box of indifferency, the same as city florists keep their flowers chilled for commercial purposes. Lady Allie, I'm sure, is fond of my little Dinkie. Yet there's a note of condescension in her affection, for even in what seems like an impulse of adoration her exclamation nearly always is "Oh, you lovable little rabbit!" or, if not that, it's likely to be "You adorable little donkey you!" She says it very prettily, of course, setting it to music almost with that melodious English drawl of hers. She is, she must be, a very fascinating woman. But at the first tee, friendship ends, as the golf-nuts say.

...I asked Peter the other day what he regarded as my besetting sin and the brute replied: "Topping the box." I told him I didn't quite get the idea. "A passion to produce a good impression," he explained, "by putting all your biggest mental strawberries on the top!"

"That sounds suspiciously like trying to be a Smart Aleck," I retorted.

"It may sound that way, but it isn't. You're so mentally alive, I mean, that you've simply got to be slightly acrobatic. And it's as natural, of course, as a child's dancing."

But Peter is wrong. I've been out of the world so long that I've a dread of impressing people as stupid, as being a clodhopper. And if trying hard not to be thought that is "topping the box," I suppose I'm guilty.

"You are also not without vanity," Peter judicially continued. "But every naturally beautiful woman has a right to that." And I proved Peter's contention by turning shell-pink even under my sunburn and feeling a warm little runway of pleasure creep up through my carcass, for the homeliest old prairie-hen that ever made a pinto shy, I suppose, loves to be told that she's beautiful.

Peter, of course, is a conscienceless liar, but I can't help liking him, and he'll always nest warm in the ashes of my heart....

There's one thing I must do, as soon as I have the chance, and that is get in to a dentist and have my teeth attended to. And now that I'm so much thinner I want a new and respectable pair of corsets. I've been studying my face in the glass, and I can see, now, what an awful Ananias Peter really is. Struthers, by the way, observed me in the midst of that inspection, and, if I'm not greatly mistaken, indulged in a sniff. To her, I suppose, I'm one of those vain creatures who fall in love with themselves as a child and perpetuate, thereby, a life romance!

Saturday the Twenty-sixth

Coming events do *not* cast their shadows before them. I was busy in the kitchen this morning, making marmalade out of what was left of Peter's oranges and contentedly humming *Oh, Dry Those Tears* when the earthquake that shook the world from under my feet occurred.

The Twins had been bathed and powdered and fed and put out in their sleeping-box, and Dinkie was having his morning nap, and Struthers was busy at the sewing-machine, finishing up the little summer shirts for Poppsy and Pee-Wee which I'd begun to make out of their daddy's discarded B. V. D.'s. It was a glorious morning with a high-arching pale blue sky and little baby-lamb cloudlets along the sky-line and the milk of life running warm and rich in the bosom of the sleeping earth. And I was bustling about in my apron of butcher's linen, after slicing oranges on my little maple-wood carving-slab until the house was aromatic with them, when the sound of a racing car-engine smote on my ear. I went to the door with fire in my eye and the long-handled preserving spoon in my hand, ready to call down destruction on the pinhead who'd dare to wake my kiddies.

My visitor, I saw, was Lady Alicia; and I beheld my broken wash-tub under the front axle of her motor-car.

I went out to her, with indignation still in my eye, but she paid no attention to either that or the tub itself. She was quite pale, in fact, as she stepped down from her driving-seat, glanced at her buckskin gauntlets, and then looked up at me.

"There's something we may as well face, and face at once," she said, with less of a drawl than usual.

I waited, without speaking, wondering if she was referring to the tub. But I could feel my heart contract, like a leg-muscle with a cramp in it. And we stood there, face to face, under the flat prairie sunlight, ridiculously like two cockerels silently estimating each other's intentions.

"I'm in love with your husband," Lady Alicia suddenly announced, with a bell-like note of challenge in her voice. "And I'd rather like to know what you're going to do about it."

I was able to laugh a little, though the sound of it seemed foolish in my own startled ears.

"That's rather a coincidence, isn't it?" I blithely admitted. "For so am I."

I could see the Scotch-granite look that came into the thick-lashed tourmaline eyes. And they'd be lovely eyes, I had to admit, if they were only a little softer.

"That's unfortunate," was her ladyship's curt retort.

"It's more than unfortunate," I agreed, "it's extremely awkward."

"Why?" she snapped, plainly annoyed at my lightness of tone.

"Because he can't possibly have both of us, you know—unless he's willing to migrate over to that Mormon colony at Red-Deer. And even there, I understand, they're not doing it now."

"I'm afraid this is something much too serious to joke about," Lady Alicia informed me.

"But it strikes me as essentially humorous," I told her.

"I'm afraid," she countered, "that it's apt to prove essentially tragic."

"But he happens to be *my* husband," I observed.

"Only in form, I fancy, if he cares for some one else," was her ladyship's deliberate reply.

"Then he has acknowledged that—that you've captured him?" I inquired, slowly but surely awakening to the sheer audacity of the lady in the buckskin gauntlets.

"Isn't that rather—er—primitive?" inquired Lady Allie, paler than ever.

"If you mean coming and squabbling over another woman's husband, I'd call it distinctly prehistoric," I said with a dangerous little red light dancing before my eyes. "It's so original that it's aboriginal. But I'm still at a loss to know just what your motive is, or what you want."

"I want an end to this intolerable situation," my visitor averred.

"Intolerable to whom?" I inquired.

"To me, to Duncan, and to *you*, if you are the right sort of woman," was Lady Alicia's retort. And still again I was impressed by the colossal egoism of the woman confronting me, the woman ready to ride rough-shod over the world, for all her sparkling veneer of civilization, as long, as she might reach her own selfish ends.

"Since you mention Duncan, I'd like to ask if you're speaking now as his cousin, or as his mistress?"

Lady Alicia's stare locked with mine. She was making a sacrificial effort, I could see, to remain calm.

"I'm speaking as some one who is slightly interested in his happiness, and his future," was her coldly intoned reply.

"And has my husband acknowledged that his happiness and his future remain in your hands?" I asked.

"I should hate to see him waste his life in a hole like this," said Lady Alicia, not quite answering my question.

"Have you brought any great improvement to it?" I parried. Yet even as I spoke I stood impressed by the thought that it was, after all, more than primitive. It was paleolithic, two prehistoric she-things in combat for their cave-man.

"That is not what I came here to discuss," she replied, with a tug at one of her gauntlets.

"I suppose it would be nearer the mark to say, since you began by being so plain-spoken, that you came here to ask me to give you my husband," I retorted as quietly as I could, not because I preferred the soft pedal, but because I nursed a strong suspicion that Struthers' attentive ear was just below the nearest window-sill.

Lady Alicia smiled forbearingly, almost pityingly.

"Any such donation, I'm afraid, is no longer your prerogative," she languidly remarked, once more mistress of herself. "What I'm more interested in is your giving your husband his liberty."

I felt like saying that this was precisely what I had been giving him. But it left too wide an opening. So I ventured, instead: "I've never heard my husband express a desire for his liberty."

"He's too honorable for that," remarked my enemy.

"Then it's an odd kind of honor," I icily remarked, "that allows you to come here and bicker over a situation that is so distinctly personal."

"Pardon me, but I'm not bickering. And I'm not rising to any heights of courage which would be impossible to your husband. It's consoling, however, to know how matters stand. And Duncan will probably act according to his own inclinations."

That declaration would have been more inflammatory, I think, if one small truth hadn't gradually come home to me. In some way, and for some reason, Lady Alicia Elizabeth Newland was not so sure of herself as she was pretending to be. She was not so sure of her position, I began to see, or she would never have thrown restraint to the winds and come to me on any such mission.

"Then that counts me out!" I remarked, with a forlorn attempt at being facetious. "If he's going to do as he likes, I don't see that you or I have much to say in the matter. But before he does finally place his happiness in your hands, I rather think I'd like to have a talk with him."

"That remains with Duncan, of course," she admitted, in a strictly qualified tone of triumph, as though she were secretly worrying over a conquest too incredibly facile.

"He knows, of course, that you came to talk this over with me?" I suggested, as though it were an after-thought.

"He had nothing to do with my coming," asserted Lady Alicia.

"Then it was your own idea?" I asked.

"Entirely," she admitted.

"Then what did you hope to gain?" I demanded.

"I wasn't considering my own feelings," imperially acknowledged her ladyship.

"That was very noble of you," I admitted, "especially when you bear in mind that you weren't considering mine, either! And what's more, Lady Newland, I may as well tell you right here, and right now, that you can't get anything out of it. I gave up my home to you, the home I'd helped make by the work of my own hands. And I gave up the hope of bringing up my children as they ought to be brought up. I even gave up my dignity and my happiness, in the hope that things could be made to come out straight. But I'm not going to give up my husband. Remember that, I'm not going to give him up. I don't care what he says or feels, at this particular moment; I'm not going to give him up to make a mess of what's left of the rest of his life. He may not know what's ahead of him, *but I do*! And now that you're shown me just what you are, and just what you're ready to do, I intend to take a hand in this. I intend to fight you to the last ditch, and to the last drop of the hat! And if that sounds primitive, as you've already suggested, it'll pay you to remember that you're out here in a primitive country where we're apt to do our fighting in a mighty primitive way!"

It was a very grand speech, but it would have been more impressive, I think, if I hadn't been suddenly startled by a glimpse of Whinstane Sandy's rock-ribbed face peering from the bunk-house window at almost the same moment that I distinctly saw the tip of Struthers' sage-green coiffure above the nearest sill of the shack. And it would have been a grander speech if I'd stood quite sure as to precisely what it meant and what I intended to do. Yet it seemed sufficiently climactic for my visitor, who, after a queenly and combative stare into what must have looked like an ecstatically excited

Fourth-of-July face, turned imperially about and swung open the door of her motor-car. Then she stepped up to the car-seat, as slowly and deliberately as a sovereign stepping up to her throne.

"It may not be so simple as it seems," she announced with great dignity, as she proceeded to start her car. And the same dignity might have attended her entire departure, but in the excitement she apparently flooded her carbureter, and the starter refused to work, and she pushed and spun and re-throttled and pushed until she was quite red in the face. And when the car finally did get under way, the running-gear became slightly involved with my broken wash-tub and it was not until the latter was completely and ruthlessly demolished that the automobile found its right-of-way undisputed and anything like dignity returned to the situation.

I stood there, with the long-handled preserving spoon still in my hand, staring after Lady Alicia and the dust that arose from her car-wheels. I stood there in a sort of trance, with all the valor gone out of my bones and that foolish declamation of mine still ringing in my ears.

I began to think of all the clever things I might have said to Lady Alicia Elizabeth Newland. But the more I thought it over the more desolated I became in spirit, so that by the time I meandered back to the shack I had a face as long as a fiddle. And there I was confronted by a bristling and voluble Struthers, who acknowledged that she'd heard what she'd heard, and could no longer keep her lips sealed, whether it was her place to speak or not, and that her ladyship was not all that she ought to be, not by any manner of means, or she would never have left England and hidden herself away in this wilderness of a colony.

I had been rather preoccupied with my own thoughts, and paying scant attention to the clattering-tongued Struthers, up to this point. But the intimation that Lady Allie was not in the West for the sake of her health brought me up short. And Struthers, when I challenged that statement, promptly announced that the lady in question was no more in search of health than a tom-cat's in search of water and no more interested in ranching than an ox is interested in astronomy, seeing as she'd 'a' been co-respondent in the Allerby and Crewe-Buller divorce case if she'd stayed where the law could have laid a hand on her, and standing more shamed than ever when Baron Crewe-Buller shut himself up in his shooting-lodge and blew his brains out three weeks before her ladyship had sailed for America, and the papers that full of the scandal it made it unpleasant for a self-respecting lady's maid to meet her friends of a morning in Finsbury Park. And as for these newer goings-on, Struthers had seen what was happening right under her nose, she had, long before she had the chance to say so openly by word of mouth, but now that the fat was in the fire she wasn't the kind to sit by and see those she should be loyal to led about by the nose. And so forth. And so forth! For just what else the irate Struthers had to unload from her turbulent breast I never did know, since at that opportune moment Dinkie awakened and proceeded to page his parent with all the strength of his impatient young lungs.

By the time I'd attended to Dinkie and finished my sadly neglected marmalade—for humans must eat, whatever happens—I'd made an effort to get some sort of order back into my shattered world. Yet it was about Duncan more than any one else that my thoughts kept clustering and centering. He seemed, at the moment, oddly beyond either pity or blame. I thought of him as a victim of his own weakness, as the prey of a predaceous and unscrupulous woman who had intrigued and would continue to intrigue against his happiness, a woman away from her own world, a self-complacent and sensual privateer who for a passing whim, for a momentary appeasement of her exile, stood ready to sacrifice the last of his self-respect. She was self-complacent, but she was also a woman with an unmistakable physical appeal. She was undeniably attractive, as far as appearances went, and added to that attractiveness was a dangerous immediacy of attack, a touch of outlawry, which only too often wins before resistance can be organized. And Dinky-Dunk, I kept reminding myself, was at that dangerous mid-channel period of a man's life where youth and age commingle, where the monotonous middle-years slip their shackles over his shoulders and remind him that his days of dalliance are ebbing away. He awakens to the fact that romance is being left behind, that the amorous adventure which once meant so much to him must soon belong to the past, that he must settle down to his jog-trot of family life. It's the age, I suppose, when any spirited man is tempted to kick up with a good-by convulsion or two of romantic adventure, as blind as it is brief and passionate, sadly like the contortions of a rooster with its head cut off.

I tried, as I sat down and struggled to think things out, to withhold all blame and bitterness. Then I tried to think of life without Dinky-Dunk. I attempted to picture my daily existence with somebody else in the place that my Diddums had once filled. But I couldn't do it. I couldn't forget the old days. I couldn't forget the wide path of life that we'd traveled together, and that he was the father of my children—my children who will always need him!—and that he and he alone had been my torch-bearer into the tangled wilderness of passion.

Then I tried to think of life alone, of going solitary through the rest of my days—and I knew that my Maker had left me too warm-blooded and too dependent on the companionship of a mate ever to turn back to single harness. I couldn't live without a man. He might be a sorry mix-up of good and bad, but I, the Eternal Female, would crave him as a mate. Most women, I knew, were averse to acknowledging such things; but life has compelled me to be candid with myself. The tragic part of it all seems that there should and could be only one man. I had been right when I had only too carelessly called myself a neck-or-nothing woman.

It wasn't until later that any definite thought of injustice to me at Dinky-Dunk's hands entered my head, since my attitude toward Dinky-Dunk seemed to remain oddly maternal, the attitude of the mother intent on extenuating her own. I even wrung a ghostly sort of consolation out of remembering that it was not a young and dewy girl who had imposed herself on his romantic imagination, for youth and innocence and chivalric obligation would have brought a much more dangerous fire to fight. But Lady Alicia, with all her carefully achieved charm, could scarcely lay claim to either youth or the other thing. Early in the morning, I knew, those level dissecting eyes of hers would look hard, and before her hair was up she'd look a little faded, and there'd be moments of stress and strain when her naively insolent drawl would jar on the nerves, like the talk of a spoiled child too intent on holding the attention of a visitor averse to precocity. And her disdain of the practical would degenerate into untidiness, and her clinging-ivyness, if it clung too much, would probably remind a man in his reactionary moments of *ennui* that there are subtler pursuits than being a wall, even though it's a sustaining wall.

And somewhere in her make-up was a strain of cruelty or she would never have come to me the way she did, and struck at me with an open claw. That cruelty, quite naturally, could never have been paraded before my poor old Dinky-Dunk's eyes. It would be, later on, after disillusionment and boredom. Then, and then only, it would dare to show its ugly head. So instead of feeling sorry for myself, I began to feel sorry for my Diddums, even though he was trying to switch me off like an electric-light. And all of a sudden I came to a decision.

I decided to write to Dinky-Dunk. That, I felt, would be safer than trying to see him. For in a letter I could say what I wanted to without being stopped or side-tracked. There would be no danger of accusations and recriminations, of anger leading to extremes, of injured pride standing in the path of honesty. It would be better than talking. And what was more, it could be done at once, for the mysterious impression that time was precious, that something ominous was in the air, had taken hold of me.

So I wrote to Dinky-Dunk. I did it on two crazy-looking pages torn out of the back of his old ranch ledger. I did it without giving much thought to precisely what I said or exactly how I phrased it, depending on my heart more than my brain to guide me in the way I should go. For I knew, in the marrow of my bones, that it was my last shot, my forlornest ultimatum, since in it went packed the last shred of my pride.

"Dear Dinky-Dunk," I wrote, "I hardly know how to begin, but I surely don't need to begin by saying we haven't been hitting it off very well of late. We seem to have made rather a mess of things, and I suppose it's partly my fault, and the fault of that stupid pride which keeps us tongue-tied when we should be honest and open with each other. But I've been feeling lately that we're both skirting a cut-bank with our eyes blindfolded, and I've faced an incident, trivial in itself but momentous in its possibilities, which persuades me that things can't go on as they are. There's too much at stake to let either ruffled nerves or false modesty—or whatever you want to call it—come between you and the very unhappy woman who still is your wife. It's time, I think, when we both ought to look everything squarely in the face, for, after all, we've only one life to live, and if you're happy, at this moment, if you're completely and tranquilly happy as I write this, then I've banked wrong, tragically wrong, on what I thought you were. For I *have* banked on you, Dinky-Dunk, banked about all my life and happiness—and it's too late to change, even if I wanted to. I'm alone in the world, and in a lonely part of the world, with three small children to look after, and that as much as anything, I suppose, drives me to plain speaking and compels me to clear thinking. But even as I write these words to you, I realize that it isn't really a matter of thought or speech. It's a matter of feeling. And the one thing I feel is that I need you and want you; that no one, that nothing, can ever take your place.... I thought I could write a great deal more. But I find I can't. I seem to have said everything. It *is* everything, really. For I love you, Dinky-Dunk, more than everything in life. Perhaps I haven't shown it very much, of late, but it's there, trying to hide its silly old ostrich-head behind a pebble of hurt pride. So let's turn the page and start over. Let's start with a clean slate, before we lose the chance. Come back to me. I'm very unhappy. I find it hard to write. It's only that big ache in my heart that allows me to write at all. And I've left a lot of things unsaid, that I ought to have said, and intended to say, but this will have to be enough. If there's nothing that speaks up to you, from between these lines, then there's nothing that can hold together, I'm afraid, what's left of your life and mine. Think this over, Dinky-Dunk, and answer the way your heart dictates. But please don't keep me waiting too long, for until I get that answer I'll be like a hen on a hot griddle or Mary Queen of Scots on the morning before she lost her head, if that's more dignified."

The hardest part of all that letter, I found, was the ending of it. It took me a long time to decide just what to sign myself, just how to pilot my pen between the rocks of candor and dignity. So I ended up by signing it "Chaddie" and nothing more, for already the fires of emotion had cooled and a perplexed little reaction of indifferency had set in. It was only a surface-stir, but it was those surface-stirs, I remembered, which played such a lamentably important part in life.

When Whinstane Sandy came in at noon for his dinner, a full quarter of an hour ahead of Peter, I had his meal all ready for him by the time he had watered and fed his team. I cut that meal short, in fact, by handing him my carefully sealed letter and telling him I wanted him to take it straight over to Casa Grande.

I knew by his face as I helped him hitch Water-Light to the buckboard— for Whinnie's foot makes it hard for him to ride horseback—that he nursed a pretty respectable inkling of the situation. He offered no comments, and he even seemed averse to having his eye meet mine, but he obviously knew what he knew.

He was off with a rattle of wheels and a drift of trail-dust even before Peter and his cool amending eyes arrived at the shack to "stoke up" as he expresses it. I tried to make Peter believe that nothing was wrong, and cavorted about with Bobs, and was able to laugh when Dinkie got some of the new marmalade in his hair, and explained how we'd have to take our mower-knives over to Teetzel's to have them ground, and did my best to direct silent reproofs at the tight-lipped and tragic-eyed Struthers, who moved about like a head-mourner not unconscious of her family obligations. But Peter, I suspect, sniffed something untoward in the air, for after a long study of my face—which made me color a little, in spite of myself—he became about as abstracted and solemn-eyed as Struthers herself.

To my dying day I shall never forget that wait for Whinnie to come back. It threatened to become an endless one. I felt like Bluebeard's wife up in the watch tower—no, it was her Sister Anne, wasn't it, who anxiously mounted the tower to search for the first sign of deliverance? At any rate I felt like Luck—now before the Relief, or a prisoner waiting for the jury to file in, or a gambler standing over an invisible roulette-table and his last throw, wondering into what groove the little ivory ball was to run. And when Whinnie finally appeared his seamed old face wore such a look of dour satisfaction that for a weak flutter or two of the heart I thought he'd brought Dinky-Dunk straight back with him.

But that hope didn't live long.

"Your maun's awa'," said Whinnie, with quite unnecessary curtness, as he held my own letter out to me.

"He's away?" I echoed in a voice that was just a wee bit trembly, as I took the note from Whinnie, "what do you mean by away?"

"He left three hours ago for Chicago," Whinstane Sandy retorted, still with that grim look of triumph in his gloomy old eyes.

"But what could be taking him to Chicago?" I rather weakly inquired.

"'Twas to see about buyin' some blooded stock for the ranch. At least, so her ladyship informed me. But that's nae more than one of her lies, I'm thinkin'."

"What did she say, Whinnie?" I demanded, doing my best to keep cool.

"Naethin'," was Whinnie's grim retort. "'Twas me did the sayin'!"

"What did you say?" I asked, disturbed by the none too gentle look on his face.

"What was needed to be said," that old sour-dough with the lack-luster eyes quietly informed me.

"What did you say?" I repeated, with a quavery feeling just under my floating ribs, alarmed at the after-light of audacity that still rested on his face, like wine-glow on a rocky mountain-tip.

"I said," Whinstane Sandy informed me with his old shoulders thrust back and his stubby forefinger pointed to within a few inches of my nose, "I said that I kenned her and her kind well, havin' watched the likes o' her ridden out o' Dawson City on a rail more times than once. I said that she was naethin' but a wanton"—only this was *not* the word Whinnie used—"a wanton o' Babylon and a temptress o' men and a corrupter o' homes out o' her time and place, bein' naught but a soft shinin' thing that was a mockery to the guid God who made her and a blight to the face o' the open prairie that she was foulin' with her presence. I said that she'd brought shame and sorrow to a home that had been filled with happiness until she crept into it like the serpent o' hell she was, and seein' she'd come into a lonely land where the people have the trick o' tryin' their own cases after their own way and takin' when need be justice into their own hands, she'd have one week, one week o' seven days and no more, to gather up what belonged to her and take herself back to the cities o' shame where she'd find more o' her kind. And if she was not disposed to hearken a friendly and timely word such as I was givin' her, I said, she'd see herself taken out o' her home, and her hoorish body stripped to the skin, and then tarred and feathered, and ridden on the cap-rail of a corral-gate out of a settlement that had small taste for her company!"

"Whinnie!" I gasped, sitting down out of sheer weakness, "you didn't say that?"

"I said it," was Whinnie's laconic retort.

"But what right had you to—"

He cut me short with a grunt that was almost disrespectful.

"I not only said it," he triumphantly affirmed, "but what's more to my likin', I made her believe it, leavin' her with the mockin' laugh dead in her eyes and her face as white as yon table-cover, white to the lips!"

Sunday the Twenty-seventh

I've been just a little mystified, to-day, by Whinstane Sandy's movements. As soon as breakfast was over and his chores were done he was off on the trail. I kept my eye on him as he went, to satisfy myself that he was not heading for Casa Grande, where no good could possibly come of his visitations.

For I've been most emphatic to Whinstane Sandy in the matter of his delightful little lynch-law program. There shall be no tarring and feathering of women by any man in my employ. That may have been possible in the Klondike in the days of the gold-rush, but it's not possible in this country and this day of grace—except in the movies. And life is not so simple that you can ride its problems away on the cap-rail from a corral. It's unfortunate that that absurd old sour-dough, for all his good intentions, ever got in touch with Lady Alicia. I have, in fact, strictly forbidden him to repeat his visit to Casa Grande, under any circumstances.

But a number of things combine to persuade me that he's not being as passive as he pretends. He's even sufficiently forgotten his earlier hostility toward Peter to engage in long and guarded conversation with that gentleman, as the two of them made a pretense of bolting the new anchor-timbers to the heel of the windmill tower. So at supper to-night I summoned up sufficient courage to ask Peter what he knew about the situation.

He replied that he knew more than he wanted to, and more than he relished. That reply proving eminently unsatisfactory, I further inquired what he thought of Lady Alicia. He somewhat startled and shocked me by retorting that according to his own personal way of thinking she ought to be spanked until she glowed.

I was disappointed in Peter about this. I had always thought of him as on a higher plane than poor old Whinnie. But he was equally atavistic, once prejudice had taken possession of him, for what he suggested must be regarded as not one whit more refined than tar and feathers. As for myself, I'd like to choke her, only I haven't the moral courage to admit it to anybody.

Thursday the First

Lady Alicia has announced, I learn through a Struthers quite pop-eyed with indignation, that it's Peter and I who possibly ought to be tarred and feathered, if our puritanical community is deciding to go in for that sort of thing! It is to laugh.

Her ladyship, I also learn, has purchased about all the small-arms ammunition in Buckhorn and toted the same back to Casa Grande in her car. There, in unobstructed view of the passers-by, she has set up a target, on which, by the hour together, she coolly and patiently practises sharpshooting with both rifle and revolver.

I admire that woman's spunk. And whatever you may do, you can't succeed in bullying the English. They have too much of the bull-dog breed in their bones. They're always at their best, Peter declares, when they're fighting. "But from an Englishwoman trying to be kittenish," he fervently added, "good Lord, deliver us all!"

And that started us talking about the English. Peter, of course, is too tolerant to despise his cousins across the Pond, but he pregnantly reminded me that Lady Allie had asked him what sort of town Saskatchewan was and he had retorted by inquiring if she was fond of Yonkers, whereupon she'd looked puzzled and acknowledged that she'd never eaten one. For Peter and Lady Allie, it seems, had had a set-to about American map-names, which her ladyship had described as both silly and unsayable, especially the Indian ones, while Peter had grimly proclaimed that any people who called Seven-Oaks *Snooks* and Belvoir *Beever* and Ruthven *Rivven* and Wrottesley *Roxly* and Marylebone *Marrabun* and Wrensfordsley *Wrensley* had no right to kick about American pronunciations.

But Peter is stimulating, even though he does stimulate you into opposition. So I found myself defending the English, and especially the Englishman, for too many of them had made me happy in their lovely old homes and too many of their sons, æons and æons ago, had tried to hold my hand.

"Your Englishman," I proclaimed to Peter, "always acts as though he quite disapproves of you and yet he'll go to any amount of trouble to do things to make you happy or comfortable. Then he conceals his graciousness by being curt about it. Then, when he's at his crankiest, he's apt to startle you by saying the divinest things point-blank in your face, and as likely as not, after treating you as he would a rather backward child of whom he rigidly disapproves, he'll make love to you and do it with a fine old Anglo-Saxon directness. He hates swank, of course, for he's a truffle-hound who prefers digging out his own delicacies. And it's ten to one, if a woman simply sits tight and listens close and says nothing, that he'll say something about her unrivaled powers of conversation!"

Sunday the Fourth

Peter, as we sat out beside the corral on an empty packing-case to-night after supper, said that civilization was a curse. "Look what it's doing to your noble Red Man right here in your midst! There was a time, when a brave died, they handsomely killed that dead brave's favorite horse, feeling he would course the plains of Heaven in peace. Now, I find, they have their doubts, and they pick out a dying old bone-yard whose day is over, or an outlaw that nobody can break and ride. And form without faith is a mockery. It's the same with us whites. Here we are, us two, with—"

But I stopped Peter. I had no wish to slide on rubber-ice just for the sake of seeing it bend.

"Can you imagine anything lovelier," I remarked as a derailer, "than the prairie at this time of the year, and this time of day?"

Peter followed my eye out over the undulating and uncounted acres of sage-green grain with an eternity of opal light behind them.

"Think of LaVérendrye, who was their Columbus," he meditated aloud. "Going on and on, day by day, week by week, wondering what was beyond that world of plain and slough and coulée and everlasting green! And they tell me there's four hundred million arable acres of it. I wonder if old Vérendrye ever had an inkling of what Whittier felt later on:

'I hear the tread of pioneers,

    Of cities yet to be—

The first low wash of waves where soon

    Shall roll a human sea.'"

Then Peter went on to say that Bryant had given him an entirely false idea of the prairie, since from the Bryant poem he'd expected to see grass up to his armpits. And he'd been disappointed, too, by the scarcity of birds and flowers.

But I couldn't let that complaint go by unchallenged. I told him of our range-lilies and foxglove and buffalo-beans and yellow crowfoot and wild sunflowers and prairie-roses and crocuses and even violets in some sections. "And the prairie-grasses, Peter—don't forget the prairie-grasses," I concluded, perplexed for a moment by the rather grim smile that crept up into his rather solemn old Peter-Panish face.

"I'm not likely to," he remarked.

For to-morrow, I remembered, Peter is going off to cut hay. He has been speaking of it as going into the wilderness for meditation. But what he's really doing is taking a team and his tent and supplies and staying with that hay until it's cut, cut and "*collected*," to use the word which the naive Lady Allie introduced into these parts.

I have a suspicion that it is the wagging of tongues that's sending Peter out into his wilderness. But I've been busy getting his grub-box ready and I can at least see that he fares well. For whatever happens, we must have hay. And before long, since we're to go in more and more for live stock, we must have a silo at Alabama Ranch. Now that the open range is a thing of the past, in this part of the country at least, the silo is the natural solution of the cattle-feed problem. It means we can double our stock, which is rather like getting another farm for nothing, especially as the peas and oats we can grow for ensilage purposes give such enormous yields on this soil of ours.

Tuesday the Sixth

For the second time the unexpected has happened. Lady Alicia has gone. She's off, bag and baggage, and has left the redoubtable Sing Lo in charge of Casa Grande.

Her ladyship waited until one full day after the time-limit imposed upon her by Whinstane Sandy in that barbarous armistice of his, and then, having saved her face, joined the Broadhursts of Montreal on a trip to Banff, where she'll be more in touch with her kind and her countrymen. From there, I understand, she intends visiting the Marquis of Anglesey ranch at Wallachie.

I don't know what she intends doing about her property, but it seems to me it doesn't show any great interest in either her crop or her cousin, to decamp at this particular time. Struthers protests that she's a born gambler, and can't live without bridge and American poker. Banff, accordingly, ought to give her what she's pining for....

But I'm too busy to worry about Lady Allie. The Big Drama of the year is opening on this sun-steeped plain of plenty, for harvest-time will soon be here and we've got to be ready for it. We're on the go from six in the morning until sun-down. We're bringing in Peter's crop of hay with the tractor, hauling three wagon-loads at a time. I make the double trip, getting back just in time to feed my babies and then hiking out again. That means we're all hitting on every cylinder. I've no time for either worries or wishes, though Peter once remarked that life is only as deep as its desires, and that the measure of our existence lies in the extent of its wants. That may be true, in a way, but I haven't time to philosophize over it. Hard work can be more than a narcotic. It's almost an anesthetic. And soil, I've been thinking, should be the symbol of life here, as it is with the peasants of Poland. I feel that I'm getting thinner, but I've an appetite that I'm ashamed of, in secret.

Dinky-Dunk, by the way, is not back yet, and there's been no word from him. Struthers is resolute in her belief that he's in hiding somewhere about the mountain-slopes of Banff. But I am just as resolute in my scorn for all such suspicions. And yet, and yet,—if I wasn't so busy I'd be tempted to hold solemn days of feasting and supplication that Lady Alicia Elizabeth Newland might wade out beyond her depth in the pellucid waters of Lake Louise.

Friday the Sixteenth

Peter surprised me yesterday by going in to Buckhorn and bringing out a machinist to work on the windmill tower. By mid-afternoon they had it ready for hoisting and rebolting to its new anchor-posts. So just before supper the team and the block-and-tackle were hitched on to that attenuated steel skeleton, Whinnie took one guide rope and I took the other, and our little Eiffel Tower slowly lifted itself up into the sky.

Peter, when it was all over, and the last nut tightened up, walked about with the triumphant smile of a Master-Builder who beholds his work completed. So I said "Hello, *Halvard Solness*!" as I stepped over to where he stood.

And he was bright enough to catch it on the wing, for he quoted back to me, still staring up at the tower-head: "From this day forward I will be a free builder."

Whereupon I carelessly retorted, "Oh, there's some parts of Ibsen that I despise."

But something in Peter's tone and his preoccupation during supper both worried and perplexed me. So as soon as I could get away from the shack I went out to the windmill tower again. And the small platform at the end of the sloping little iron ladder looked so tempting and high above the world that I started up the galvanized rungs.

When I was half-way up I stopped and looked down. It made me dizzy, for prairie life gives you few chances of getting above the flat floor of your flat old world. But I was determined to conquer that feeling, and by keeping my eyes turned up toward the windmill head I was able to reach the little platform at the top and sit there with my feet hanging over and my right arm linked through one of the steel standards.

I suppose, as windmills go, it wasn't so miraculously high, but it was amazing how even that moderate altitude where I found myself could alter one's view-point. I felt like a sailor in a crow's-nest, like a sentinel on a watch-tower, like an eagle poised giddily above the world. And such a wonderful and wide-flung world it was, spreading out beneath me in mottled patches of grape-leaf green and yellow and gold, with a burgundian riot of color along the western sky-line where the last orange rind of the sun had just slipped down out of sight.

As I stared down at the roof of our shack it looked small and pitiful, tragically meager to house the tangled human destinies it was housing. And the fields where we'd labored and sweated took on a foreign and ghostly coloring, as though they were oblongs on the face of an alien world, a world with mystery and beauty and unfathomable pathos about it.

I was sitting there, with my heels swinging out in space and an oddly consoling sense of calmness in my heart, when Peter came out of the shack and started to cross toward the corral. I couldn't resist the temptation to toss my old straw hat down at him.

He stopped short as it fell within twenty paces of him, like a meteor out of the sky. Then he turned and stared up at me. The next minute I saw him knock out his little briar pipe, put it away in his pocket, and cross over to the tower.

I could feel the small vibrations of the steel structure on which I sat poised, as he mounted the ladder toward me. And it felt for all the world like sitting on the brink of Heaven, like a blessed damozel the second, watching a sister-soul coming up to join you in your beatitude.

"I say, isn't this taking a chance?" asked Peter, a little worried and a little out of breath, as he clambered up beside me.

"It's glorious!" I retorted, with a nod toward the slowly paling sky-line.

That far and lonely horizon looked as though a fire of molten gold burned behind the thinnest of mauve and saffron and purple curtains, a fire that was too subdued to be actual flame, but more an unearthly and ethereal radiance, luring the vision on and on until it brought an odd little sense of desolation to the heart and made me glad to remember that Peter was swinging his lanky legs there at my side out over empty space.

"I find," he observed, "that this tower was sold to a tenderfoot, by the foot. That's why it went over. It was too highfalutin! It was thirty feet taller than it had any need to be."

Then he dropped back into silence.

I finally became conscious of the fact that Peter, instead of staring at the sunset, was staring at me. And I remembered that my hair was half down, trailing across my nose, and that three distinctly new freckles had shown themselves that week on the bridge of that same nose.

"O God, but you're lovely!" he said in a half-smothered and shamefaced sort of whisper.

"*Verboten!*" I reminded him. "And not so much the cussing, Peter, as the useless compliments."

He said nothing to that, but once more sat staring out over the twilight prairie for quite a long time. When he spoke again it was in a quieter and much more serious tone.

"I suppose I may as well tell you," he said without looking at me, "that I've come into a pretty clear understanding of the situation here at Alabama Ranch."

"It's kind of a mix-up, isn't it?" I suggested, with an attempt at lightness.

Peter nodded his head.

"I've been wondering how long you're going to wait," he observed, apparently as much to himself as to me.

"Wait for what?" I inquired.

"For what you call your mix-up to untangle," was his answer.

"There's nothing for me to do but to wait," I reminded him.

He shook his head in dissent.

"You can't waste your life, you know, doing that," he quietly protested.

"What else can I do?" I asked, disturbed a little by the absence of color from his face, apparent even in that uncertain light.

"Nothing's suggested itself, I suppose?" he ventured, after a silence.

"Nothing that prompts me into any immediate action," I told him. "You see, Peter, I'm rather anchored by three little hostages down in that little shack there!"

That left him silent for another long and brooding minute or two.

"I suppose you've wondered," he finally said, "why I've stuck around here as long as I have?"

I nodded, not caring to trust myself to words, and then, realizing I was doing the wrong thing, I shook my head.

"It's because, from the morning you found me in that mud-hole, I've just wanted to be near you, to hear your voice when you spoke, to see the curve of your lips and the light come and go in your eyes when you laugh," were the words that came ever so slowly from Peter. "I've wanted that so much that I've let about everything else in life go hang. Yet in a way, and in my own world, I'm a man of some little importance. I've been cursed with enough money, of course, to move about as I wish, and loaf as I like. But that sort of life isn't really living. I'm not in the habit, though, of wanting the things I can't have. So what strikes me as the tragic part of it all is that I couldn't have met and known you when you were as free as I am now. In a way, you *are* free, or you ought to be. You're a woman, I think, with arrears of life to make up. You've struck me, from the very first, as too alive, too sensitive, too responsive to things, to get the fullest measure out of life by remaining here on the prairie, in what are, after all, really pioneer conditions. You've known the other kind of life, as well as I have, and it will always be calling to you. And if that call means anything to you, and the—the change we've spoken of is on its way, or for some unexpected reason has to come, I'm—well, I'm going to take the bit in my teeth right here and tell you that I love you more than you imagine and a good deal more, I suppose, than the law allows!"

He pushed my hand aside when I held it up to stop him.

"I may as well say it, for this is as good a time and place as we'll ever have, and I can't go around with my teeth shut on the truth any longer. I know you've got your three little tots down there, and I love 'em about as much as you do. And it would seem like giving a little meaning and purpose to life to know that I had the chance of doing what I could to make you and to make them happy. I've—"

But I couldn't let him go on.

"It's no use, Peter," I cried with a little choke in my voice which I couldn't control. "It's no earthly use. I've known you liked me, and it's given me a warm little feeling down in one corner of my heart. But I could never allow it to be more than a corner. I like you, Peter, and I like you a lot. You're wonderful. In some ways you're the most adorable man I've ever known in all my life. That's a dangerous thing to say, but it's the truth and I may as well say it. It even hurts a little to remember that I've traded on your chivalry, though that's the one thing in life you *can* trade on without reproof or demand for repayment. But as I told you before, I'm one of those neck-or-nothing women, one of those single-track women, who can't have their tides of traffic going two ways at once. And if I'm in a mix-up, or a maelstrom, or whatever you want to call it, I'm in it. That's where I belong. It would never, never do to drag an innocent outsider into that mixed-up mess of life, simply because I imagined it could make me a little more comfortable to have him there."

Peter sat thinking over what I'd said. There were no heroics, no chest-pounding, no suggestion of romantically blighted lives and broken hearts.

"That means, of course, that I'll have to climb out," Peter finally and very prosaically remarked.

"Why?" I asked.

"Because it's so apt to leave one of us sailing under false colors," was his somewhat oblique way of explaining the situation. "I might have hung on until something happened, I suppose, if I hadn't shown my hand. And I hadn't quite the right to show my hand, when you take everything into consideration. But you can't always do what you intend to. And life's a little bigger than deportment, anyway, so what's the use of fussing over it? There's just one thing, though, I want to say, before we pull down the shutters again. I want you to feel that if anything does happen, if by any mischance things should take a turn for the worse, or you're worried in any way about the outcome of all this"—he indulged in a quiet but comprehensive hand-wave which embraced the entire ranch that lay in the gray light at our feet—"I want you to feel that I'd be mighty happy to think you'd turn to me for—for help."

It was getting just a little too serious again, I felt, and I decided in a bit of a panic to pilot things back to shallower water.

"But you *have* helped, Peter," I protested. "Look at all that hay you cut, and the windmill here, and the orange marmalade that'll make me think of you every morning!"

He leaned a little closer and regarded me with a quiet and wistful eye. But I refused to look at him.

"That's nothing to what I'd like to do, if you gave me the chance," he observed, settling back against the tower-standard again.

"I know, Peter," I told him, "And it's nice of you to say it. But the nicest thing of all is your prodigious unselfishness, the unselfishness that's leaving this talk of ours kind of—well, kind of hallowed, and something we'll not be unhappy in remembering, when it could have so easily turned into something selfishly mean and ugly and sordid. That's where you're *big*. And that's what I'll always love you for!"

"Let's go down," said Peter, all of a sudden. "It's getting cold."

I sat staring down at the world to which we had to return. It seemed a long way off. And the ladder that led down to it seemed a cobwebby and uncertain path for a lady whose heart was still slipping a beat now and then. Peter apparently read the perplexity on my face.

"Don't worry," he said. "I'll go down one rung ahead of you. Even if you did slip, then, I'll be there to hold you up. Come on."

We started down, with honest old Peter's long arms clinging to the ladder on either side of me and my feet following his, step by step, as we went like a newfangled sort of quadruped down the narrow steel rungs.

We were within thirty feet of the ground when I made ever so slight a misstep and brought Peter up short. The next moment he'd caught me up bodily in his right arm, and to steady myself I let my arms slip about his neck. I held on there, tight, even after I knew what I was doing, and let my cheek rest against the bristly side of his head as we went slowly down to the bottom of the tower.

It wasn't necessary, my holding my arms about Peter's neck. It wasn't any more necessary than it was for him to pick me up and carry me the rest of the way down. It wasn't true-to-the-line fair play, even, when you come to think of it in cold blood, and it wasn't by any manner of means just what sedately married ladies should do.

But, if the terrible truth must be told, *it was nice*. I think both our hearts were a little hungry for the love which didn't happen to be coming our way, which the law of man and his Maker alike prohibited. So we saved our dignity and our self-respect, oddly enough, by resorting to the shallowest of subterfuges. And I don't care much if it wasn't true-to-the-line ethics. I liked the feel of Peter's arm around me, holding me that way, and I hope he liked that long and semi-respectable hug I gave him, and that now and then, later on, in the emptier days of his life, he'll remember it pleasantly, and without a bit of bitterness in his heart.

For Alabama Ranch, of course, is going to lose Peter as soon as he can get away.

Tuesday the Twenty-fourth

Peter is no longer with us. He went yesterday, much to the open grief of an adoring and heart-broken Struthers. I stood in the doorway as he drove off, pretending to mop my eyes with my hankie and then making a show of wringing the brine out of it. He laughed at this bit of play-acting, but it was rather a melancholy laugh. Struthers, however, was quite snappy for the rest of the morning, having apparently construed my innocent pantomime as a burlesque of her tendency to sniffle a little.

I never quite knew how much we'd miss Peter until he was gone, and gone for good. Even Dinkie was strangely moody and downcast, and showed his depression by a waywardness of spirit which reached its crowning misdemeanor by poking a bean into his ear.

This seemed a trivial enough incident, at first. But the heat and moisture of that little pocket of flesh caused the bean to swell, and soon had Dinkie crying with pain. So I renewed my efforts to get that bean out of the child's ear, for by this time he was really suffering. But I didn't succeed. There was no way of getting behind it, or getting a hold on it. And poor Dinkie bawled bitterly, ignorant of why this pain should be inflicted on him and outraged that his own mother should add to it by probing about the already swollen side of his head.

I was, in fact, getting a bit panicky, and speculating on how long it would take to get Dinkie in to Buckhorn and a doctor, when Struthers remembered about a pair of toilet tweezers she'd once possessed herself of, for pulling out an over-punctual gray-hair or two. Even then I had to resort to heroic measures, tying the screaming child's hands tight to his side with a bath-towel and having the tremulous Struthers hold his poor little head flat against the kitchen table.

It was about as painful, I suppose, as extracting a tooth, but I finally got a grip on that swollen legume and pulled it from its inflamed pocket of flesh. I felt as relieved and triumphant as an obstetrician after a hard case, and meekly handed over to Dinkie anything his Royal Highness desired, even to his fifth cookie and the entire contents of my sewing-basket, which under ordinary circumstances is strictly taboo. But once the ear-passage was clear the pain went away, and Dinkie, at the end of a couple of hours, was himself again.

But Peter has left a hole in our lives. I keep feeling that he's merely out on the land and will be coming in with that quiet and remote smile of his and talking like mad through a meal that I always had an incentive for making a little more tempting than the ordinary grub-rustling of a clodhopper.

The only person about Alabama Ranch who seems undisturbed by Peter's departure is Whinstane Sandy. He reminds me of a decrepit but robustious old rooster repossessing himself of a chicken-run after the decapitation of an arrogant and envied rival. He has with a dour sort of blitheness connected up the windmill pump, in his spare time, and run a pipe in through the kitchen wall and rigged up a sink, out of a galvanized pig-trough. It may not be lovely to the eye, but it will save many a step about this shack of ours. And the steps count, now that the season's work is breaking over us like a Jersey surf!

Thursday the Twenty-sixth

I've got Struthers in jumpers, and she's learning how to handle a team. Whinnie laughed at her legs, and said they made him think a-muckle o' a heron. But men are scarce in this section, and it looks as though Alabama Ranch was going to have a real wheat crop. Whinnie boasts that we're three weeks ahead of Casa Grande, which, they tell me, is taking on a neglected look.

I've had no message from my Dinky-Dunk, and no news of him. All day long, at the back of my brain, a nervous little mouse of anxiety keeps nibbling and nibbling away. Last night, when she was helping me get the Twins ready for bed, Struthers confided to me that she felt sure Lady Alicia and my husband had been playmates together in England at one time, for she's heard them talking, and laughing about things that had happened long ago. But it's not the things that happened long ago that are worrying me. It's the things that may be happening now.

I wonder what the fair Lady Alicia intends doing about getting her crop off. Sing Lo will scarcely be the man to master that problem.... The Lord knows I'm busy enough, but I seem to be eternally waiting for something. I wonder if every woman's life has a larval period like this? I've my children and Bobs. Over my heart, all day long, should flow a deep and steady current of love. But it's not the kind I've a craving for. There's something missing. I've been wondering if Dinky-Dunk, even though he were here at my side, would still find any "kick" in my kisses. I can't understand why he never revealed to me the fact that he and Lady Allie were playmates as children. In that case, she must be considerably older than she looks. But old or young, I wish she'd stayed in England with her croquet and pat-tennis and broom-stick-cricket, instead of coming out here and majestically announcing that nothing was to be expected of a country which had no railway porters!

Wednesday the First

The departed Peter has sent back to us a Victrola and a neatly packed box of records. Surely that was kind of him. I suppose he felt that I needed something more than a banjo to keep my melodious soul alive. He may be right, for sometimes during these long and hot and tiring days I feel as though my spirit had been vitrified and macadamized. But I haven't yet had time to unpack the music-box and get it in working-order, though I've had a look through the records. There are quite a number of my old favorites. I notice among them a song from *The Bohemian Girl*. It bears the title of *Then You'll Remember Me*. Poor old Peter! For when I play it, I know I'll always be thinking of another man.

Sunday the Fifth

Life is a club from which Cupid can never be blackballed. I notice that Struthers, who seems intent on the capture of a soul-mate, has taken to darning Whinstane Sandy's socks for him. And Whinnie, who is a bit of a cobbler as well as being a bit of renegade to the ranks of the misogynists, has put new heels and soles on the number sevens which Struthers wears at the extremities of her heron-like limbs. Thus romance, beginning at the metatarsus, slowly but surely ascends to the diastolic region!

Wednesday the Eighth

I've just had a nice little note from Peter, written from the Aldine Club in Philadelphia, saying he'd neglected to mention something which had been on his mind for some time. He has a slightly rundown place in the suburbs of Pasadena, he went on to explain, and as his lazy summer would mean he'd have to remain in the East and be an ink-coolie all winter, the place was at my disposal if it so turned out that a winter in California seemed desirable for me and my kiddies. It would, in fact, be a God-send—so he protested—to have somebody dependable lodged in that empty house, to keep the cobwebs out of the corners and the mildew off his books and save the whole disintegrating shebang from the general rack and ruin which usually overtakes empty mansions of that type. He gave me the name and address of the caretaker, on Euclid Avenue, and concluded by saying it wasn't very much of a place, but might be endured for a winter for the sake of the climate, if I happened to be looking for a sunnier corner of the world than Alabama Ranch. He further announced that he'd give an arm to see little Dinkie's face when that young outlaw stole his first ripe orange from the big Valencia tree in the *patio*. And Peter, in a post-script, averred that he could vouch for the flavor of the aforementioned Valencias.

Tuesday the Fourteenth

Whinstane Sandy about the middle of last week brought home the startling information that Sing Lo had sold Lady Allie's heavy work-team to Bud O'Malley for the paltry sum of sixty dollars. He further reported that Sing Lo had decamped, taking with him as rich a haul as he could carry.

I was in doubt on what to do, for a while. But I eventually decided to go in to Buckhorn and send a telegram to the owner of Casa Grande. I felt sure, if Lady Allie was in Banff, that she'd be at the C. P. R. hotel there, and that even if she had gone on to the Anglesey Ranch my telegram would be forwarded to Wallachie. So I wired her: "Chinaman left in charge has been selling ranch property. Advise me what action you wish taken."

A two-day wait brought no reply to this, so I then telegraphed to the hotel-manager asking for information as to her ladyship. I was anxious for that information, I'll confess, for more personal reasons than those arising out of the activities of Sing Lo.

When I went in for my house supplies on Friday there was a message there from the Banff hotel-manager stating that Lady Newland had left, ten days before, for the Empress Hotel in Victoria. So I promptly wired that hotel, only to learn that my titled wanderer might be found in San Francisco, at the Hotel St. Francis. So I repeated my message; and yesterday morning Hy Teetzel, homeward bound from Buckhorn in his tin Lizzie, brought the long-expected reply out to me. It read:

"Would advise consulting my ranch manager on the matter mentioned in your wire," and was signed "Alicia Newland."

There was a sense of satisfaction in having located the lady, but there was a distinctly nettling note in the tenor of that little message. I decided, accordingly, to give her the retort courteous by wiring back to her: "Kindly advise me of ranch manager's present whereabouts," and at the bottom of that message inscribed, "Mrs. Duncan Argyll McKail."

And I've been smiling a little at the telegram which has just been sent on to me, for now that I come to review our electric intercourse in a cooler frame of mind it looks suspiciously like back-biting over a thousand miles of telegraph-wire. This second message from San Francisco said: "Have no knowledge whatever of the gentleman's movements or whereabouts."

It was, I found, both a pleasant and a puzzling bit of information, and my earlier regrets at wasting time that I could ill spare betrayed a tendency to evaporate. It was satisfying, and yet it was not satisfying, for morose little doubts as to the veracity of the lady in question kept creeping back into my mind. It also left everything pretty much up in the air, so I've decided to take things in my own hand and go to Casa Grande and look things over.

Thursday the Sixteenth

I didn't go over to Casa Grande, after all. For this morning the news came to me that Duncan had been back since day before yesterday. And he is undoubtedly doing anything that needs to be done.

But the lady lied, after all. That fact now is only too apparent. And her equerry has been hurried back to look after her harried estate. The live stock, I hear, went without water for three whole days, and the poultry would all have been in kingdom-come if Sing Lo, in choosing a few choice birds for his private consumption, hadn't happened to leave the run-door unlatched....

I was foolish enough to expect, of course, that Duncan might nurse some slight curiosity as to his family and its welfare. This will be his third day back, and he has neither put in an appearance nor sent a word. He's busy, of course, with that tangle to unravel—but where there's a will there's usually a way. And hope dies hard. Yet day by day I find less bitterness in my heart. Those earlier hot tides of resentment have been succeeded, not by tranquillity or even indifference, but by a colder and more judicial attitude toward things in general. I've got a home and a family to fight for—not to mention a baby with prickly-heat—and they must not be forgotten. I have the consolation, too, of knowing that the fight doesn't promise to be a losing one. I've banked on wheat, and old Mother Earth is not going to betray me. My grain has ripened miraculously during these last few weeks of hot dry weather. It's *too* hot, in fact, for my harvest threatens to come on with a rush. But we'll scramble through it, in some way.

Sunday the Nineteenth

It's only three days since I wrote those last lines. But it seems a long time back to last Thursday. So many, many things have happened since then.

Friday morning broke very hot, and without a breath of wind. By noon it was stifling. By mid-afternoon I felt strangely tired, and even more strangely depressed. I even attempted to shake myself together, arguing that my condition was purely mental, for I had remembered that it was unmistakably Friday, a day of ill-omen to the superstitious.

I was surprised, between four and five, to see Whinstane Sandy come in from his work and busy himself about the stables. When I asked him the reason for this premature withdrawal he pointed toward a low and meek-looking bank of clouds just above the southwest sky-line and announced that we were going to have a "blow," as he called it.

I was inclined to doubt this, for the sun was still shining, there was no trace of a breeze, and the sky straight over my head was a pellucid pale azure. But, when I came to notice it, there was an unusual, small stir among my chickens, the cattle were restless, and one would occasionally hold its nose high in the air and then indulge in a lowing sound. Even Bobs moved peevishly from place to place, plainly disturbed by more than the flies and the heat. I had a feeling, myself, of not being able to get enough air into my lungs, a depressed and disturbed feeling which was nothing more than the barometer of my body trying to tell me that the glass was falling, and falling forebodingly.

By this time I could see Whinnie's cloud-bank rising higher above the horizon and becoming more ragged as it mushroomed into anvil-shaped turrets. Then a sigh or two of hot air, hotter even than the air about us, disturbed the quietness and made the level floor of my yellowing wheat undulate a little, like a breast that has taken a quiet breath or two. Then faint and far-off came a sound like the leisurely firing of big guns, becoming quicker and louder as the ragged arch of the storm crept over the sun and marched down on us with strange twistings and writhings and up-boilings of its tawny mane.

"Ye'd best be makin' things ready!" Whinnie called out to me. But even before I had my windows down little eddies of dust were circling about the shack. Then came a long and sucking sigh of wind, followed by a hot calm too horrible to be endured, a hot calm from the stifling center of which your spirit cried out for whatever was destined to happen to happen at once. The next moment brought its answer to that foolish prayer, a whining and whistling of wind that shook our little shell of a house on its foundations, a lurid flash or two, and then the tumult of the storm itself.

The room where I stood with my children grew suddenly and uncannily dark. I could hear Struthers calling thinly from the kitchen door to Whinnie, who apparently was making a belated effort to get my chicken-run gate open and my fowls under cover. I could hear a scattering drive of big rain-drops on the roof, solemn and soft, like the fall of plump frogs. But by the time Whinnie was in through the kitchen door this had changed. It had changed into a passionate and pulsing beat of rain, whipped and lashed by the wind that shook the timbers about us. The air, however, was cooler by this time, and it was easier to breathe. So I found it hard to understand why Whinnie, as he stood in the half-light by one of the windows, should wear such a look of protest on his morose old face which was the color of a pigskin saddle just under the stirrup-flap.

Even when I heard one solitary thump on the roof over my head, as distinct as the thump of a hammer, I failed to understand what was worrying my hired man. Then, after a momentary pause in the rain, the thumps were repeated. They were repeated in a rattle which became a clatter and soon grew into one continuous stream of sound, like a thousand machine-guns all going off at once.

I realized then what it meant, what it was. It was hail. And it meant that we were being "hailed out."

We were being cannonaded with shrapnel from the skies. We were being deluged with blocks of ice almost the size of duck-eggs. So thunderous was the noise that I had no remembrance when the window-panes on the west side of the house were broken. It wasn't, in fact, until I beheld the wind and water blowing in through the broken sashes that I awakened to what had happened. But I did nothing to stop the flood. I merely sat there with my two babes in my arms and my Dinkie pressed in close between my knees, in a foolishly crouching and uncomfortable position, as though I wanted to shield their tender little bodies with my own. I remember seeing Struthers run gabbing and screaming about the room and then try to bury herself under her mattress, like the silly old she-ostrich she was, with her number sevens sticking out from under the bedding. I remember seeing Whinnie picking up one of the white things that had rolled in through the broken window. It was oblong, and about as big as a pullet's egg, but more irregular in shape. It was clear on the outside but milky at the center, making me think of a half-cooked globe of tapioca. But it was a stone of solid ice. And thousands and thousands of stones like that, millions of them, were descending on my wheat, were thrashing down my half-ripened oats, were flailing the world and beating the life and beauty out of my crops.

The storm ended almost as abruptly as it had begun. The hammers of Thor that were trying to pound my lonely little prairie-house to pieces were withdrawn, the tumult stopped, and the light grew stronger. Whinstane Sandy even roused himself and moved toward the door, which he opened with the hand of a sleep-walker, and stood staring out. I could see reflected in that seamed old face the desolation which for a minute or two I didn't have the heart to look upon. I knew, even before I got slowly up and followed him toward the door, that our crop was gone, that we had lost everything.

I stood in the doorway, staring out at what, only that morning, had been a world golden with promise, rich and bountiful and beautiful to the eye and blessed in the sight of God. And now, at one stroke, it was all wiped out. As far as the eye could see I beheld only flattened and shredded ruin. Every acre of my crop was gone. My year's work had been for nothing, my blind planning, my petty scheming and contriving, my foolish little hopes and dreams, all, all were there, beaten down into the mud.

Yet, oddly enough, it did not stir in me any quick and angry passion of protest. It merely left me mute and stunned, staring at it with the eyes of the ox, with a dull wonder in my heart and a duller sense of deprivation away off at the back of my brain. I scarcely noticed when little Dinkie toddled out and possessed himself of a number of the larger hailstones, which he promptly proceeded to suck. When a smaller one melted in the warmth of his hand, he stared down at the emptiness between his little brown fingers, wondering where his pretty pebble had vanished to, just as I wondered where my crop had gone.

But it's gone. There's no doubt of that. The hail went from southwest to northeast, in a streak about three miles wide, like a conquering army, licking up everything as it went. Whinnie says that it's the will of God. Struthers, resurrected from her mattress, proclaims that it's Fate punishing us for our sins. My head tells me that it's barometric laws, operating along their own ineluctable lines. But that doesn't salve the sore.

For the rest of the afternoon we stood about like Italian peasants after an earthquake, possessed of a sort of collective mutism, doing nothing, saying nothing, thinking nothing. Even my seven dead pullets, which had been battered to death by the hail, were left to lie where they had fallen. I noticed a canvas carrier for a binder which Whinnie had been mending. It was riddled like a sieve. If this worried me, it worried me only vaguely. It wasn't until I remembered that there would be no wheat for that binder to cut and no sheaves for that carrier to bear, that the extent of what had befallen

Alabama Ranch once more came fully home to me. It takes time to digest such things, just as it takes time to reorganize your world. The McKails, for the second time, have been cleaned to the bones. We ought to be getting used to it, for it's the second time we've gone bust in a year!

It wasn't until yesterday morning that any kind of perspective came back to us. I went to bed the night before wondering about Dinky-Dunk and hoping against hope that he'd come galloping over to make sure his family were still in the land of the living. But he didn't come. And before noon I learned that Casa Grande had not been touched by the hail. That at least was a relief, for it meant that Duncan was safe and sound.

In a way, yesterday, there was nothing to do, and yet there was a great deal to do. It reminded me of the righting up after a funeral. But I refused to think of anything beyond the immediate tasks in hand. I just did what had to be done, and went to bed again dog-tired. But I had nightmare, and woke up in the middle of the night crying for all I was worth. I seemed alone in an empty world, a world without meaning or mercy, and there in the blackness of the night when the tides of life run lowest, I lay with my hand pressed against my heart, with the feeling that there was nothing whatever left in existence to make it worth while. Then Pee-Wee stirred and whimpered, and when I lifted him into my bed and held him against my breast, the nearness of his body brought warmth and consolation to mine, and I remembered that I was still a mother....

It was this morning (Sunday) that Dinky-Dunk appeared at Alabama Ranch. I had looked for him and longed for him, in secret, and my heart should have leapt up with gladness at the sight of him. But it didn't. It couldn't. It was like asking a millstone to pirouette.

In the first place, everything seemed wrong. I had a cold in the head from the sudden drop in the temperature, and I was arrayed in that drab old gingham wrapper which Dinkie had cut holes in with Struthers' scissors, for I hadn't cared much that morning when I dressed whether I looked like a totem-pole or a Stoney squaw. And the dregs of what I'd been through during the last two days were still sour in the bottom of my heart. I was a Job in petticoats, a mutineer against man and God, a nihilist and an I. W. W. all in one. And Dinky-Dunk appeared in Lady Alicia's car, in *her* car, carefully togged out in his Sunday best, with that strangely alien aspect which citified clothes can give to the rural toiler when he emerges from the costume of his kind.

But it wasn't merely that he came arrayed in this outer shell of affluence and prosperity. It was more that there was a sense of triumph in his heart which he couldn't possibly conceal. And I wasn't slow to realize what it meant. I was a down-and-outer now, and at his mercy. He could have his way with me, without any promise of protest. And whatever he might have done, or might yet do, it was ordained that I in my meekness should bow to the yoke. All that I must remember was that he stood my lord and master. I had made my foolish little struggle to be mistress of my own destiny, and now that I had failed, and failed utterly, I must bend to whatever might be given to me.

"It's hard luck, Chaddie," he said, with a pretense at being sympathetic. But there was no real sorrow in his eye as he stood there surveying my devastated ranch.

"Nix on that King Cophetua stuff!" I curtly and vulgarly proclaimed.

"Just what do you mean?" he asked, studying my face.

"Kindly can the condescension stuff!" I repeated, taking a wayward satisfaction out of shocking him with the paraded vulgarity of my phrasing.

"That doesn't sound like you," he said, naturally surprised, I suppose, that I didn't melt into his arms.

"Why not?" I inquired, noticing that he no longer cared to meet my eye.

"It sounds hard," he said.

"Well, some man has said that a hard soil makes a hard race," I retorted, with a glance about at my ruined wheatlands. "Did you have a pleasant time in Chicago?"

He looked up quickly.

"I wasn't in Chicago," he promptly protested.

"Then that woman lied, after all," I remarked, with a lump of Scotch granite where my heart ought to have been. For I could see by his face that he knew, without hesitation, the woman I meant.

"Isn't that an unnecessarily harsh word?" he asked, trying, of course, to shield her to the last. And if he had not exactly winced, he had done the next thing to it.

"What would _you_ call it?" I countered. It wouldn't have taken a microphone, I suppose, to discover the hostility in my tone. "And would it be going too far to inquire just where you were?" I continued as I saw he had no intention of answering my first question.

"I was at the Coast," he said, compelling himself to meet my glance.

"I'm sorry that I cut your holiday short," I told him.

"It was scarcely a holiday," he remonstrated.

"What would you call it then?" I asked.

"It was purely a business trip," he retorted.

There had, I remembered, been a great deal of that business during the past few months. And an ice-cold hand squeezed the last hope of hope out of my heart. *She* had been at the Coast.

"And this belated visit to your wife and children, I presume, is also for business purposes?" I inquired. But he was able to smile at that, for all my iciness.

"*Is* it belated?" he asked.

"Wouldn't you call it that?" I quietly inquired.

"But I had to clear up that case of the stolen horses," he protested, "that Sing Lo thievery."

"Which naturally comes before one's family," I ironically reminded him.

"But courts are courts, Chaddie," he maintained, with a pretense of patience.

"And consideration is consideration," I rather wearily amended.

"We can't always do what we want to," he next remarked, apparently intent on being genially axiomatic.

"Then to what must the humble family attribute this visit?" I inquired, despising that tone of mockery into which I had fallen yet seeming unable to drag myself out of its muck-bottom depths.

"To announce that I intend to return to them," he asserted, though it didn't seem an easy statement to make.

It rather took my breath away, for a moment. But Reason remained on her throne. It was too much like sticking spurs into a dead horse. There was too much that could not be forgotten. And I calmly reminded Dinky-Dunk that the lightest of heads can sometimes have the longest of memories.

"Then you don't want me back?" he demanded, apparently embarrassed by my lack of hospitality.

"It all depends on what you mean by that word," I answered, speaking as judicially as I was able. "If by coming back you mean coming back to this house, I suppose you have a legal right to do so. But if it means anything more, I'm afraid it can't be done. You see, Dinky-Dunk, I've got rather used to single harness again, and I've learned to think and act for myself, and there's a time when continued unfairness can kill the last little spark of friendliness in any woman's heart. It's not merely that I'm tired of it all. But I'm *tired of being tired*, if you know what that means. I don't even know what I'm going to do. Just at present, in fact, I don't want to think about it. But I'd much prefer being alone until I am able to straighten things out to my own satisfaction."

"I'm sorry," said Dinky-Dunk, looking so crestfallen that for a moment I in turn felt almost sorry for him.

"Isn't it rather late for that?" I reminded him.

"Yes, I suppose it is," he admitted, with a disturbing new note of humility. Then he looked up at me, almost defiantly. "But you need my help."

It was masterful man, once more asserting himself. It was a trivial misstep, but a fatal one. It betrayed, at a flash, his entire misjudgment of me, of my feelings, of what I was and what I intended to be.

"I'm afraid I've rather outlived that period of Bashi-Bazookism," I coolly and quietly explained to my lord and master. "You may have the good luck to be confronting me when I seem to be floored. I've been hailed out, it's true. But that has happened to other people, and they seem to have survived. And there are worse calamities, I find, than the loss of a crop."

"Are you referring to anything that I have done?" asked Dinky-Dunk, with a slightly belligerent look in his eye.

"If the shoe fits, put it on," I observed.

"But there are certain things I want to explain," he tried to argue, with the look of a man confronted by an overdraft on his patience.

"Somebody has said that a friend," I reminded him, "is a person to whom one need never explain. And any necessity for explanation, you see, removes us even from the realm of friendship."

"But, hang it all, I'm your husband," protested my obtuse and somewhat indignant interlocutor.

"We all have our misfortunes," I found the heart, or rather the absence of heart, to remark.

"I'm afraid this isn't a very good beginning," said Dinky-Dunk, his dignity more ruffled than ever.

"It's not a beginning at all," I reminded him. "It's more like an ending."

That kept him silent for quite a long while.

"I suppose you despise me," he finally remarked.

"It's scarcely so active an emotion," I tried to punish him by retorting.

"But I at least insist on explaining what took me to the Coast," he contended.

"That is scarcely necessary," I told him.

"Then you know?" he asked.

"I imagine the whole country-side does," I observed.

He made a movement of mixed anger and protest.

"I went to Vancouver because the government had agreed to take over my Vancouver Island water-front for their new shipbuilding yards. If you've forgotten just what that means, I'd like to remind you that there's———"

"I don't happen to have forgotten," I interrupted, wondering why news which at one time would have set me on fire could now leave me quite cold. "But what caused the government to change its mind?"

"Allie!" he said, after a moment's hesitation, fixing a slightly combative eye on mine.

"She seems to have almost unlimited powers," I observed as coolly as I could, making an effort to get my scattered thoughts into line again.

"On the contrary," Dinky-Dunk explained with quite painful politeness, "it was merely the accident that she happened to know the naval officer on the Imperial Board. She was at Banff the week the board was there, and she was able to put in a good word for the Vancouver Island site. And the Imperial verdict swung our own government officials over."

"You were lucky to have such an attractive wirepuller," I frigidly announced.

"The luck wasn't altogether on my side," Dinky-Dunk almost as frigidly retorted, "when you remember that it was giving her a chance to get rid of a ranch she was tired of!"

I did my best to hide my surprise, but it wasn't altogether a success. The dimensions of the movement, apparently, were much greater than my poor little brain had been able to grasp.

"Do you mean it's going to let you take Casa Grande off her ladyship's hands?" I diffidently inquired.

"That's already arranged for," Dinky-Dunk quite casually informed me. We were a couple of play-actors, I felt, each deep in a rôle of his own, each stirred much deeper than he was ready to admit, and each a little afraid of the other.

"You are to be congratulated," I told Dinky-Dunk, chilled in spite of myself, never for a moment quite able to forget the sinister shadow of Lady Alicia which lay across our trodden little path of everyday life.

"It was you and the kiddies I was thinking of," said my husband, in a slightly remote voice. And the mockery of that statement, knowing what I knew, was too much for me.

"I'm sorry you didn't think of us a little sooner," I observed. And I had the bitter-sweet reward of seeing a stricken light creep up into Dinky-Dunk's eyes.

"Why do you say that?" he asked.

But I didn't answer that question of his. Instead, I asked him another.

"Did you know that Lady Alicia came here and announced that she was in love with you?" I demanded, resolved to let the light in to that tangled mess which was fermenting in the silo of my soul.

"Yes, I know," he quietly affirmed, as he hung his head. "She told me about it. And it was *awful*. It should never have happened. It made me ashamed even—even to face you!"

"That was natural," I agreed, with my heart still steeled against him.

"It makes a fool of a man," he protested, "a situation like that."

"Then the right sort of man wouldn't encourage it," I reminded him, "wouldn't even permit it." And still again I caught that quick movement of impatience from him.

"What's that sort of thing to a man of my age?" he demanded. "When you get to where I am you don't find love looming so large on the horizon. What—"

"No, it clearly doesn't loom so large," I interrupted.

"What you want then," went on Dinky-Dunk, ignoring me, "is power, success, the consolation of knowing you're not a failure in life. *That's* the big issue, and that's the stake men play big for, and play hard for."

It was, I remembered in my bitterness of soul, what I myself had been playing hard for—but I had lost. And it had left my heart dry. It had left my heart so dry that my own Dinky-Dunk, standing there before me in the open sunlight, seemed millions of miles removed from me, mysteriously depersonalized, as remote in spirit as a stranger from Mars come to converse about an inter-stellar telephone-system.

"Then you've really achieved your ambition," I reminded my husband, as he stood studying a face which I tried to keep tranquil under his inspection.

"Oh, no," he corrected, "only a small part of it."

"What's the rest?" I indifferently inquired, wondering why most of life's victories, after all, were mere Pyrrhic victories.

"You," declared Dinky-Dunk, with a reckless light in his eyes, "You, and the children, now that I'm in a position to give them what they want."

"But *are* you?" I queried.

"Well, that's what I'm coming back to demonstrate," he found the courage to assert.

"To them?" I asked.

"To all of you!" he said with a valiant air of finality.

I told him it was useless, but he retorted that he didn't propose to have that stop him. I explained to him that it would be embarrassing, but he parried that claim by protesting that sacrifice was good for the soul. I asserted that it would be a good deal of a theatricality, under the circumstances, but he attempted to brush this aside by stating that what he had endured for years might be repeated by patience.

So Dinky-Dunk is coming back to Alabama Ranch! It sounds momentous, and yet, I know in my heart, that it doesn't mean so very much. He will sleep under the same roof with me as remote as though he were reposing a thousand miles away. He will breakfast and go forth to his work, and my thoughts will not be able to go with him. He will return with the day's weariness in his bones, but a weariness which I can neither fathom nor explain in my own will keep my blood from warming at the sound of his voice through the door. Being still his wife, I shall have to sew and mend and cook for him. *That* is the penalty of prairie life; there is no escape from propinquity.

But that life can go on in this way, indefinitely, is unthinkable. What will happen, I don't know. But there will have to be a change, somewhere. There will have to be a change, but I am too tired to worry over what it will be. I'm too tired even to think of it. That's something which lies in the lap of Time.

Saturday the Twenty-fifth

Dinky-Dunk is back. At least he sleeps and breakfasts at home, but the rest of the time he is over at Casa Grande getting his crop cut. He's too busy, I fancy, to pay much attention to our mutual lack of attention. But the compact was made, and he seems willing to comply with it. The only ones who fail to regard it are the children. I hadn't counted on them. There are times, accordingly, when they somewhat complicate the situation. It didn't take them long to get re-acquainted with their daddy. I could see, from the first, that he intended to be very considerate and kind with them, for I'm beginning to realize that he gets a lot of fun out of the kiddies. Pee-Wee will go to him, now, from anybody. He goes with an unmistakable expression of "Us-men-have-got-to-stick-together" satisfaction on his little face.

But Dinky-Dunk's intimacies, I'm glad to say, do not extend beyond the children. Three days ago, though, he asked me about turning his hogs in on my land. It doesn't sound disturbingly emotional. But if what's left of my crop, of course, is any use to Duncan, he's welcome to it....

I looked for that letter which I wrote to Dinky-Dunk several weeks ago, looked for it for an hour and more this morning, but haven't succeeded in finding it. I was sure that I'd put it between the pages of the old ranch journal. But it's not there.

Last night before I turned in I read all of Meredith's *Modern Love*. It was nice to remember that once, at Box Hill, I'd felt the living clasp of the hand which had written that wonderful series of poems. But never before did I quite understand that elaborated essay in love-moods. It came like a friendly voice, like an understanding comrade who knows the world better than I do, and brought me comfort, even though the sweetness of it was slightly acidulated, like a lemon-drop. And as for myself, I suppose I'll continue to

"............sit contentedly

And eat my pot of honey on the grave."

Sunday the Second

I have written to Uncle Carlton again, asking him about my Chilean Nitrate shares. If the company's reorganized and the mines opened again, surely my stock ought to be worth something.

The days are getting shorter, and the hot weather is over for good, I hope. I usually like autumn on the prairie, but the thought of fall, this year, doesn't fill me with any inordinate joy. I'm unsettled and atonic, and it's just as well, I fancy, that I'm weaning the Twins.

It's not the simple operation I'd expected, but the worst is already over. Pee-Wee is betraying unmistakable serpentine powers, and it's no longer safe to leave him on a bed. Poppsy is a fastidious little lady, and apparently a bit of a philosopher. She is her father's favorite. Whinstane Sandy is loyal to little Dinkie, and, now that the evenings are longer, regales him on stories, stories which the little tot can only half understand. But they must always be about animals, and Whinnie seems to run to wolves. He's told the story of the skater and the wolves, with personal embellishments, and Little Red Riding-Hood in a version all his own, and last night, I noticed, he recounted the tale of the woman in the sleigh with her children when the pack of wolves pursued her. And first, to save herself and her family, she threw her little baby out to the brutes. And when they had gained on her once more, she threw out her little girl, and then her little boy, and then her biggest boy of ten. And when she reached a settlement and told of her deliverance, the Oldest Settler took a wood-ax and clove her head clear down to the shoulder-blades—the same, of course, being a punishment for saving herself at the expense of her little ones.

My Dinkie sat wriggling his toes with delight, the tale being of that gruesome nature which appeals to him. It must have been tried on countless other children, for, despite Whinnie's autobiographical interjections, the yarn is an old and venerable one, a primitive Russian folk-tale which even Browning worked over in his *Ivan Ivanovitch*.

Dinky-Dunk, wandering in on the tail end of it, remarked: "That's a fine story, that is, with all those coyotes singing out there!"

"The chief objection to it," I added, "is that the lady didn't drop her husband over first."

Dinky-Dunk looked down at me as he filled his pipe.

"But the husband, as I remember the story, had been left behind to do what a mere husband could to save their home," my spouse quietly reminded me.

Monday the Tenth

There was a heavy frost last night. It makes me feel that summer is over. Dinky-Dunk asked me yesterday why I disliked Casa Grande and never ventured over into that neighborhood. I evaded any answer by announcing that there were very few things I liked nowadays....

Only once, lately, have we spoken of Lady Allie. It was Dinky-Dunk, in fact, who first brought up her name in speaking of the signing of the transfer-papers.

"Is it true," I found the courage to ask, "that you knew your cousin quite intimately as a girl?"

Dinky-Dunk laughed as he tamped down his pipe.

"Yes, it *must* have been quite intimately," he acknowledged. "For when she was seven and I was nine we went all the way down Teignmouth Hill together in an empty apple-barrel—than which nothing that I know of could possibly be more intimate!"

I couldn't join him in his mirth over that incident, for I happened to remember the look on Lady Alicia's face when she once watched Dinky-Dunk mount his mustang and ride away. "Aren't men lawds of creation?" she had dreamily inquired. "Not after you've lived with them for a couple of years," I had been heartless enough to retort, just to let her know that I didn't happen to have a skin like a Douglas pine.

Sunday the Sixteenth

I've just had a letter from Uncle Carlton. It's a very long and businesslike letter, in which he goes into details as to how our company has been incorporated in *La Association de Productores de Salitre de Chile*, with headquarters at Valparaiso. It's a new and rather unexpected arrangement, but he prophesies that with nitrate at ten shillings per Spanish quintal the returns on the investment, under the newer conditions, should be quite satisfactory. He goes on to explain how nitrate is shipped in bags of one hundred kilos, and the price includes the bags, but the weight is taken on the nitrate only, involving a deduction from the gross weight of seven-tenths per cent. Then he ambles off into a long discussion of how the fixation method from the air may eventually threaten the stability of our entire amalgamated mines, but probably not during his life-time or even my own. And I had to read the letter over for the third time before I winnowed from it the obscure but essential kernel that my shares from this year forward should bring me in an annual dividend of at least two thousand, but more probably three, and possibly even four, once the transportation situation is normalized, but depending largely, of course, on the labor conditions obtaining in Latin America—and much more along the same lines.

That news of my long-forgotten and long-neglected nest-egg should have made me happy. But it didn't. I couldn't quite react to it. As usual, I thought of the children first, and from their standpoint it did bring a sort of relief. It was consoling, of course, to know that, whatever happened, they could have woolens on their little tummies and shoe-leather on their little piggies. But the news didn't come with sufficient force to shock the dull gray emptiness out of existence. I've even been wondering if there's any news that could. For the one thing that seems always to face me is the absence of intensity from life. Can it be, I found myself asking to-day, that it's youth, golden youth, that is slipping away from me?

It startled me a little, to have to face that question. But I shake my fist in the teeth of Time. I refuse to surrender. I shall not allow myself to become antiquated. I'm on the wrong track, in some way, but before I dry up into a winter apple I'm going to find out where the trouble is, and correct it. I never was much of a sleep-walker. I want life, Life—and oodles of it....

Among other things, by the way, which I've been missing are books. They at least are to be had for the buying, and I've decided there's no excuse for letting the channels of my mind get moss-grown. I've had a "serious but not fatal wound," as the newspapers say, to my personal vanity, but there's no use in letting go of things, at my time of life. Pee-Wee, I'm sure, will never be satisfied with an empty-headed old frump for a mother, and Dinkie is already asking questions that are slightly disturbing. Yesterday, in his bath, he held his hand over his heart. He held it there for quite a long time, and then he looked at me with widening eyes. "Mummy," he called out, "I've got a m'sheen inside me!" And Whinnie's explorations are surely worth emulating. I too have a machine inside me which some day I'll be compelled to rediscover. It is a machine which, at present, is merely a pump, though the ancients, I believe, regarded it as the seat of the emotions.

Saturday the Twenty-ninth

Dinky-Dunk is quite subtle. He is ignoring me, as a modern army of assault ignores a fortress by simply circling about its forbidding walls and leaving it in the rear. But I can see that he is deliberately and patiently making love to my children. He is entrenching himself in their affection.

He is, of course, their father, and it is not for me to interfere. Last night, in fact, when Pee-Wee cried for his dad, poor old Dinky-Dunk's face looked almost radiumized. He has announced that on Tuesday, when he will have to go in to Buckhorn, he intends to carry along the three kiddies and have their photograph taken. It reminded me that I had no picture whatever of the Twins. And that reminded me, in turn, of what a difference there is between your first child and the tots who come later. Little Dinkie, being a novelty, was followed by a phosphorescent wake of diaries and snap-shots and weigh-scales and growth-records, with his birthdays duly reckoned, not by the year, but by the month.

It's not that I love the Twins less. It's only that the novelty has passed. And in one way it's a good thing, for over your second and third baby you worry less. You know what is needed, and how to do it. You blaze your trail, as a mother, with your first-born. You build your road, and after that you are no longer a pioneer. You know the way you have to go, henceforth, and you follow it. It is less a Great Adventure, perhaps, but, on the other hand, the double-pointed tooth of Anxiety does not rowel quite so often at the core of your heart.... I've been wondering if, with the coming of the children, there is not something which slips away from the relationship between husband and wife. That there is a difference is not to be denied. There was a time when I resented this and tried to fight against it. But I wasn't big enough, I suppose, to block the course of Nature. And it *was* Nature, you have to admit when you come to look it honestly in the face, Nature in her inexorable economy working out her inexorable ends. If I hadn't loved Dinky-Dunk, fondly, foolishly, abandonedly, there would have been no little Dinkie and Poppsy and Pee-Wee. They would have been left to wander like disconsolate little ghosts through that lonely and twilit No-Man's Land of barren love and unwanted babes. And the only thing that keeps me human, nowadays, that keeps me from being a woman with a dead soul, a she-being of untenanted hide and bones and dehydrated ham-strings, is my kiddies. The thought of them, at any time of the day, can put a cedilla under my heart to soften it....

Struthers, who is to go in to Buckhorn with the children when they have their picture taken, is already deep in elaborating preparations for that expedition. She is improvising an English nurse's uniform and has asked if there might be one picture of her and the children.

Tuesday the Fifteenth

The children have been away for a whole day, the first time in family history. And oh, what a difference it makes in this lonely little prairie home of ours! The quietness, the emptiness, the desolation of it all was something quite beyond my imagination. I know now that I could never live apart from them. Whatever happens, I shall not be separated from my kiddies....

I spent my idle time in getting Peter's music-box in working order. Dinky-Dunk, who despises it, thoughtlessly sat on the package of records and broke three of them. I've been trying over the others. They sound tinny and flat, and I'm beginning to suspect I haven't my sound-box adjusted right. I've a hunger to hear good music. And without quite knowing it, I've been craving for city life again, for at least a taste of it, for even a chocolate cream-soda at a Huyler counter. Dinky-Dunk yesterday said that I was a cloudy creature, and accused me of having a mutinous mouth. Men seem to think that love should be like an eight-day clock, with a moment or two of industrious winding-up rewarded by a long week of undeviating devotion.

Sunday the Twenty-seventh

The thrashing outfits are over at Casa Grande, and my being a mere spectator of the big and busy final act of the season's drama reminds me of three years ago, just before Dinkie arrived. Struthers, however, is at Casa Grande and in her glory, the one and only woman in a circle of nine active-bodied men.

I begin to see that it's true what Dinky-Dunk said about business looming bigger in men's lives than women are apt to remember. He's working hard, and his neck's so thin that his Adam's apple sticks out like a push-button, but he gets his reward in finding his crop running much higher than he had figured. He's as keen as ever he was for power and prosperity. He wants success, and night and day he's scheming for it. Sometimes I wonder if he didn't deliberately *use* his cousin Allie in this juggling back of Casa Grande into his own hands. Yet Dinky-Dunk, with all his faults, is not, and could not be, circuitous. I feel sure of that.

He became philosophical, the other day when I complained about the howling of the coyotes, and protested it was these horizon-singers that kept the prairie clean. He even argued that the flies which seem such a pest to the cattle in summer-time are a blessing in disguise, since the unmolested animals over-eat when feed is plentiful and get black-rot. So out of suffering comes wisdom and out of endurance comes fortitude!

Thursday the Sixth

On Tuesday morning we had our first snow of the season, or, rather, before the season. It wasn't much of a snow-storm, but Dinkie was greatly worked up at the sight of it and I finally put on his little reefer and his waders and let him go out in it. But the weather had moderated, the snow turned to slush, and when I rescued Dinkie from rolling in what looked to him like a world of ice-cream he was a very wet boy.

On Tuesday night Dinkie, usually so sturdy and strong, woke up with a tight little chest-cough that rather frightened me. I went over to his crib and covered him up. But when he wakened me again, a couple of hours later, the cough had grown tighter. It turned into a sort of sharp bark. And this time I found Dinkie hot and feverish. So I got busy, rubbing his chest with sweet oil and turpentine until the skin was pink and giving him a sip or two of cherry pectoral which I still had on the upper shelf of the cupboard.

When morning came he was no better. He seemed in a stupor, rousing only to bark into his pillow. I called Dinky-Dunk in, before he left in the pouring rain for Casa Grande, and he said, almost indifferently, "Yes, the boy's got a cold all right." But that was all.

When breakfast was over I tried Dinkie with hot gruel, but he declined it. He refused to eat, in fact, and remembering what Peter had once said about my first-born being pantophagous, I began to suspect that I had a very sick boy on my hands.

At noon, when he seemed no better, I made a mild mustard-plaster and put it on the upper part of his little chest. I let it burn there until he began to cry with the discomfort of it. Then I tucked a double fold of soft flannel above his thorax.

As night came on he was more flushed and feverish than ever, and I wished to heaven that I'd a clinic thermometer in the house. For by this time I was more than worried: I was panicky. Yet Duncan, when he came in, and got out of his oil-skins, didn't seem very sympathetic. He flatly refused to share my fears. The child, he acknowledged, had a croupy little chest-cold, but all he wanted was keeping warm and as much water as he could drink. Nature, he largely protested, would attend to a case like that.

I was ready to turn on him like a she-tiger, but I held myself in, though it took an effort. I saw Duncan go off to bed, dog-tired, of course, but I felt that to go to sleep, under the circumstances, would be criminal. Dinkie, in the meantime, was waking every now and then and barking like a baby-coyote. I could have stood it, I suppose, if that old Bobs of ours hadn't started howling outside, in long-drawn and dreary howls of unutterable woe. I remembered about a dog always howling that way when somebody was going to die in the house. And I concluded, with an icy heart, that it was the death-howl. I tried to count Dinkie's pulse, but it was so rapid and I was so nervous that I lost track of the beats. So I decided to call Dinky-Dunk.

He came in to us kind of sleepy-eyed and with his hair rumpled up, and asked, without thinking, what I wanted.

And I told him, with a somewhat shaky voice, what I wanted. I said I wanted antiphlogistine, and a pneumonia-jacket, and a doctor, and a trained nurse, and just a few of the comforts of civilization.

Dinky-Dunk, staring at me as though I were a madwoman, went over to Dinkie's crib, and felt his forehead and the back of his neck, and held an ear against the boy's chest, and then against his shoulder-blades. He said it was all right, and that I myself ought to be in bed. As though in answer to that Dinkie barked out his croupy protest, tight and hard, barked as I'd never heard a child bark before. And I began to fuss, for it tore my heart to think of that little body burning up with fever and being denied its breath.

"You might just as well get back to bed," repeated Dinky-Dunk, rather impatiently. And that was the spark which set off the mine, which pushed me clear over the edge of reason. I'd held myself in for so long, during weeks and weeks of placid-eyed self-repression, that when the explosion did come I went off like a Big Bertha. I turned on my husband with a red light dancing before my face and told him he was a beast and a heartless brute. He tried to stop me, but it was no use. I even said that this was a hell of a country, where a white woman had to live like a Cree squaw and a child had to die like a sick hound in a coulée. And I said a number of other things, which must have cut to the raw, for even in the uncertain lamplight I could see that Dinky-Dunk's face had become a kind of lemon-color, which is the nearest to white a sunburned man seems able to turn.

"I'll get a doctor, if you want one," he said, with an over-tried-patience look in his eyes.

"*I* don't want a doctor," I told him, a little shrill-voiced with indignation. "It's the child who wants one."

"I'll get your doctor," he repeated as he began dressing, none too quickly. And it took him an interminable time to get off, for it was raining cats and dogs, a cold, sleety rain from the northeast, and the shafts had to be taken off the buckboard and a pole put in, for it would require a team to haul anything on wheels to Buckhorn, on such a night.

It occurred to me, as I stood at the window and saw Dinky-Dunk's lantern wavering about in the rain while he was getting the team and hooking them on to the buckboard, that it would be only the decent thing to send him off with a cup of hot coffee, now that I had the kettle boiling. But he'd martyrize himself, I knew, by refusing it, even though I made it. And he was already sufficiently warmed by the fires of martyrdom.

Yet it was an awful night, I realized when I stood in the open door and stared after him as he swung out into the muddy trail with the stable lantern lashed to one end of his dashboard. And I felt sorry, and a little guilty, about the neglected cup of coffee.

I went back to little Dinkie, and found him asleep. So I sat down beside him. I sat there wrapped up in one of Dinky-Dunk's four-point Hudson-Bays, deciding that if the child's cough grew tighter I'd rig up a croup-tent, as I'd once seen Chinkie's doctor do with little Gimlets. But Dinkie failed to waken. And I fell asleep myself, and didn't open an eye until I half-tumbled out of the chair, well on toward morning.

By the time Dinky-Dunk got back with the doctor, who most unmistakably smelt of Scotch whisky, I had breakfast over and the house in order and the Twins fed and bathed and off for their morning nap. I had a fresh nightie on little Dinkie, who rather upset me by announcing that he wanted to get up and play with his Noah's Ark, for his fever seemed to have slipped away from him and the tightness had gone from his cough. But I said nothing as that red-faced and sweet-scented doctor looked the child over. His stethoscope, apparently, tickled Dinkie's ribs, for after trying to wriggle away a couple of times he laughed out loud. The doctor also laughed. But Dinky-Dunk's eye happened to meet mine.

It would be hard to describe his expression. All I know is that it brought a disagreeable little sense of shame to my hypocritical old heart, though I wouldn't have acknowledged it, for worlds.

"Why, those lungs are clear," I heard the man of medicine saying to my husband. "It's been a nasty little cold, of course, but nothing to worry over."

His optimism struck me as being rather unprofessional, for if you travel half a night to a case, it seems to me, it ought not to be brushed aside with a laugh. And I was rather sorry that I had such a good breakfast waiting for them. Duncan, it's true, did not eat a great deal, but the way that red-faced doctor lapped up my coffee with clotted cream and devoured bacon and eggs and hot muffins should have disturbed any man with an elementary knowledge of dietetics. And by noon Dinkie was pretty much his old self again. I half expected that Duncan would rub it in a little. But he has remained discreetly silent.

Next time, of course, I'll have a better idea of what to do. But I've been thinking that this exquisite and beautiful animalism known as the maternal instinct can sometimes emerge from its exquisiteness. Children are a joy and a glory, but you pay for that joy and glory when you see them stretched out on a bed of pain, with the shadow of Death hovering over them.

When I tried to express something like this to Dunkie last night, somewhat apologetically, he looked at me with an odd light in his somber old Scotch Canadian eye.

"Wait until you see him really ill," he remarked, man-like, stubbornly intent on justifying himself. But I was too busy saying a little prayer, demanding of Heaven that such a day might never come, to bother about delivering myself of the many laboriously concocted truths which I'd assembled for my bone-headed lord and master. I was grateful enough for things as they were, and I could afford to be generous.

Sunday the Ninth

For the first time since I came out on the prairie, I dread the thought of winter. Yet it's really something more than the winter I dread, since snow and cold have no terrors for me. I need only to look back about ten short months and think of those crystal-clear winter days of ours, with the sleigh piled up with its warm bear-robes, the low sun on the endless sea of white, the air like champagne, the spanking team frosted with their own breath, the caroling sleigh-bells, and the man who still meant so much to me at my side. Then the homeward drive at night, under violet clear skies, over drifts of diamond-dust, to the warmth and peace and coziness of one's own hearth! It was often razor-edge weather, away below zero, but we had furs enough to defy any threat of frost-nip.

We still have the furs, it's true, but there's the promise of a different kind of frost in the air now, a black frost that creeps into the heart which no furs can keep warm....

We still have the furs, as I've already said, and I've been looking them over. They're so plentiful in this country that I've rather lost my respect for them. Back in the old days I used to invade those mirrored and carpeted *salons* where a trained and deferential saleswoman would slip sleazy and satin-lined moleskin coats over my arms and adjust baby-bear and otter and ermine and Hudson-seal next to my skin. It always gave me a very luxurious and Empressy sort of feeling to see myself arrayed, if only experimentally, in silver-fox and plucked beaver and fisher, to feel the soft pelts and observe how well one's skin looked above seal-brown or shaggy bear.

But I never knew what it cost. I never even considered where they came from, or what they grew on, and it was to me merely a vague and unconfirmed legend that they were all torn from the carcasses of far-away animals. Prairie life has brought me a little closer to that legend, and now that I know what I do, it makes a difference.

For with the coming of the cold weather, last winter, Francois and Whinstane Sandy took to trapping, to fill in the farm-work hiatus. They made it a campaign, and prepared for it carefully, concocting stretching-rings and cutting-boards and fashioning rabbit-snares and overhauling wicked-looking iron traps, which were quite ugly enough even before they became stained and clotted and rusted with blood.

They had a very successful season, but even at the first it struck me as odd to see two men, not outwardly debased, so soberly intent on their game of killing. And in the end I got sick of the big blood-rusted traps and the stretching-rings and the blood-smeared cutting-boards and the smell of pelts being cured. For every pelt, I began to see, meant pain and death. In one trap Francois found only the foot of a young red fox: it had gnawed its leg off to gain freedom from those vicious iron jaws that had bitten so suddenly into its flesh and bone and sinew. He also told me of finding a young bear which had broken the anchor-chain of a twelve-pound trap and dragged it over one hundred miles. All the fight, naturally, was gone out of the little creature. It was whimpering like a woman when Francois came up with it—poor little tortured broken-hearted thing! And some empty-headed heiress goes mincing into the Metropolitan, on a Caruso night, very proud and peacocky over her new ermine coat, without ever dreaming it's a patchwork of animal sufferings that is keeping her fat body warm, and that she's trying to make herself beautiful in a hundred tragedies of the wild.

If women only thought of these things! But we women have a very convenient hand-made imagination all our own, and what upsets us as perfect ladies we graciously avoid. Yet if the petticoated Vandal in that ermine coat were compelled to behold from her box-chair in the Metropolitan, not a musty old love-affair set to music, but the spectacle of how each little animal whose skin she has appropriated had been made to suffer, the hours and sometimes days of torture it had endured, and how, if still alive when the trapper made the rounds of his sets, it had been carefully strangled to death by that frugal harvester, to the end that the pelt might not be bloodied and reckoned only as a "second"—if the weasel-decked lady, I repeat, had to witness all this with her own beaded eyes, our wilderness would not be growing into quite such a lonely wilderness.

Or some day, let's put it, as one of these beaver-clad ladies tripped through the Ramble in Central Park, supposing a steel-toothed trap suddenly and quite unexpectedly snapped shut on her silk-stockinged ankle and she writhed and moaned there in public, over the week-end. Then possibly her cries of suffering might make her sisters see a little more light. But the beaver, they tell me, is trapped under the ice, always in running water. A mud-ball is placed a little above the waiting trap, to leave the water opaque, and when the angry iron jaws have snapped shut on their victim, that victim drowns, a prisoner. Francois used to contend shruggingly that it was an easy death. It may be easy compared with some of the other deaths imposed on his furry captives. But it's not my idea of bliss, drowning under a foot or two of ice with a steel trap mangling your ankle for full measure!

"We live forward, but we understand backward." I don't know who first said it. But the older I grow the more I realize how true it is.

Sunday the Umptieth

I've written to Peter, reminding him of his promise, and asking about the Pasadena bungalow.

It seems the one way out. I'm tired of living like an Alpine ibex, all day long above the snow-line. I'm tired of this blind alley of inaction. I'm tired of decisions deferred and threats evaded. I want to get away to think things over, to step back and regain a perspective on the over-smudged canvas of life.

To remain at Alabama Ranch during the winter can mean only a winter of discontent and drifting—and drifting closer and closer to uncharted rocky ledges. There's no ease for the mouth where one tooth aches, as the Chinese say.

Dinky-Dunk, I think, has an inkling of how I feel. He is very thoughtful and kind in small things, and sometimes looks at me with the eyes of a boy's dog which has been forbidden to follow the village gang a-field. And it's not that I dislike him, or that he grates on me, or that I'm not thankful enough for the thousand and one little kind things he does. But it's rubbing on the wrong side of the glass. It can't bring back the past. My husband of to-day is not the Dinky-Dunk I once knew and loved and laughed with. To go back to dogs, it reminds me of Chinkie's St. Bernard, "Father Tom," whom Chinkie petted and trained and loved almost to adoration. And when poor old Father Tom was killed Chinkie in his madness insisted that a taxidermist should stuff and mount that dead dog, which stood, thereafter, not a quick and living companion but a rather gruesome monument of a vanished friendship. It was, of course, the shape and color of the thing he had once loved; but you can't feed a hungry heart by staring at a pair of glass eyes and a wired tail without any wag in it.

Saturday the Ninth

Struthers and I have been busy making clothes, during the absence of Dinky-Dunk, who has been off duck-shooting for the last three days. He complained of being a bit tuckered out and having stood the gaff too long and needing a change. The outing will do him good. The children miss him, of course, but he's promised to bring Dinkie home an Indian bow-and-arrow. I can see death and destruction hanging over the glassware of this household.... The weather has been stormy, and yesterday Whinnie and Struthers put up the stove in the bunk-house. They were a long time about it, but I was reluctant to stop the flutterings of Cupid's wings.

Tuesday the Twelfth

I had a brief message from Peter stating the Pasadena house is entirely at my disposal.... Dinky-Dunk came back with a real pot-hunter's harvest of wild ducks, which we'll pick and dress and freeze for winter use. I'm taking the breast-feathers for my pillows and Whinstane Sandy is taking what's left for a sleeping-bag—from which I am led to infer that he's still reconciled to a winter of solitude. Struthers, I know, could tell him of a warmer bag than that, lined with downier feathers from the pinions of Eros. But, as I've said before, Fate, being blind, weaves badly.

Friday the Fifteenth

I've just told Dinky-Dunk of my decision to take the kiddies to California for the winter months. He rather surprised me by agreeing with everything I suggested. He feels, I think, as I do, that there's danger in going aimlessly on and on as we have been doing. And it's really a commonplace for the prairie rancher—when he can afford it—to slip down to California for the winter. They go by the thousand, by the train-load.

Friday the Sixth

It's three long weeks since I've had time for either ink or retrospect. But at last I'm settled, though I feel as though I'd died and ascended into Heaven, or at least changed my world, as the Chinks say, so different is Pasadena to the prairie and Alabama Ranch. For as I sit here on the *loggia* of Peter's house I'm bathed in a soft breeze that is heavy with a fragrance of flowers, the air is the air of our balmiest midsummer, and in a pepper-tree not thirty feet away a mocking-bird is singing for all it's worth. It seems a poignantly beautiful world. And everything suggests peace. But it was not an easy peace to attain.

In the first place, the trip down was rather a nightmare. It brought home to me the fact that I had three young barbarians to break and subjugate, three untrained young outlaws who went wild with their first plunge into train-travel and united in defiance of Struthers and her foolishly impressive English uniform which always makes me think of Regent Park. I have a suspicion that Dinky-Dunk all the while knew of the time I'd have, but sagely held his peace.

I had intended, when I left home, to take the boat at Victoria and go down to San Pedro, for I was hungry for salt water and the feel of a rolling deck under my feet again. But the antics of my three little outlaws persuaded me, before we pulled into Calgary, that it would be as well to make the trip south as short a one as possible. Dinkie disgraced me in the dining-car by insisting on "drinking" his mashed potatoes, and made daily and not always ineffectual efforts to appropriate all the fruit on the table, and on the last day, when I'd sagaciously handed him over to the tender mercies of Struthers, I overheard this dialogue:

"I want shooder in my soup!"

"But little boys don't eat sugar in their soup."

"I want shooder in my soup!"

"But, darling, mommie doesn't eat sugar in her soup!"

"Shooder! Dinkie wants shooder, shooder in his soup!"

"Daddy never eats shooder in his soup, Sweetness."

"I want shooder!"

"But really nice little boys don't ask for sugar in their soup," argued the patient-eyed Struthers.

"*Shooder!*" insisted the implacable tyrant. And he got it.

There was an exceptional number of babies and small children on board and my unfraternal little prairie-waifs did not see why every rattle and doll and automatic toy of their little fellow travelers and sister tourists shouldn't promptly become their own private property. And traveling with twins not yet a year old is scarcely conducive to rest.

And yet, for all the worry and tumult, I found a new peace creeping into my soul. It was the first sight of the Rockies, I think, which brought the change. I'd grown tired of living on a billiard-table, without quite knowing it, tired of the trimly circumscribed monotony of material life, of the isolating flat contention against hunger and want. But the mountains took me out of myself. They were Peter's windmill, raised to the Nth power. They loomed above me, seeming to say: "We are timeless. You, puny one, can live but a day." They stood there as they had stood from the moment God first whispered: "Let there be light"—and there was light. But no, I'm wrong there, as Peter would very promptly have told me, for it was only in the Cambrian Period that the cornerstone of the Rockies was laid. The geologic clock ticked out its centuries until the swamps of the Coal Period were full of Peter's Oldest Inhabitants in the form of Dinosaurs and then came the Cretaceous Period and the Great Architect looked down and bade the Rockies arise, and tooled them into beauty with His blue-green glaciers and His singing rivers, and touched the lordliest peaks with wine-glow and filled the azure valleys with music and peace. And we threaded along those valley-sides on our little ribbons of steel, skirted the shouting rivers and plunged into tiny twisted tubes of darkness, emerging again into the light and once more hearing the timeless giants, with their snow-white heads against the sunset, repeat their whisper: "We live and are eternal. Ye, who fret about our feet, dream for a day, and are forgotten!"

But we seemed to be stepping out into a new world, by the time we got to Pasadena. It was a summery and flowery and holiday world, and it impressed me as being solely and scrupulously organized for pleasure. Yet all minor surprises were submerged in the biggest surprise of Peter's bungalow, which is really more like a *château*, and strikes me as being singularly like Peter himself, not amazingly impressive to look at, perhaps, but hiding from the world a startlingly rich and luxurious interior. The house itself, half hidden in shrubbery, is of weather-stained stucco, and looks at first sight a little gloomy, with the *patina* of time upon it. But it is a restful change from the spick-and-spanness of the near-by millionaire colony, so eloquent of the paint-brush and the lawn-valet's shears, so smug and new and strident in its paraded opulence. Peter's gardens, in fact, are a rather careless riot of color and line, a sort of achieved genteel roughness, like certain phases of his house, as though the wave of refinement driven too high had broken and tumbled over on itself.

The house, which is the shape of an "E" without the middle stroke, has a green-sodded *patio* between the two wings, with a small fountain and a stained marble basin at the center. There are shade-trees and date-palms and shrubs and Romanesque-looking stone seats about narrow walks, for this is the only really formalized portion of the entire property. This leads off into a grove and garden, a confusion of flowers and trees where I've already been able to spot out a number of orange trees, some of them well fruited, several lemon and fig trees, a row of banana trees, or plants, whichever they should be called, besides pepper and palm and acacia and a long-legged double-file of eucalyptus at the rear. And in between is a pergola and a mixture of mimosa and wistaria and tamarisk and poppies and trellised roses and one woody old geranium with a stalk like a crab-apple trunk and growth enough to cover half a dozen prairie hay-stacks.

But, as I've already implied, it was the inside of the house that astonished me. It is much bigger than it looks and is crowded with the most gorgeous old things in copper and brass and leather and mahogany that I ever saw under one roof. It has three open fireplaces, a huge one of stone in the huge living-room, and rough-beamed ceilings of redwood, and Spanish tiled floors, and chairs upholstered with cowhide with the ranch-brand still showing in the tanned leather, and tables of Mexican mahogany set in redwood frames, and several convenient little electric heaters which can be carried from room to room as they are needed.

Pinshaw, Peter's gardener and care-taker, had before our arrival picked several clumps of violets, with perfume like the English violets, and the house was aired and everything waiting and ready when we came, even to two bottles of certified milk in the icebox for the babies and half a dozen Casaba melons for their elders. My one disturbing thought is that it will be a hard house to live up to. But Struthers, who is not untouched with her *folie de grandeur*, has the slightly flurried satisfaction of an exile who has at last come into her own. One of the first things I must do, however, is to teach my kiddies to respect Peter's belongings. In one cabinet of books, which is locked, I have noticed several which are by "Peter Ketley" himself. Yet that name meant nothing to me, when I met it out on the prairie and humiliated its owner by converting him into one of my hired hands. *Ce monde est plein de fous.*

Monday the Sixteenth

This is a great climate for meditation. And I have been meditating. Back at Alabama Ranch, I suppose, there's twenty degrees of frost and a northwest wind like a search-warrant. Here there's a pellucid blue sky, just enough breeze to rustle the bamboo-fronds behind me, and a tall girl in white lawn, holding a pale green parasol over her head and meandering slowly along the sun-steeped boulevard, which smells of hot tar.

I've been sitting here staring down that boulevard, with the strong light making me squint a little. I've been watching the two rows of date-palms along the curb, with their willow-plume head-dress stirring lazily in the morning breeze. Well back from the smooth and shining asphalt, as polished as ebony with its oil-drip and tire-wear, is a row of houses, some shingled and awninged, some Colonial-Spanish, and stuccoed and bone-white in the sun, some dark-wooded and vine-draped and rose-grown, but all immaculate and finished and opulent. The street is very quiet, but half-way down the block I can see a Jap gardener in brown denim sedately watering a well-barbered terrace. Still farther away, somebody, in one of the deep-shadowed porches, is tinkling a ukelele, and somebody that I can't see is somewhere beating a rug. I can see a little rivulet of water that flows sparkling down the asphalted runnel of the curb. Then the clump of bamboos back by Peter's bedroom window rustles crisply again and is quiet and the silence is broken by a nurse-maid calling to a child sitting in a toy motor-wagon. Then a touring-car purrs past, with the sun flashing on its polished metal equipment, and the toy motor child being led reluctantly homeward by the maid cries shrilly, and in the silence that ensues I can hear the faint hiss of a spray-nozzle that builds a transient small rainbow just beyond the trellis of Cherokee roses from which a languid white petal falls, from time to time.

It's a *dolce-far-niente* day, as all the days seem to be here, and the best that I can do is sit and brood like a Plymouth Rock with a full crop. But I've been thinking things over. And I've come to several conclusions.

One is that I'm not so contented as I thought I was going to be. I am oppressed by a shadowy feeling of in some way sailing under false colors. I am also hounded by an equally shadowy impression that I'm a convalescent. Yet I find myself vulgarly healthy, my kiddies have all acquired a fine coat of tan, and only Struthers is slightly off her feed, having acquired a not unmerited attack of cholera morbus from over-indulgence in Casaba melon. But I keep wondering if Dinky-Dunk is getting the right sort of things to eat, if he's lonely, and what he does in his spare time.

And another conclusion I've come to is that men, much as I hate to admit it, are built of a stronger fiber than women. They seem able to stand shock better than the weaker sex. They are not so apt to go down under defeat, to take the full count, as I have done. For I still have to face the fact that I was a failure. Then I turned tail and fled from the scene of my collapse. That flight, it is true, has brought me a certain brand of peace, but it is not an enduring peace, for you can't run away from what's in your own heart. And already I'm restless and ill-at-ease. It's not so much that I'm dissatisfied; it's more that I'm unsatisfied. There still seems to be something momentous left out of the plan of things. I have the teasing feeling of confronting something which is still impending, which is being withheld, which I can not reach out for, no matter how I try, until the time is ripe.... Those rustling bamboos so close to the room where I sleep have begun to bother me so much that I'm migrating to a new bedroom to-night. "There's never anything without something!"

Tuesday the Twenty-fourth

Little Dinky-Dunk has adventured into illicit knowledge of his first orange from the bough. It was one of Peter's low-hanging Valencias, and seems to have left no ill-effects, though I prefer that all inside matter be carefully edited before consumption by that small Red. So Struthers hereafter must stand the angel with the flaming sword and guard the gates that open upon that tree of forbidden fruit. Her own colic, by the way, is a thing of the past, and at present she's extremely interested in Pinshaw, who, she tells me, was once a cabinet-maker in England, and came out to California for his health. Struthers, as usual, is attempting to reach the heart of her new victim by way of the stomach, and Pinshaw, apparently, is not unappreciative, since he appears a little more punctually at his watering and raking and gardening and has his ears up like a rabbit for the first inkling of his lady-love's matutinal hand-out. And poor old Whinstane Sandy, back at Alabama Ranch, is still making sheep's eyes at the patches which Struthers once sewed on his breeks, like as not, and staring with a moonish smile at the atrabilious photograph which the one camera-artist of Buckhorn made of Struthers and my three pop-eyed kiddies....

These are, without exception, the friendliest people I have ever known. The old millionaire lumberman from Bay City, who lives next door to me, pushes through the hedge with platefuls of green figs and tid-bits from his gardens, and delightful girls whose names I don't even know come in big cars and ask to take little Dinkie off for one of their lawn *fêtes*. It even happened that a movie-actor—who, I later discovered, was a drug-addict— insisted on accompanying me home and informed me on the way that I had a dream of a face for camera-work. It quite set me up, for all its impertinence, until I learned to my sorrow that it had flowered out of nothing more than an extra shot in the arm.

They are a friendly and companionable folk, and they'd keep me on the go all the time if I'd let 'em. But I've only had energy enough to run over to Los Angeles twice, though there are a dozen or two people I must look up in that more frolicsome suburb. But I can't get away from the feeling, the truly rural feeling, that I'm among strangers. I can't rid myself of the extremely parochial impression that these people are not my people. And there's a valetudinarian aspect to the place which I find slightly depressing. For this seems to be the one particular point where the worn-out old money-maker comes to die, and the antique ladies with asthma struggle for an extra year or two of the veranda rocking-chair, and rickety old *beaux* sit about in Panamas and white flannels and listen to the hardening of their arteries. And I haven't quite finished with life yet—not if I know it—not by a long shot!

But one has to be educated for idleness, I find, almost as much as for industry. I knew the trick once, but I've lost the hang of it. The one thing that impresses me, on coming straight from prairie life to a city like this, is how much women-folk can have done for them without quite knowing it. The machinery of life here is so intricate and yet so adequate that it denudes them of all the normal and primitive activities of their grandmothers, so they have to invent troubles and contrive quite unnecessary activities to keep from being bored to extinction. Everything seems to come to them ready-made and duly prepared, their bread, their light and fuel and water, their meat and milk. All that, and the daily drudgery it implies, is made ready and performed beyond their vision, and they have no balky pumps to prime and no fires to build, and they'd probably be quite disturbed to think that their roasts came from a slaughter-house with bloody floors and that their breakfast rolls, instead of coming ready-made into the world, are mixed and molded in bake-rooms where men work sweating by night, stripped to the waist, like stokers.

Wednesday the Second

Dinky-Dunk's letter, which reached me Monday, was very short and almost curt. It depressed me for a day. I tried to fight against that feeling, when it threatened to return yesterday, and was at Peter's piano shouting to the kiddies:

"Coon, Coon, Coon, I wish my color'd fade!

Coon, Coon, Coon, I'd like a different shade!"

when Struthers carried in to me, with a sort of triumphant and tight-lipped I-told-you-so air, a copy of the morning's *Los Angeles Examiner*. She had it folded so that I found myself confronting a picture of Lady Alicia Newland, Lady Alicia in the "Teddy-Bear" suit of an aviator, with a fur-lined leather jacket and helmet and heavy gauntlets and leggings and the same old audacious look out of the quietly smiling eyes, which were squinting a little because of the sunlight.

Lady Allie, I found on perusing the letter-press, had been flying with some of the North Island officers down in San Diego Bay. And now she and the Right Honorable Lieutenant-Colonel Brereton Ainsley-Brook, of the British Imperial Commission to Canada, were to attempt a flight to Kelly Field Number Two, at San Antonio, in Texas, in a De Haviland machine. She had told the *Examiner* reporter who had caught her as she stood beside a naval sea-plane, that she "loved" flying and loved taking a chance and that her worst trouble was with nose-bleed, which she'd get over in time, she felt sure. And if the Texas flight was a success she would try to arrange for a flight down to the Canal at the same time that the Pacific fleet comes through from Colon.

"Isn't that 'er, all over?" demanded Struthers, forgetting her place and her position and even her aspirate in the excitement of the moment. But I handed back the paper without comment. For a day, however, Lady Allie has loomed large in my thoughts.

Sunday the Thirteenth

It will be two weeks to-morrow since I've had a line from Dinky-Dunk. The world about me is a world of beauty, but I'm worried and restless and Edna Millay's lines keep running through my head:

"...East and West will pinch the heart

That can not keep them pushed apart;

And he whose soul is flat—the sky

Will cave in on him by and by!"

Wednesday the Sixteenth

Peter has written to me saying that unless he hears from me to the contrary he thinks he can arrange to "run through" to the Coast in time for the Rose Tournament here on New Year's Day. He takes the trouble to explain that he'll stay at the Alexandria in Los Angeles, so there'll be no possible disturbance to me and my family routine.

That's so like Peter!

But there's been no word from Dinky-Dunk. The conviction is growing in my mind that he's not at Alabama Ranch.

Monday the Twenty-first

A letter has just come to me this morning from Whinstane Sandy, written in lead-pencil. It said, with an orthography all its own, that Duncan had been in bed for two weeks with what they thought was pneumonia, but was up again and able to eat something, and not to worry. It seemed a confident and cheerful message at first, but the oftener I read it the more worried I became. So one load was taken off my heart only to make room for another. My first decision was to start north at once, to get back to Alabama Ranch and my Dinky-Dunk as fast as steam could take me. I was still the sharer of his joys and sorrows, and ought to be with him when things were at their worst. But on second thought it didn't seem quite fair to the kiddies, to dump them from midsummer into shack-life and a sub-zero climate. And always, always, always, there were the children to be considered. So I wired Ed Sherman, the station-agent at Buckhorn, asking him to send out a message to Duncan, saying I was waiting for him in Pasadena and to come at once....

I wonder what his answer will be? It's surrender, on my part. It's capitulation, and Dinky-Dunk, of course, will recognize that fact. Or he ought to. But it's not this I'm worrying over. It's Duncan himself, and his health. It gives me a guilty feeling.... I once thought that I was made to heal hearts. But about all I can do, I find, is to bruise them.

Thursday the Twenty-fourth

A telegram of just one word has come from Duncan, dated at Calgary. It said: "Coming." I could feel a little tremble in my knees as I read it. He must be better, or he'd never be able to travel. To-morrow will be Christmas Day, but we've decided to postpone all celebration until the kiddies' daddy is on the scene. It will never seem much like Christmas to us Eskimos, at eighty-five in the shade. And we're temporarily subduing that red-ink day to the eyes of the children by carefully secreting in one of Peter's clothes-closets each and every present that has come for them.

Sunday the Twenty-seventh

Dinky-Dunk is here. He arrived this morning, and we were all at the station in our best bib-and-tucker and making a fine show of being offhanded and light-hearted. But when I saw the porter helping down my Diddums, so white-faced and weak and tired-looking, something swelled up and burst just under my floating ribs and for a moment I thought my heart had had a blow-out like a tire and stopped working for ever and ever. Heaven knows I held my hands tight, and tried to be cheerful, but in spite of everything I could do, on the way home, I couldn't stop the tears from running slowly down my cheeks. They kept running and running, as though I had nothing to do with it, exactly as a wound bleeds. The poor man, of course, was done out by the long trip. He was just *blooey*, and saved himself from being pitiful by shrinking back into a shell of chalky-faced self-sufficiency. He has said very little, and has eaten nothing, but had a sleep this afternoon for a couple of hours, out in the *patio* on a *chaise-longue*. It hurt him, I think, to find his own children look at him with such cold and speculative eyes. But he has changed shockingly since they last saw him. And they have so much to fill up their little lives. They haven't yet reached the age when life teaches them they'd better stick to what's given them, even though there's a bitter tang to its sweetness!

Wednesday the Thirtieth

It is incredible, what three days of rest and forced feeding at my implacable hands, have done for Dinky-Dunk. He is still a little shaky on his pins, if he walks far, and the noonday sun makes him dizzy, but his eyes don't look so much like saucers and I haven't heard the trace of a cough from him all to-day. Illness, of course, is not romantic, but it plays its altogether too important part in life, and has to be faced. And there is something so disturbingly immuring and depersonalizing about it! Dinky-Dunk appears rather in a world by himself. Only once, so far, has he seemed to step back to our every-day old world. That was when he wandered into the Blue Room in the East Wing where little Dinkie has been sleeping. I was seated beside his little lordship's bed singing:

"The little pigs sleep with their tails curled up,"

and when that had been exhausted, rambling on to

"The sailor being both tall and slim,

The lady fell in love with him,"

when *pater familias* wandered in and inquired, "Whyfore the cabaret?"

I explained that Dinkie, since coming south, had seemed to demand an even-song or two before slipping off.

"I see that I'll have to take our son in hand," announced Dinky-Dunk—but there was just the shadow of a smile about his lips as he went slowly out and closed the door after him.

To-night, when I told Dinky-Dunk that Peter would in all likelihood be here to-morrow, he listened without batting an eyelash. But he asked if I'd mind handing him a cigarette, and he studied my face long and intently. I don't know what he saw there, or what he concluded, for I did my best to keep it as noncommittal as possible. If there is any move, it must be from him. That sour-inked Irishman called Shaw has said that women are the wooers in this world. A lot he knows about it!... Yet something has happened, in the last half-hour, which both disturbs and puzzles me. When I was unpacking Dinky-Dunk's second trunk, which had stood neglected for almost four long days, I came across the letter which I thought I'd put away in the back of the ranch ledger and had failed to find.... And he had it, all the time!

The redoubtable Struthers, it must be recorded, to-day handed me another paper, and almost as triumphantly as the first one. She'd picked it up on her way home from the druggist's, where she went for aspirin for Dinky-Dunk. On what was labeled its "Woman's Page" was yet another photographic reproduction of the fair Lady Allie in aviation togs and a head-line which read: "Insists On Tea Above The Clouds." But I plainly disappointed the expectant Struthers by promptly handing the paper back to her and by declining to make any comment.

Thursday the Thirty-first

Peter walked in on us to-day, a little less spick and span, I'm compelled to admit, than I had expected of one in his position, but as easy and unconcerned as though he had dropped in from across the way for a cigarette and a cup of tea. And I played up to that pose by having Struthers wheel the tea-wagon out into the *patio*, where we gathered about it in a semicircle, as decorously as though we were sitting in a curate's garden to talk over the program for the next meeting of the Ladies' Auxiliary.

There we sat, Dinky-Dunk, my husband who was in love with another woman; Peter, my friend, who was in love with me, and myself, who was too busy bringing up a family to be in love with anybody. There we sat in that beautiful garden, in that balmy and beautiful afternoon sunlight, with the bamboos whispering and a mocking-bird singing from its place on the pepper-tree, stirring our small cups and saying "Lemon, please," or "Just one lump, thank you." It may not be often, but life *does* occasionally surprise us by being theatrical. For I could not banish from my bones an impression of tremendous reservations, of guarded waiting and watching from every point of that sedate and quiet-mannered little triangle. Yet for only one moment had I seen it come to the front. That was during the moment when Dinky-Dunk and Peter first shook hands. On both faces, for that moment, I caught the look with which two knights measure each other. Peter, as he lounged back in his wicker chair and produced his familiar little briar pipe, began to remind me rather acutely of that pensive old *picador* in Zuloaga's *The Victim of The Fête*, the placid and plaintive and only vaguely hopeful knight on his bony old Rosinante, not quite ignorant of the fact that he must forage on to other fields and look for better luck in newer ventures, yet not quite forgetful that life, after all, is rather a blithe adventure and that the man who refuses to surrender his courage, no matter what whimsical turns the adventure may take, is still to be reckoned the conqueror. But later on he was jolly enough and direct enough, when he got to showing Dinky-Dunk his books and curios. I suppose, at heart, he was about as interested in those things as an aquarium angel-fish is in a Sunday afternoon visitor. But if it was pretense, and nothing more, there was very actual kindliness in it. And there was nothing left for me but to sit tight, and refill the little lacquered gold cups when necessary, and smile non-committally when Dinky-Dunk explained that my idea of Heaven was a place where husbands were served *en brochette*, and emulate the Priest and the Levite by passing by on the other side when Peter asked me if I'd ever heard that the West was good for mules and men but hard on horses and women. And it suddenly struck me as odd, the timidities and reticences which nature imposes on our souls. It seemed so ridiculous that the three of us couldn't sit there and unbosom our hearts of what was hidden away in them, that we couldn't be open and honest and aboveboard and say just what we felt and thought, that we couldn't quietly talk things out to an end and find where each and all of us stood. But men and women are not made that way. Otherwise, I suppose, life would be too Edenic, and we'd part company with a very old and venerable interest in Paradise!

"She's not dead?" I asked in a breath

Saturday the Second

Peter had arranged to come for us with a motor-car and carry us all off to the Rose Tournament yesterday morning, "for I do want to be sitting right next to that little tike of yours," he explained, meaning Dinkie, "when he bumps into his first brass band!"

But little Dinkie didn't hear his brass band, and we didn't go to the Rose Tournament, although it was almost at our doors and some eighty thousand crowded automobiles foregathered here from the rest of the state to get a glimpse of it. For Peter, who is staying at the Greene here instead of at the Alexandria over in Los Angeles, presented himself before I'd even sat down to breakfast and before lazy old Dinky-Dunk was even out of bed.

Peter, I noticed, had a somewhat hollow look about the eye, but I accepted it as nothing more than the after-effects of his long trip, and blithely commanded him to sit down and partake of my coffee.

Peter, however, wasn't thinking about coffee.

"I'm afraid," he began, "that I'm bringing you rather—rather bad news."

We stood for a moment with our gazes locked. He seemed appraising me, speculating on just what effect this message of his might have on me.

"What is it?" I asked, with that forlorn tug at inner reserves which life teaches us to send over the wire as we grow older.

"I've come," explained Peter, "simply because this thing would have reached you a little later in your morning paper—and I hated the thought of having it spring out at you that way. So you won't mind, will you? You'll understand the motive behind the message?"

"But what is it?" I repeated, a little astonished by this obliquity in a man customarily so direct.

"It's about Lady Newland," he finally said. And the solemnity of his face rather frightened me.

"She's not dead?" I asked in a breath.

Peter shook his head from side to side.

"She's been rather badly hurt," he said, after several moments of silence. "Her plane was winged yesterday afternoon by a navy flier over San Diego Bay. She didn't fall, but it was a forced landing and her machine had taken fire before they could get her out of her seat."

"You mean she was burnt?" I cried, chilled by the horror of it.

And, inapposite as it seemed, my thoughts flashed back to that lithe and buoyant figure, and then to the picture of it charred and scorched and suffering.

"Only her face," was Peter's quiet and very deliberate reply.

"Only her face," I repeated, not quite understanding him.

"The men from the North Bay field had her out a minute or two after she landed. But practically the whole plane was afire. Her heavy flying coat and gauntlets saved her body and hands. But her face was unprotected. She—"

"Do you mean she'll be *disfigured?*" I asked, remembering the loveliness of that face with its red and wilful lips and its ever-changing tourmaline eyes.

"I'm afraid so," was Peter's answer. "But I've been wiring, and you'll be quite safe in telling your husband that she's in no actual danger. The Marine Hospital officials have acknowledged that no flame was inhaled, that it's merely temporary shock, and, of course, the face-burn."

"But what can they do?" I asked, in little more than a whisper.

"They're trying the new ambersine treatment, and later on, I suppose, they can rely on skin-grafting and facial surgery," Peter explained to me.

"Is it that bad?" I asked, sitting down in one of the empty chairs, for the mere effort to vision any such disfigurement had brought a Channel-crossing and Calais-packet feeling to me.

"It's very sad," said Peter, more ill-at-ease than I'd ever seen him before, "But there's positively no danger, remember. It won't be so bad as your morning paper will try to make it out. They've sensationalized it, of course. That's why I wanted to be here first, and give you the facts. They are distressing enough, God knows, without those yellow reporters working them over for wire consumption."

I was glad that Peter didn't offer to stay, didn't even seem to wish to stay. I wanted quietness and time to think the thing over. Dinky-Dunk, I realized, would have to be told, and told at once. It would, of course, be a shock to him. And it would be something more. It would be a sudden crowding to some final issue of all those possibilities which lay like spring-traps beneath the under-brush of our indifference. I had no way of knowing what it was that had attracted him to Lady Alicia. Beauty of face, of course, must have been a factor in it. And that beauty was now gone. But love, according to the Prophets and the Poets, overcometh all things. And in her very helplessness, it was only too plain to me, his Cousin Allie might appeal to him in a more personal and more perilous way. My Diddums himself, of late, had appealed more to me in his weakness and his unhappiness than in his earlier strength and triumph. There was a time, in fact, when I had almost grown to hate his successes. And yet he was my husband. He was *mine*. And it was a human enough instinct to fight for what was one's own. But that wild-bird part of man known as his will could never be caged and chained. If somewhere far off it beheld beauty and nobility it must be free to wing its way where it wished. The only bond that held it was the bond of free-giving and goodness. And if it abjured such things as that, the sooner the flight took place and the colors were shown, the better. If on the home-bough beside him nested neither beauty nor nobility, it was only natural that he should wander a-field for what I had failed to give him. And now, in this final test, I must not altogether fail him. For once in my life, I concluded, I had to be generous.

So I waited until Dinky-Dunk emerged. I waited, deep in thought, while he splashed like a sea-lion in his bath, and called out to Struthers almost gaily for his glass of orange-juice, and shaved, and opened and closed drawers, and finished dressing and came out in his cool-looking suit of cricketer's flannel, so immaculate and freshly-pressed that one would never dream it had been bought in England and packed in mothballs for four long years.

I heard him asking for the kiddies while I was still out in the *patio* putting the finishing touches to his breakfast-table, and his grunt that was half a sigh when he learned that they'd been sent off before he'd had a glimpse of them. And I could see him inhale a lungful of the balmy morning air as he stood in the open doorway and stared, not without approval, at me and the new-minted day.

"Why the clouded brow, Lady-Bird?" he demanded as he joined me at the little wicker table.

"I've had some rather disturbing news," I told him, wondering just how to begin.

"The kiddies?" he asked, stopping short.

I stared at him closely as I shook my head in answer to that question. He looked leaner and frailer and less robustious than of old. But in my heart of hearts I liked him that way. It left him the helpless and unprotesting victim of that run-over maternal instinct of mine which took wayward joy in mothering what it couldn't master. It had brought him a little closer to me. But that contact, I remembered, was perhaps to be only something of the moment.

"Dinky-Dunk," I told him as quietly as I could, "I want you to go down to San Diego and see Lady Allie."

It was a less surprised look than a barricaded one that came into his eyes.

"Why?" he asked as he slowly seated himself across the table from me.

"Because I think she needs you," I found the courage to tell him.

"Why?" he asked still again.

"There has been an accident," I told him.

"What sort of accident?" he quickly inquired, with one hand arrested as he went to shake out his table-napkin.

"It was an air-ship accident. And Lady Allie's been hurt."

"Badly?" he asked, as our glances met.

"Not badly, in one way," I explained to him. "She's not in any danger, I mean. But her plane caught fire, and she's been burned about the face."

His lips parted slightly, as he sat staring at me. And slowly up into his colorless face crept a blighted look, a look which brought a vague yet vast unhappiness to me as I sat contemplating it.

"Do you mean she's disfigured," he asked, "that it's something she'll always—"

"I'm afraid so," I said, when he did not finish his sentence.

He sat looking down at his empty plate for a long time.

"And you want me to go?" he finally said.

"Yes," I told him.

He was silent for still another ponderable space of time.

"But do you understand—" he began. And for the second time he didn't finish his sentence.

"I understand," I told him, doing my best to sit steady under his inquisitorial eye. Then he looked down at the empty plate again.

"All right," he said at last. He spoke in a quite flat and colorless tone. But it masked a decision which we both must have recognized as being momentous. And I knew, without saying anything further, that he would go.

Sunday the Third

Dinky-Dunk left Friday night and got back early this morning before I was up. This naturally surprised me. But what surprised me more was the way he looked. He was white and shaken and drawn about the eyes. He seemed so wretched that I couldn't help feeling sorry for him.

"*She wouldn't see me!*" was all he said as I stopped him on the way to his room.

But he rather startled me, fifteen minutes later, by calling up the Greene and asking for Peter. And before half an hour had dragged past Peter appeared in person. He ignored the children, and apparently avoided me, and went straight out to the pergola, where he and Dinky-Dunk fell to pacing slowly up and down, with the shadows dappling their white-clad shoulders like leopards as they walked up and down, up and down, as serious and solemn as two ministers of state in a national crisis. And something, I scarcely knew what, kept me from going out and joining them.

It was Peter himself who finally came in to me. He surprised me, in the first place, by shaking hands. He did it with that wistful wandering-picador smile of his on his rather Zuloagaish face.

"I've got to say good-by," I found him saying to me.

"Peter!" I called out in startled protest, trying to draw back so I could see him better. But he kept my hand.

"I'm going east to-night," he quite casually announced. "But above all things I want you and your Dinky-Dunk to hang on here as long as you can. *He* needs it. I'm stepping out. No, I don't mean that, exactly, for I'd never stepped in. But it's a fine thing, in this world, for men and women to be real friends. And I know, until we shuffle off, that we're going to be that!"

"Peter!" I cried again, trying not to choke up with the sudden sense of deprivation that was battering my heart to pieces. And the light in faithful old Peter's eyes didn't make it any easier.

But he dropped my hand, of a sudden, and went stumbling rather awkwardly over the Spanish tiling as he passed out to the waiting car. I watched him as he climbed into it, stiffly yet with a show of careless bravado, for all the world like the lean-jowled knight of the vanished fête mounting his bony old Rosinante.

It was nearly half an hour later that Dinky-Dunk came into the cool-shadowed living-room where I was making a pretense of being busy at cutting down some of Dinkie's rompers for Pee-Wee, who most assuredly must soon bid farewell to skirts.

"Will you sit down, please?" he said with an abstracted sort of formality. For he'd caught me on the wing, half-way back from the open window, where I'd been glancing out to make sure Struthers was on guard with the children.

My face was a question, I suppose, even when I didn't speak.

"There's something I want you to be very quiet and courageous about," was my husband's none too tranquillizing beginning. And I could feel my pulse quicken.

"What is it?" I asked, wondering just what women should do to make themselves quiet and courageous.

"It's about Allie," answered my husband, speaking so slowly and deliberately that it sounded unnatural. "She shot herself last night. She—she killed herself, with an army revolver she'd borrowed from a young officer down there."

I couldn't quite understand, at first. The words seemed like half-drowned things my mind had to work over and resuscitate and coax, back into life.

"This is terrible!" I said at last, feebly, foolishly, as the meaning of it all filtered through my none too active brain.

"It's terrible for me," acknowledged Dinky-Dunk, with a self-pity which I wasn't slow to resent.

"But why aren't you there?" I demanded. "Why aren't you there to keep a little decency about the thing? Why aren't you looking after what's left of her?"

Dinky-Dunk's eye evaded mine, but only for a moment.

"Colonel Ainsley-Brook is coming back from Washington to take possession of the remains," he explained with a sort of dry-lipped patience, "and take them home."

"But why should an outsider like—"

Dinky-Dunk stopped me with a gesture.

"He and Allie were married, a little over three weeks ago," my husband quietly informed me. And for the second time I had to work life into what seemed limp and sodden words.

"Did you know about that?" I asked.

"Yes, Allie wrote to me about it, at the time," he replied with a sort of coerced candor. "She said it seemed about the only thing left to do."

"Why should she say that?"

Dinky-Dunk stared at me with something strangely like a pleading look in his haggard eye.

"Wouldn't it be better to keep away from all that, at a time like this?" he finally asked.

"No," I told him, "this is the time we *can't* keep away from it. She wrote you that because she was in love with you. Isn't that the truth?"

Dinky-Dunk raised his hand, as though he were attempting a movement of protest, and then dropped it again. His eyes, I noticed, were luminous with a sort of inward-burning misery. But I had no intention of being merciful. I had no chance of being merciful. It was like an operation without ether, but it had to be gone through with. It had to be cut out, in some way, that whole cancerous growth of hate and distrust.

"Isn't that the truth?" I repeated.

"Oh, Tabby, don't turn the knife in the wound!" cried Dinky-Dunk, with his face more than ever pinched with misery.

"Then it *is* a wound!" I proclaimed in dolorous enough triumph. "But there's still another question, Dinky-Dunk, you must answer," I went on, speaking as slowly and precisely as I could, as though deliberation in speech might in some way make clearer a matter recognized as only too dark in spirit. "And it must be answered honestly, without any quibble as to the meaning of words. Were you in love with Lady Allie?"

His gesture of repugnance, of seeming self-hate, was both a prompt and a puzzling one.

"That's the hideous, the simply hideous part of it all," he cried out in a sort of listless desperation.

"Why hideous?" I demanded, quite clear-headed, and quite determined that now or never the overscored slate of suspicion should be wiped clean. I still forlornly and foolishly felt, I suppose, that he might yet usher before me some miraculously simple explanation that would wipe his scutcheon clean, that would put everything back to the older and happier order. But as I heard his deep-wrung cry of "Oh, what's the good of all this?" I knew that life wasn't so romantic as we're always trying to make it.

"I've got to know," I said, as steel-cold as a surgeon.

"But can't you see that it's—that it's worse than revolting to me?" he contended, with the look of a man harried beyond endurance.

"Why should it be?" I exacted.

He sank down in the low chair with the ranch-brand on its leather back. It was an oddly child-like movement of collapse. But I daren't let myself feel sorry for him.

"Because it's all so rottenly ignoble," he said, without looking at me.

"For whom?" I asked, trying to speak calmly.

"For me—for you," he cried out, with his head in his hands. "For you to have been faced with, I mean. It's awful, to think that you've had to stand it!" He reached out for me, but I was too far away for him to touch. "Oh, Tabby, I've been such an awful rotter. And this thing that's happened has just brought it home to me."

"Then you cared, that much?" I demanded, feeling the bottom of my heart fall out, for all the world like the floor of a dump-cart.

"No, no; that's the unforgivable part of it," he cried in quick protest. "It's not only that I did you a great wrong, Tabby, but I did *her* a worse one. I coolly exploited something that I should have at least respected. I manipulated and used a woman I should have been more generous with. There wasn't even bigness in it, from my side of the game. I traded on that dead woman's weakness. And my hands would be cleaner if I could come to you with the claim that I'd really cared for her, that I'd been swept off my feet, that passion had blinded me to the things I should have remembered." He let his hands fall between his knees. Knowing him as the man of reticence that he was, it seemed an indescribably tragic gesture. And it struck me as odd, the next moment, that he should be actually sobbing. "Oh, my dear, my dear, the one thing I was blind to was your bigness, was your goodness. The one thing I forgot was how true blue you could be."

I sat there staring at his still heaving shoulders, turning over what he had said, turning it over and over, like a park-squirrel with a nut. I found a great deal to think about, but little to say.

"I don't blame you for despising me," Dinky-Dunk said, out of the silence, once more in control of himself.

"I was thinking of *her*," I explained. And then I found the courage to look into my husband's face. "No, Dinky-Dunk, I don't despise you," I told him, remembering that he was still a weak and shaken man. "But I pity you. I do indeed pity you. For it's selfishness, it seems to me, which costs us so much, in the end."

He seemed to agree with me, by a slow movement of the head.

"That's the only glimmer of hope I have," he surprised me by saying.

"But why hope from *that?*" I asked.

"Because you're so utterly without selfishness," that deluded man cried out to me. "You were always that way, but I didn't have the brains to see it. I never quite saw it until you sent me down to—to *her.*" He came to a stop, and sat staring at the terra-cotta Spanish floor-tiles. "*I* knew it was useless, tragically useless. You didn't. But you were brave enough to let my weakness do its worst, if it had to. And that makes me feel that I'm not fit to touch you, that I'm not even fit to walk on the same ground with you!"

I tried my best to remain judicial.

"But this, Dinky-Dunk, isn't being quite fair to either of us," I protested, turning away to push in a hair-pin so that he wouldn't see the tremble that I could feel in my lower lip. For an unreasonable and illogical and absurdly big wave of compassion for my poor old Dinky-Dunk was welling up through my tired body, threatening to leave me and all my make-believe dignity as wobbly as a street-procession Queen of Sheba on her circus-float. I was hearing, I knew, the words that I'd waited for, this many a month. I was at last facing the scene I'd again and again dramatized on the narrow stage of my woman's imagination. But instead of bringing me release, it brought me heart-ache; instead of spelling victory, it came involved with the thin humiliations of compromise. For things could never be the same again. The blot was there on the scutcheon, and could never be argued away. The man I loved had let the grit get into the bearings of his soul, had let that grit grind away life's delicate surfaces without even knowing the wine of abandoned speed. He had been nothing better than the passive agent, the fretful and neutral factor, the cheated one without even the glory of conquest or the tang of triumph. But he had been saved for me. He was there within arm's reach of me, battered, but with the wine-glow of utter contrition on his face.

"Take me back, *Babushka*," I could hear his shaken voice imploring. "I don't deserve it—but I can't go on without you. I can't! I've had enough of hell. And I need you more than anything else in this world!"

That, I had intended telling him, wasn't playing quite fair. But when he reached out his hands toward me, exactly as I've seen his own Dinky do at nightfall when a darkening room left his little spirit hungry for companionship, something melted like an overlooked chocolate *mousse* in my crazy old maternal heart, and before I was altogether aware of it I'd let my hands slip over his shoulders as he knelt with his bowed head in my lap. The sight of his colorless and unhappy face with that indescribable homeless-dog look in his eyes was too much for me. I gave up. I hugged his head to my breast-bone as though it were my only life-buoy in an empty and endless Atlantic and only stopped when I had to rub the end of my nose, which I couldn't keep a collection of several big tears from tickling.

"I'm a fool, Dinky-Dunk, a most awful fool," I tried to tell him, when he gave me a chance to breathe again. "And I've got a temper like a bob-cat!"

"No, no, Beloved," he protested, "it's not foolishness—it's nobility!"

I couldn't answer him, for his arms had closed about me again. "And I love you, Tabbie, I love you with every inch of my body!"

Women are weak. And there is no such thing, so far as I know, as an altogether and utterly perfect man. So we must winnow strength out of our weakness, make the best of a bad bargain, and over-scroll the walls of our life-cell with the illusions which may come to mean as much as the stone and iron that imprison us. All we can do, we who are older and wiser, is wistfully to overlook the wobble where the meshed perfection of youth has been bruised and abused and loosened, tighten up the bearings, and keep as blithely as we can to the worn old road. For life, after all, is a turn-pike of concession deep-bedded with compromise. And our To-morrows are only our To-days over again.... So Dinky-Dunk, who keeps saying in unexpected and intriguing ways that he can't live without me, is trying to make love to me as he did in the old days before he got salt-and-peppery above the ears. And I'm blockhead enough to believe him. I'm like an old shoe, I suppose, comfortable but not showy. Yet it's the children we really have to think of. Our crazy old patch-work of the Past may be our own, but the Future belongs to them. There's a heap of good, though, in my humble-eyed old Dinky-Dunk, too much good ever to lose him, whatever may have happened in the days that are over.

Sunday the Twenty-fourth

Dinky-Dunk, whom I actually heard singing as he took his bath this morning, is exercising his paternal prerogative of training little Dinkie to go to bed without a light. He has peremptorily taken the matter out of my hands, and is, of course, prodigiously solemn about it all.

"I'll show that young Turk who's boss around this house!" he magisterially proclaims almost every night when the youthful wails of protest start to come from the Blue Room in the East Wing.

And off he goes, with his Holbein's Astronomer mouth set firm and the fiercest of frowns on his face.

It had a tendency to terrify me, at first. But now I know what a colossal old fraud and humbug this same soft-hearted and granite-crusted specimen of humanity can be. For last night, after the usual demonstration, I slipped out to the Blue Room and found big Dunkie kneeling down beside little Dinkie's bed, with Dinkie's small hand softly enclosed in his dad's big paw, and Dinkie's yellow head nestled close against his dad's salt-and-peppery pate.

It made me gulp a little, for some reason or other. So I tiptoed away, without letting my lord and master know I'd discovered the secret of that stern mastery of his. And later on Dinky-Dunk himself tiptoed into Peter's study, farther down the same wing, so that he could, with a shadow of truth, explain that he'd been looking over some of the Spanish manuscripts there, when I happened to ask him, on his return, just what had kept him away so long!

THE END

9 789361 478116